McCOMB PUBLIC LIBRARY
McCOMB, OHIO

D0720803

No Accident

LAURA BATES

sourcebooks
fire

Copyright © 2021, 2022 by Laura Bates
Cover and internal design © 2020 by Sourcebooks
Cover design and lettering by Stephanie Gafron/Sourcebooks
Cover photos © MonishM/Getty Images, Andrii Lutsyk/Ascent Media/Getty
Images, Avesun/Shutterstock

Sourcebooks and the colophon are registered trademarks of Sourcebooks.

All rights reserved. No part of this book may be reproduced in any form or by
any electronic or mechanical means including information storage and retrieval
systems—except in the case of brief quotations embodied in critical articles or
reviews—without permission in writing from its publisher, Sourcebooks.

The characters and events portrayed in this book are fictitious or are used
fictitiously. Any similarity to real persons, living or dead, is purely coincidental and
not intended by the author.

All brand names and product names used in this book are trademarks, registered
trademarks, or trade names of their respective holders. Sourcebooks is not
associated with any product or vendor in this book.

Published by Sourcebooks Fire, an imprint of Sourcebooks
P.O. Box 4410, Naperville, Illinois 60567–4410
(630) 961-3900
sourcebooks.com

Originally published as *The Trial* in 2021 in Great Britain by Simon & Schuster,
an imprint of Simon & Schuster UK Ltd.

Cataloging-in-Publication Data is on file with the Library of Congress.

Printed and bound in Canada.
MBP 10 9 8 7 6 5 4 3 2 1

FOR GRACE

CONTENT WARNING

This book deals with issues including rape, coercive control, and sexual bullying.

DAY 1

A FLAMING SOCK.

It seems like such a ridiculous thing. But that's what Hayley is looking at as she lies flat on her back, staring at the bright, blue sky. A smoldering gym sock, twirling in slow motion, trailing a smudge of smoke as it floats gently down toward her.

Hayley tries hard to swallow but there is something wrong with her throat, with her eyes. She can't move her arms or her legs. She isn't meant to be here—this isn't right. *Concentrate, Hayley. You aren't here, you can't be. You're on a plane. Think back.*

Bing!

The seat belt signs were turned off and Brian was first out of his seat, lumbering down the aisle toward the bathroom next to the cockpit. The back of his neck looked even paler than usual beneath his ruddy curls, freckles standing out like a smattering of fawn paint drops flicked off a brush.

"Actually, Brian, please take your seat for a moment." Coach Erickson ushered him back toward the rest of the team. Hayley saw Brian's eyes bulge a little. Was it just the artificial overhead lights or did he look faintly green?

"I really need to get in there, Coach," Brian mumbled, gesturing toward the bathroom door.

"This will just take a moment, son." Coach Erickson grinned, clapping his weathered hands to attract everyone's attention. Brian collapsed reluctantly into a free seat, cradling his stomach.

Erickson ran a hand through his thinning hair. Graying now, but the same floppy cut he'd sported since the grainy photos in the school trophy case that showed him lifting the all-state high school basketball championship cup forty years before. His face had leathered since, decades of working outdoors sending tiny red thread veins crisscrossing his nose so he looked permanently flushed with enthusiasm.

From her seat over the wing, Hayley twisted to look toward the back of the small private plane. May and Jessa were fast asleep, their backs pressed together, knees drawn up. May's glossy black hair spilled forward over a blanket clutched in her arms. Jessa's long, plump twists were draped over May's chest as her head lolled back onto her best friend's shoulder. Across the aisle, Shannon was looking out the window, her back poker straight, one foot automatically rotating and pointing through a complicated series of flexibility exercises.

The boys looked vaguely disinterested. Jason was lounging back in his seat with his legs stretched out across the aisle, playing a game on his phone. Elliot was sitting a little apart from the others, as always, bent over a sketchbook, his eyes flicking up and down at the other kids as his hand moved quickly back and forth across the page. Brian looked like he was focusing all his energy on keeping his mouth closed.

"Guys, I need your attention for a second." Slight irritation flashed across the usually placid face of the coach. He put his fingers in his mouth and let out a shrill whistle so that all eyes swiveled toward him. May and Jessa reluctantly disentangled themselves, yawning.

"Jeez, you guys. Do we need to talk about what happened last night?" There was a sudden silence, the air practically crackling. Jason shot a glance toward Shannon, who continued to look doggedly out the window. Hayley thought she saw Jessa jerk as she sat up straighter. Elliot's hand froze on the page.

Erickson gave a sly smile. "Oh-ho, you think a coach doesn't know what happens on the last night of tour? You think this is my first rodeo?"

Brian convulsed slightly and started fumbling in the seat pocket in front of him for a sick bag. Hayley watched curiously as May leaned toward Jessa and whispered loudly, "Where did you go last night? I lost you halfway through the party…"

Erickson beamed and waved his hand dismissively. "Hell, you can all relax. What goes on tour stays on tour and all that. I know about the 'rave.'" He sketched quote marks in the air with his fingers, and Hayley cringed for him as his shirt rode up a little, exposing a hint of late middle-age spread. She'd never seen anyone look less like they knew the details of what happened at a "rave."

"I just wanted to tell you all how proud I am of you," Erickson went on, smiling at them. "I know not all of you are here, but I've already said a few words to the players who went back on the other flight. Of course, we're very grateful to the Angel family for extending the use of their company planes." He nodded toward Jason, who grinned and tipped a small bag of salted peanuts into his mouth.

Erickson cleared his throat. "Now, I know the off-season prep tour isn't the be-all and end-all of tournaments, but it's an important lead-in to our main season, and you showed up and gave it your all. Ladies"—he tipped an imaginary hat to the back of the plane—"your enthusiasm and athleticism were outstanding, as always. A team is nothing without its cheerleaders. And guys...well, what can I say? Not many of you know this, but this is actually my very last tour. I'll be retiring at the end of next semester."

Hayley watched Coach Erickson carefully, her chin resting on a cupped hand. Were his eyes getting a little misty? Erickson was a "drop and gimme twenty" kind of coach, the sort of old-school educator who'd never owned a cell phone and believed there was no problem in life that couldn't be solved by a brisk run and a hot shower. She began to reach for her notebook. That was a good line. There'd be a tribute in the school paper, maybe even a piece in the local press. "Drop-and-gimme-twenty coach comes to the end of his last lap." She should get that down before she forg—

It happened so suddenly, it was like a light going out. One second, Erickson was talking, his back to the cockpit door, the students staring at him from several rows away. The next, everything moved at once. The seats dropped out from underneath them as if they'd been snatched away by an invisible hand. The windows that should have been to the left and right were suddenly on the ceiling, then spinning around to appear beneath her. Backpacks, water bottles, plastic food trays, shoes, paper cups, phones, magazines—everything was whizzing through the air like the inside of a snow globe, flying debris smashing into elbows and scratching faces. Limbs crashed and tangled into each other, spines bowed, heads whipped helplessly from side to side.

The noise was deafening. A crunching, screeching shriek of grinding metal; the roar of machinery; the din of alarms all blaring at once. And over the top of it, screaming and screaming.

There wasn't time to think. No time to wonder what was happening, to process or brace or react. There was only sensation. The lurching, roiling lightness in the stomach. The clench of panicked eyes flashing open, scrunching closed, and sharp scratches sparking hot and angry against the face and forearms. A strange sort of emptiness in the brain, like air pushing against the inside of your skull. No real pain, not yet. Then darkness.

And, presumably some time later, a flaming sock. Floating down toward Hayley as she lies on her back, unable to move. There isn't any sound. It's like watching a muted TV. The sock drifts in and out of focus. Hayley blinks, and it has fallen away somewhere else, the screen all blue again. Then a shadow obscures the blue and she thinks, ludicrously, that the signal has gone, but then her eyes begin to sting and she realizes it is smoke.

When it hits the back of her throat, it's like the world has been turned back on. She chokes and starts to retch, acrid fumes thickening in her mouth, her eyes streaming. She vomits, her head twisting automatically to the side. She finds that she can move and that her whole body is throbbing with pain.

The shock feels like a heavy blanket, weighing down every limb, clouding the air around her, making it almost impossible to see. Slowly, Hayley raises her head, her neck screaming in protest. She lifts a hand to shield her eyes from the white glare of the sun and registers distantly, as if she were looking at someone else's fingers, that there is a deep wound across the back of her wrist, that her skin is streaked with something black and sticky, that one of her fingernails is ripped and half hanging off. The hand is shaking.

There is sand everywhere. Grittiness in her eyes, between her teeth. Granules between her fingers, prickling the backs of her knees.

In the years afterwards, when Hayley thinks back to that

afternoon, she will only ever be able to see it in snatches, like photographs laid out in a line. Moments and sensations, jumbled and out of order, some so vivid she can taste them, others so alien she doesn't know if they really happened at all.

Black skin a yard or two away, streaked with red. Jessa. A jam-like sticky goo on the side of her arm, every muscle in Hayley's body straining not to look at it.

A twisted carcass of metal, unrecognizable. Wires hanging like streamers. Little fires crackling with sparks.

Bodies scattered in the sand. Some moving. Some not. Shannon's narrow, sheet-white face inches from hers, her hands gripping Hayley's shoulders, shaking lightly, her voice, distorted like she's underwater, saying something.

Relief like a liquid gush when Shannon moves to Jessa, puts two long fingers in the hollow under her chin, and says, "There's a pulse."

The weirdest sensation of hysterical laughter somewhere deep in her chest as she watches Shannon bending over Jessa, and a singsong voice in her head intones, "A head cheerleader never cracks under pressure."

Stumbling to her feet, a clean, hot pain flashes through Hayley's ankle and she drops to the ground again, crawling now instead.

Elliot is sitting up, spitting into the sand. He looks at her, nodding mutely and waving her past with a blood-streaked hand as she moves from body to body, the sand burning her knees raw.

Sobs, shuddering, screaming grind into Hayley's ears like someone scraping the inside of her head with a metal spoon. She wants them to stop so she can think, so she can breathe. She isn't here, she's on a plane. She is meant to be on a plane.

May sits up slowly, the side of her face sharply grazed. Her pupils are like lagoons. Jessa's body shakes and convulses as she screams, her arm sticking out at the wrong angle, black oil running down it and mixing with blood and torn skin.

One day, when she thinks back, Hayley will remember how her Girl Scout first aid training flashed into her mind as she knelt next to Jessa. How strange it felt to remember a smiling nurse in mint-green overalls, a blue plastic dummy on the floor.

Brain numb. Clogged, heavy with cotton wool. Something about breathing? And circulation? ABC? Or ACE? But that smooth, clinical blue plastic had looked nothing like this. It wasn't meant to be ugly and dirty, sand and blood and a mess like congealed pudding. It was meant to be clean and pleasant. Time for mistakes and starting over and asking for tips. Do I put my hands here or here? How many breaths again? Comforting, firm hands on top of hers, mint overalls swishing.

Someone says they need to set Jessa's arm and holds Jessa down. Elliot pulls, like ripping at a butcher's carcass. Hayley feels useless kneeling there, trying to remember her Girl Scout acronyms. She holds Jessa's other hand instead, letting her grip hard, painfully squeezing sand into Hayley's open cuts.

Even years later, she will know that the noises Jessa made

then caused Hayley to vomit again and again onto her own feet. But her brain won't let her remember them.

Time moves strangely. She knows they are on a beach. She knows that the front of the plane is missing, that there is no sign of Coach Erickson or the pilot. She can't remember how she knows this or who told her. Her ankle throbs and rages and when she tries to walk again; she still can't get very far. Sometimes she looks down and sees, to her surprise, that her arms and legs are shaking.

She doesn't know how long it is before Jason staggers out of the line of trees along the top of the beach, dragging Brian's motionless body.

"He's alive," he says grimly, preempting the unasked question on all of their faces.

Jason lets Brian slump limply to the ground and runs to Shannon, wraps her in his arms, stroking her long, curly dark hair like a child. "My baby," he murmurs. Seeing the two of them entwined like that makes Hayley feel terrifyingly alone. But there's a stiffness in Shannon's back. Her arms hang at her sides, and she doesn't return the embrace.

Time jumps forward again.

Hayley is sitting at the base of a palm where the beach meets the tree line, rough bark reassuringly solid behind her back. A few yards to her right, in the shade of another tree, Jessa is lying, mercifully asleep, her head in May's lap. May is stroking the baby hairs on Jessa's forehead with the tips of her fingers. Jessa usually gels them flat, but they've started to curl wispily at the roots in the humid air. It makes her look younger, more vulnerable somehow. Jason puts his hands under Brian's armpits, heaving him over to lie next to Jessa. Thick bushes and palm trees with shiny, rubbery leaves that Hayley doesn't recognize spread behind them in a dense tangle. The beach stretches out uninterrupted to the left and right like a smooth slick of butter. The smoldering wreck of the plane is hunched, gargoyle-esque, twenty feet away, its wing forced deep into the sand. Elliot encouraged them to get away from it in case there was a fuel explosion, but the flames have died down. It isn't the whole plane but a torn-off hunk, one wing and the tube of its body, the tail ripped and twisted to one side. There is no sign of the nose or the front third. The beach is strewn with parts as if the carcass of the plane has been ravaged by scavengers, trailing its innards across the sand. Ripped seat cushions dribbling foam stuffing, metal panels and glass shards littering the beach. A piece of tasteful beige carpet flaps listlessly in the breeze.

In the distance, beyond the wreckage, is a shimmering swipe of pale golden turquoise that must be sea, hough the tide is so far out that Hayley can't make out where the sand ends and the water begins. The chances of them landing on an island rather than plunging into the sea were infinitesimally small, Hayley realizes. Lucky. An odd way to look at it—but they are.

"I shouldn't be here," Hayley says to no one in particular, a stream of giggles burbling suddenly and unstoppably out of her. It seems hopelessly, ridiculously funny. Things like this do not happen to Hayley Larkin; everything in her life is perfect, controlled and calculated down to the very last detail. Or at least that's what it looks like from the outside. She wouldn't be here at all if it weren't for the unwelcome revelation from her guidance counselor that even being on track for valedictorian and maintaining a flawless GPA wasn't enough to guarantee admission to an Ivy League college without diverse extracurriculars to boost her application.

Her head feels light somehow, as if there's too much air inside her skull, and she can't keep hold of her thoughts. Suddenly she's back in that drab, airless office, its gray walls closing in on her even as the sun beats down around her.

She expects the appointment be a formality, a check-in on her excellent progress, a pat on the back. She is on track for Princeton or Harvard; she has ticked every box. A major in English with a stint on the college paper, then internships at the *New York Times* or the *Washington Post* in her junior year and a position as a cub reporter at a local outlet when she graduates. She has it all planned out. So it's a shock when Mr. Curtis looks at her file and frowns. "Right now, on paper, you look like a very...*solitary* candidate. What you need is something that shouts *team player!*"

She hopefully suggests debate club and reminds Mr. Curtis she is already editor of the *Oak Ridge Tribune*, but he frowns and kindly proposes something "a little further from your comfort zone...less academic."

"It needn't be long term," he adds, catching her expression of dismay as she mentally tries to work out how she will cram anything else into her already-packed schedule. "It might even be fun. What's the worst that could happen?"

And suddenly, she is on a windy field one Monday at lunch, tugging her cycling shorts out of her crotch and trying to remember to smile while she high kicks her way awkwardly through her audition routine.

Which (thanks to two dropouts and a nasty bout of strep throat) lets her scrape into the bottom of the cheerleading squad. Which, in turn, leads her here. To this beach.

And suddenly she is back on it, this beach covered in vomit and blood and twisted metal.

Hayley Larkin does not belong on this beach.

The strange thing is that she cannot seem to move. Distantly, she is aware of activity around her. Shannon is moving purposefully from Brian to Jessa, lifting their wrists to check pulses, bending down low to feel their breath on her cheek. Jason has wrapped a wet basketball jersey around his face as a makeshift smoke mask and is diving in and out of the plane's wreckage, pulling out anything that might be useful or edible and piling it high on the beach. With the sun shining on his muscular, lightly tanned arms and swept-back blond hair, he looks like something out of a superhero movie.

I always thought I would be the unlikely superhero, Hayley thinks vaguely, as she feels the sand prickle the backs of her thighs. Sure, she might be the weakest link in the squad, the last one invited to social events, more likely to attend prom as a student reporter than somebody's date. But she's always somehow believed that when it came down to it, when "real life" started, she'd show them all. She'd secretly pictured herself one day becoming the front-page story instead of the person who wrote it. Graciously accepting her Pulitzer for blowing a sex trafficking ring or a corruption scandal wide open while the cheerleaders, weirdly still in their teens, stood by, mouths open, pom-poms hanging limply. She'd daydreamed it in the long, tedious hours sitting in hotel rooms on the tour, pretending to be glad to have the time to study while she listened to the other girls shrieking with laughter at TikToks of cats dubbed to look like they were singing pop songs.

Yet still she cannot move. She wants to sit here with the solid tree against her back for as long as it takes until things don't feel like they are spinning out of control anymore.

She sees May gently ease Jessa's head onto a folded sweatshirt and walk over to help Jason sort through the growing heap of supplies next to the plane. Her willowy frame bends and straightens, bends and straightens as she goes through the items.

Hayley watches as May stacks a small tower of those foil-covered trays of plane food, watches as they slide down in all directions, crashing into the sand. She sees the exasperation on May's face as she wipes beads of sweat from the bridge of her nose, running her hand over her perfectly groomed black eyebrows. Numbly, Hayley thinks that the food shouldn't be left there in the sun. Someone should carry it into the shade. But she can't move.

"It'll spoil so quickly in this heat," her mom tuts unexpectedly in her head.

Mom.

Hayley sees her walking toward the front door, frowning, glancing at her watch. Taking off her glasses, wiping them automatically on her sleeve and tucking them into the collar of her sweater. Swiping her dark blond hair back over her shoulder with one hand as she reaches for the doorknob with the other. Sees the panic flicker on her face as red-and-blue lights cross her forehead. Sees Dad appear behind her at the open front door, place a hand on her shoulder, start barking urgent questions at the police officer as Mom stays silent. Sees the tension in the tendons of his neck, stiffening beneath the short salt-and-pepper hair, jaw clenching, dark brown skin carefully clean shaven.

"A phone," she croaks, surprised to find how sore her throat is. "Does anyone still have their phone?" Shannon looks up from where she's kneeling beside Brian, one dark eyebrow raised in the sort of patronizing expression Hayley has become far too accustomed to in cheer practice.

"Don't you think we've already tried? No signal," she replies curtly, tossing her phone into the sand at Hayley's feet with a soft thud. Shannon and Jason grin cheesily in the lock screen picture, all wide white smiles, his teeth practically sparkling. They look like an ad for all-American high school sweethearts. Shannon's right. No bars.

Shannon moves practiced hands to Hayley's ankle, rotating it expertly as Hayley winces and draws a sharp breath. "It's swollen, but it's probably just a sprain. You wouldn't be able to put any weight on it if it was broken." And Hayley's so grateful that someone is taking charge, touching her with firm, confident fingers that show her limbs where to move and when, that she doesn't find Shannon's know-it-all tone as annoying as usual. "The soreness in your chest is probably from smoke inhalation," Shannon adds, almost smugly. "Lucky I got my first aid extension certificate last month."

"Or bruising from the crash?" Hayley asks, indicating a nasty bruise blooming below Shannon's collarbone.

"Maybe," Shannon agrees, handing Hayley an open bottle of water. She takes it and swigs great gulps, then suddenly stops, the bottle still raised to her lips.

"Should we be…" It sounds so silly, so melodramatic. "Should we be saving our water?" she asks uncertainly.

"I don't think it's going to come to starvation rations." Shannon smirks. "It's the Gulf of Mexico, not the Bermuda Triangle—I'd be surprised if someone hasn't found us by sunset." She bustles off again.

"Speaking of sunset…" Hayley glances at the horizon. The sun pulses egg-yolk orange, lower in the sky now, and the incoming tide, while still distant, has crept closer, so that she can see a faint white line where the frothy edges of the waves meet the shore.

Hayley passes the water bottle to Jason and he swigs thirstily, wiping his lip with the back of his hand, his eyes on Shannon, who is hovering over Jessa again.

"So," he says, sitting down in the sand with his legs out in front of him, knees bent. Hayley notices little grains of sand hanging on to his sun-bleached blond leg hairs. They all turn toward him instinctively. It's as if, with Coach Erickson gone, he's the natural source of authority. As if being captain on the court has anything at all to do with this. As if a carefully crafted defensive play is going to help them now. Hayley feels giggles fizzing inside her again. It is all so completely absurd.

Jason holds up seven fingers. "Shannon, Hayley, May, me—all okay or near enough." He nods at each of them, folding down his fingers one by one as he checks them off.

"Elliot too, though I don't know where he's gone." He folds down the thumb, leaving a curled fist and two fingers still sticking up on the other hand. "Jessa—hurt but conscious." They all turn to look at Jessa, curled in a fetal position, her long, glossy twists splayed on the sand, lips slightly parted to reveal the gap between her front teeth. There's some swelling around her shoulder, but the blood on her upper arm has congealed to a dark paste.

A small fly lands inquisitively at the edge of the dark blood. May brushes it away angrily, glaring at the others as if all this is their fault. Jessa has always been hers, as long as anyone can remember. They've been a pair since day one of first grade, fingers interlaced in a wordless playground pact before the bell even rang. Jessa's gentle, considered thoroughness and May's spiky, scrappy boldness somehow fit together and made a whole.

"The mouth on that girl," Hayley's mom had gasped, half admiring, half disapproving, after she'd stopped by to pick up Hayley after practice one night just in time to hear May unleash a stream of profanities in the direction of a truck that had blocked her in the parking lot. Hayley has never seen May without a comeback. But she looks shrunken and lost without Jessa awake and alert by her side. Her straight black hair hangs around her shoulders like a silk curtain, like she's already in mourning. Her delicate features look crumpled, long black eyelashes shining with tears.

They all stare at the seventh unchecked finger. Jason doesn't need to say it. Brian lies motionless in the shade, his meaty calves and forearms limp, his thick neck looking strangely delicate and vulnerable.

Only a short while ago, they'd been teasing him on the plane for having to wear his basketball jersey because he'd run out of clean clothes two days before the end of the tour. He grinned proudly and started explaining how underwear lasts twice as long if you turn it inside out, at which point Hayley very deliberately stopped listening.

Now Brian's arms and legs glow an angry red, his fair skin already burning under the relentless sun. The pale brown freckles that usually dust his round cheeks have been swallowed by the new rose pallor, which clashes with the ginger of his messy curls.

"He's breathing," Jason says, a little too loudly. "Maybe he just needs to sleep it off." Hayley resists the urge to point out that he hasn't regained consciousness yet; the situation is significantly more serious than an extended nap. She looks at Brian's slack face again and feels a wave of nausea rise in the base of her throat. She swallows it down and looks away.

"OH MY GOD, NAKED TWIN LESBIANS!" Jason shouts suddenly, leaning toward Brian and shaking his leg. Brian's head lolls a little, his eyes remaining closed.

"Yeah, he's genuinely unconscious." Jason smirks, apparently oblivious to the fact that he's the only one who seems to find this amusing.

"We queer women don't only exist for your amusement, Jason, you might be shocked to hear," May mutters without looking up. And Jason at least has the grace to look awkward, though he doesn't apologize.

"Has anybody seen Coach Erickson? Or the pilot?" Hayley asks.

Jason shakes his head. "I walked pretty deep into the trees looking for Brian. He must have been thrown farther from the wreckage because he wasn't wearing his seat belt. But there was no sign of anyone else or the front of the plane."

"It probably broke away much earlier," Shannon says grimly, looking out to sea. Her pale, angular face is serious, dark circles making her eye sockets look hollow and gaunt where usually she exudes an unusual kind of sharp glamour. "That grinding, screeching noise started a good minute or two before we crashed. The rest of the plane could be miles away."

"Or it could be somewhere else on the island," May snaps. "They could be injured, or worse—they might need our help."

"I don't think so, May," says a quiet voice, and Elliot steps out of the bushes, his curly, chestnut-brown hair wild, his arms piled with sticks and twigs. There's a thin diagonal cut across his right cheekbone, and his knee-length khaki shorts are torn.

He bends down, carefully piling the wood on the sand. "There's a pretty steep incline to the north." He jerks his head back toward the trees and to the right. "I climbed up far enough to get a sense of the whole island, and I didn't see anybody else or anything that looked like it was from the plane. There's a lot of tree cover across the center of the island, so I guess it's possible there's something I didn't spot if part of the plane went down there…but I'd still expect to see some debris, broken branches…something. I think Shannon's right. We're on our own."

There's a surprised silence. Hayley isn't sure she's ever heard Elliot talk uninterrupted for that long. She sees a sudden flash of him skulking into the first joint practice at the start of the semester, head bowed, not meeting anyone's eye.

Then the reality of what he has said hits her like a cold blast. *On our own.* Stranded. Stuck. The enormity of it is so great she almost can't think about it at all. She looks down at her bloodied hand and notices her torn fingernail is beginning to throb. Somehow it's easier to focus on that one small thing, the immediate pain, than it is to contemplate what Elliot has told them. There's a wave of panic hovering, threatening to completely overwhelm her. She picks at the nail and earns herself a sharp stab of pain. The panic recedes a little.

"How do you know that's north?" May blurts it at Elliot like she wants to pick a fight. Hayley looks at May's dark, glinting eyes and knows she isn't the only one at risk of being swept away by that wave of fear.

Elliot holds out his arm, showing them a worn leather watch whose soft, threadbare strap is the same sandy golden brown as his skin. "You can work it out by pointing the hour hand at the sun. A line drawn between the hour hand and twelve points south." The others stare at him. "My family camps. A lot," he adds awkwardly.

"Anyway." Elliot crouches and starts arranging little twigs and scraps of wood in a pyramid. "It's going to get dark and cold pretty quickly once the sun goes down. And if anyone comes looking for us, a fire is the best way to get their attention."

Hayley feels like an idiot. They've been here for hours—why didn't any of them think of a fire?

"Nobody has a lighter," Jason scoffs, shifting his weight forward like he wants to draw the others back toward him. Heads obediently swivel in his direction. On the court, Elliot might've ducked his head in embarrassment, danced to Jason's tune, but here he ignores him, walking over to the pile of supplies by the plane.

"I said there aren't any lighters or matches, man," Jason repeats, a tougher note in his voice daring Elliot to contradict him.

Elliot picks up a plastic water bottle, murmurs to himself, and starts walking up and down the beach, sifting through the debris. With a grunt of satisfaction, he pulls his sketchbook out from under a pile of clothes and shoes, flicking past a half-finished picture of them sitting in the back of the plane, and carefully rips out a piece of paper covered in dark pencil lines.

Hayley leans forward to watch, wondering how he can manage to stay so calm. Bending close to the tepee of twigs, Elliot folds the paper in two and holds it in his left hand, then slowly tilts the water bottle back and forth using his right hand. A bright spot of light appears on the paper, a circle that grows and shrinks as he experimentally moves the bottle around. When the light is at its brightest, a tiny concentrated pinprick, he holds it still, and almost immediately the paper begins to smolder and smoke. A dime-size circle scorches out from the center, the edges curling white. Jason raises his eyebrows and puts his arm around Shannon's waist. "Nice trick, Cub Scout."

Elliot's lip twitches with a tiny smile as he gently waves the paper back and forth, feeding it oxygen, patiently encouraging it until an orange flame flickers up. He pokes it between the twigs he's arranged, pulling a handful of dry, dead grass from his pocket and stuffing it into the gaps.

Elliot puts his cheek to the sand and blows, and a little spiral of bluish smoke rises up again, chased by tiny tongues of flame licking at the twigs.

There's a low whistle. "Impressive," croaks a voice. Brian is struggling to raise himself up on one elbow.

Hayley feels the relief thrum warm in her chest.

"Fuck's sake, Brian. Do you have any idea how long you've been out?" Jason's voice is rough—accusing, even. He wipes his hand swiftly across his face and frowns at Brian like he's committed five fouls in a game.

Brian grins sheepishly. "Where are we? What happened?" He looks around, taking in his surroundings, and mutters, "Jesus." He raises his hand to the back of his head with a wince and then gulps greedily from the water bottle Jason shoves toward him.

"The plane crashed," Shannon says simply. "We're on an island."

"Is everyone okay?"

"Everyone except Jessa. She's been conscious, but her arm is hurt. We don't know about Coach Erickson and the pilot. We think they went down somewhere else."

Brian's gaze wanders from the fire to the trees to the plane, then out over the beach toward the sea. The heat of the sun is waning now, a breeze rushing up the beach and into the canopy above them as if to whisper that the sea is coming, coming. They can smell it—the wet, fresh scent of salt and seaweed that tethers Hayley to reality, forces her to acknowledge that this is actually happening.

Brian is eyeing Jessa. "Is it just her arm? Because I saw something like this on *Grey's Anatomy* where they thought the guy was totally fine because he was awake and talking, but then he had a delayed brain hemorrhage and he just died." Brian snaps his fingers. "Like that."

"Oh, good." Shannon rolls her eyes. "I didn't realize we had a qualified brain doctor with us."

May's eyes shoot daggers at Brian as he shuffles into a sitting position, wincing and rotating his head from side to side.

"What? They have medical advisers to make it realistic, you know."

It's quiet around the fire as they peel back the metal foil from the food trays and start picking at the contents with plastic forks. Cold macaroni and cheese isn't exactly appealing, but at least it fills their stomachs. Hayley pulls the plastic wrapper off a small bread roll and is about to take a bite when Elliot walks out of the trees carrying another large armful of sticks, which he dumps in a pile near the fire.

"What are you all doing?" Elliot pants, gaping at them.

They blink at him, this new, different Elliot who isn't sitting on the sidelines with his patched backpack guarding the seat next to him, listening silently to post-practice pep talks, emerging from the locker room like a ghost after the other boys have tumbled out in a loud group. They are so used to not noticing him that nobody even saw him go, and his return takes them by surprise.

"What do you mean, what are we doing?" Shannon looks at her macaroni and wrinkles her nose "We're eating dinner, if you can call it that."

"Guys," Elliot speaks urgently, angrily. "You can't just eat everything. We have no idea how long we're going to be stuck here. We need to ration our food and liquids."

"Oh, come on, man," Jason drawls, taking a bite of a candy bar he has helped himself to from the supply pile.

"No, 'man,' *you* come on," Elliot shoots back. "The plane only had enough food on board for one meal, plus whatever snacks people had on them. That's it. How long do you think we're going to last if we eat it all at once?"

There's an uncomfortable silence.

"It's only a matter of time till someone finds us," Jason says dismissively. "My parents are going to have people out looking, believe me."

"I'm sure they will," Elliot retorts drily. "But do you have any idea how big the Gulf of Mexico is? How long it could take? We're talking about more than a million square miles."

"They know our flight path," Hayley points out, swallowing a gelatinous mouthful of macaroni and trying to quell the rising fear Elliot's words are igniting in her stomach. "Houston to Miami. That'll narrow it down."

"Sure, if we'd stayed on it. But who knows how far we zigzagged or what went off course with the plane? We have no idea whether the radio transmitter was still working, whether the pilot was able to issue a Mayday call…" Elliot frowns. "Even in the act of falling out of the sky, the plane could have covered miles and miles! And they might have lost track of us long before we went down."

"Aren't we on a barrier island?" May asks uncertainly. "I assumed we were somewhere close to land, just not close enough to see it."

Elliot shakes his head. "I've been fishing off some of the barrier islands with my dad. They're basically just big sandbars. They're flat, grassy." He waves his hand at the thick trees behind them and the darkening shadow where the land rises to the right. "Nothing like this."

"Right." Jason claps his hands loudly, speaking over Elliot. "I think we need a plan. Let's assume it could be a few days before we're rescued. We need to do an inventory of our supplies and ration them out."

There are six untouched, foil-covered plane dinners left in the pile and a smattering of squashed snacks.

"Each tray has a carton of macaroni, a salad, a bread roll, crackers, and cheese," Jason announces. "Let's call that four portions of food." He pauses, and Hayley physically bites her tongue to stop herself from doing the sum for him. "Twenty-four portions in all. There's seven of us, so that's enough for three days if we each eat just one portion per day. Plus two Snickers, a Slim Jim, and three bags of Cheetos. There's no way it'll take them more than three days to find us."

"They better find us faster," Brian mutters. "This puny salad is not a day's worth of calories. Although," he says, brightening, "if Jessa doesn't wake up tomorrow, I call her macaroni."

"What?" he asks defensively as the others look at him in horror. "I'm not saying I don't *want* her to wake up...I'm just saying there'll be more food to go around if she doesn't. It's a simple fact."

"What about water?" Hayley interrupts. "It's more important than food, isn't it?"

They separate the pile of supplies into four sections. Food, liquids, clothing, and things like cushions and towels that they can use for bedding. There are twelve unopened bottles of water left. Hayley feels her chest tightening as she does the math. Four bottles a day if they're rescued in the next three days. Four between seven. Less than a bottle each per day.

"We should keep the water all in one place," Shannon says as Jason stuffs the rest of the candy bar in his mouth. "Make sure it's shared out fairly."

"Good idea, sweetie." Jason nods. "You be in charge of that, okay?"

Shannon doesn't reply. She begins stacking the water bottles methodically. "And we should stay out of the sun," Hayley adds, "then we'll dehydrate less quickly."

She feels an automatic rush of relief that she's thought of something to contribute, then realizes how ridiculous the impulse is. It's not debate club. Nobody here is being graded. "That's all settled, then," Hayley says. "Nobody eats or drinks alone. We'll put the food and water in the bushes to keep it cool."

"What about animals?" May's voice is uncharacteristically small and uncertain. "How do we know it won't get eaten by wild animals?" she repeats, slumping down next to Jessa and pulling her knees to her chest. "How do we even know it's safe to sleep out here?" She gestures to the beach, where the tide has crept much closer, little waves running up the sand and stopping about thirty yards away. "Who's going to keep Jessa safe in the night? What if something smells her blood—" Her voice is rising, and there are tears in her throat though her eyes look fierce. Hayley wants to hug her, to tell her it'll all be okay. Except that she doesn't know whether it will be, and she knows that May would hate a hug, shrugging off the pity as if it burned her skin.

And underneath her sympathy, her urge to comfort, there's a colder, selfish part of her that just wants May to shut up, to stop pointing out problems. She wants Elliot to stop going on about search areas, wants to stop counting bottles of water over and over again in her head. A part of her that doesn't want to accept what has happened or start thinking about the reality of what it means. And a part of her that really, really doesn't want to think about wild animals.

"It's okay, May." Jessa has woken and is suddenly sitting up next to her best friend, looking shaken but awake, uninjured arm around May's waist, where anyone else's would have been scornfully rejected. The very fact that she's conscious is the shot of relief they all desperately need. "We can sleep in shifts."

"Here's what we should do." Jason stands up, and Brian instinctively lumbers to his feet, leaning toward him, wheezing a little. It almost looks as if they're going into a tactical huddle on the deserted beach.

Jason grabs Elliot's arm, and Hayley realizes he's the only one with an old-school wristwatch. Jessa and Jason both have Apple watches, and the others just rely on their phones. It won't be long before the batteries die.

"It's just after seven," Jason says, "and sunset probably isn't far off." Elliot looks as if he's about to say something but doesn't. "So, Brian and I will stay awake until ten, then wake Elliot. He can take the next shift until one, then wake us. We'll keep watch until four then switch again." The others nod in agreement.

"And what are we, chopped liver?" Hayley asks, taking herself by surprise. The boys blink at her.

"No offense but this is a guy's job." Jason laughs. "Are you really going to chase off a wild dog or a boar or whatever with no weapon?"

"Are *you*?" Hayley retorts, her confidence growing. "What are you going to do, flirt it to death?"

"They're offering to protect us," Shannon mutters. "There's no need to start burning our bras. We should just be grateful." Jason grins, reaching out a hand to touch her hair.

"We need weapons. We can sharpen some sticks from the

forest," Brian suggests enthusiastically as Hayley glowers. He crashes off into the undergrowth, followed by Jason, leaving Elliot with the girls.

"The tide won't come up much higher," he says to May, as if the last few minutes' conversation never happened. "You see the line of debris just there?" He walks down the beach beyond the plane, a few yards from where the waves are rushing up the sand. When they look closely, there's a line of broken shells, little pieces of driftwood, and scraps of seaweed stretching the length of the beach. "That shows you where the tide was at its highest point," Elliot explains. "It won't reach us if we sleep up near the trees."

May nods with a nonchalance Hayley suspects might be fake.

"As for animals, I don't think it's likely there are any large predators on this island." Elliot looks back into the forest. "I've been quite far into the trees and haven't seen any tracks, and the island isn't very big. You could cover the whole thing in a few hours. Animals aren't what we need to be worrying about."

"What do we need to be worrying about, Elliot?" Hayley asks in a low voice.

"Dehydration," Elliot replies simply. "We can survive weeks without food but only a few days without water. And I'm really glad everyone's so optimistic, I hope you're right, but honestly, we have no guarantee of when we might be found. If it looks like we're going to run out of water, we need to do something about it before that happens—plan ahead before it's too late."

There's a long silence. Hayley knows he is right. But the others look skeptical. None of them are used to hearing Elliot speak, let alone taking orders from him. She wants to back him up, tell them they have to listen. But that means letting in the fears at the very edges of her mind, the ones tap-tap-tapping to get in and willing her to absolutely lose her shit. Hayley Larkin doesn't lose her shit. She doesn't panic or lose control. So she stands there, looking at Elliot, and says nothing.

"Fine." Elliot spits the word out sharply, but it's swallowed by the sand's softness. He turns on his heel and starts rifling through the supplies, tugging at something. It's the plastic drawstring bag that held the practice balls, except the balls are all long gone. For a moment, Hayley pictures them raining from the sky, dropping into the waves like cannonballs. But then she sees other things dropping, like Coach Erickson's body, and feeling sick, she turns away. Elliot disappears again into the trees.

Night comes suddenly, just as Elliot said it would. It's not a slow, lingering beach sunset like the ones in the movies. The night swallows them whole. And it's cold—colder than they could possibly have imagined. Elliot hasn't come back when Hayley curls into herself under a coat, huddling near the fire and waiting for sleep to come. Through her eyelashes, she watches Jason marching up and down, clutching a freshly broken branch, his strides long and his knuckles clenched.

But sleep doesn't arrive. And the island comes alive at

night, becomes a roiling, writhing, terrible thing, outraged at their presence. The sand belches tiny flies that tap-dance across Hayley's flesh with heels like tiny needles. They want to claim her body and gnaw away at it until the beach is smooth and untouched once again. She can't say when the noise starts exactly, only that suddenly it's around her and inside her all at once, a rhythmic, vibrating denseness that she can feel in the back of her jaw, in her teeth.

She shifts uncomfortably, trying to find a position where her shoulder blades and hip bones aren't grinding uncomfortably against the sand. Listening to the steady *thud, thud, thud* of Jason's footsteps as they recede and approach. The sea seems to be farther away again, its cycles governed by a timetable she doesn't recognize, its low, uneven whispering like a conversation just out of earshot, leaving her straining to hear. And the feeling that the island is closing ranks against her—the sand and the sea and the invisible chorus of rasping, scuttling creatures all united in harmony—is all too familiar.

Suddenly, she's back in the school gym, echoing with shoe squeaks and rank with the smell of rubber and slightly damp tumbling mats. Standing awkwardly in the corner, panic slowly rising as she realizes she's wearing the wrong thing. Tugging down the edges of the purple nylon pleated skirt, wishing the tank top emblazoned with the Oak Ridge crest came below her belly button. Everyone else is in leggings, oversize T-shirts, or slouchy sweaters. May in a graceful front split position, back arched forwards, arms extended. Shannon pacing out a new routine, her face lined with concentration.

Jessa puts a gentle hand on Hayley's shoulder and hands her a spare T-shirt. "Sweats are fine for practice. You'll know for next time."

"Looking good, new girl." Jason wolf whistles. "Didn't know it was dress-up Friday!" Hayley glances instinctively at Shannon, but her back is turned, hunched over some complicated diagrams. Brian and some of the other boys snigger appreciatively, circling Hayley like hyenas.

"Knock it off, pigs," Jessa shouts, rolling her eyes.

"She might like it, Jessa." Brian leers, his eyes creeping up Hayley's thighs. "Not every cheerleader's as uptight as the Virgin Mary." He gestures to the crucifix hanging on a fine silver chain around Jessa's neck, and she stiffens, flipping it under her top.

"The Virgin Mary got knocked up outside marriage, you tool." Jason takes careful aim and bounces a basketball off the back of Brian's head before catching it and dribbling up the court to shoot. Brian stumbles, cursing, behind him.

"Uh, it was an immaculate conception," Hayley mutters, unable to stop herself.

"Impractical come what now?" Brian mimics her, his voice high and reedy.

"Never mind," Hayley mumbles, grateful for the interruption when Coach Erickson arrives, gesturing the boys over to the benches, and Coach Robinson walks in behind him to start cheer practice.

"Thanks," Hayley murmurs as Jessa stands next to her in the huddle.

"Let us know if you're going to need a babysitter every practice," Shannon whispers. "We'll need to know in advance if we've got to bring an extra squad member with us to hold your hand."

Hayley's stomach curls up at the edges, shrinking in humiliation.

Trying to block out the memory, Hayley looks around the circle. She can hear a soft, repetitive whisper, almost like a chant. May and Jessa are a couple of yards away, flickering in and out of view as the flames from the campfire rise and fall. They're curled together in a tight nest fashioned from spare pieces of clothing. Behind them, she can just see the curve of Shannon's back, unmoving. May is fast asleep, her face smooth and peaceful, her breathing slow and steady. Hayley watches the smooth, light fawn skin rise and fall beneath her collarbones. But Jessa is staring into the fire, her necklace grasped between her fingers, murmuring the same prayer over and over again.

DAY 2

THERE'S GENTLE WARMTH, A SOFT SWISHING NOISE, AND the rich, savory smell of woodsmoke. Just for a moment, Hayley is lying in her own bed with her eyes closed, the warm weekend sun streaming through her window, her stomach awakened by the smell of Dad barbecuing bacon outside. In a minute, she'll stretch and open her eyes, pull on a fluffy robe, and slouch downstairs to perch on a high stool by the breakfast bar, sipping orange juice while she watches Mom flip perfect, plump pancakes. She'll slide them onto a serving plate in a great warm pile, and they'll head outside. Dad'll take the plate and make the same joke he always does: "Thanks, but what are you two going to eat?"

But she can't stay there; her body won't let her linger. The illusion disperses like smoke as the physical pull of pain drags her back to the here and now. Something hard is sticking into her back. Her ankle throbs and her hands are sore. She itches all over. There are aches in places she didn't even know could ache, and for someone who went from a total nonathlete to a member of a cheer squad (okay, the weakest member, but still) in less than two months, that is really saying something.

Screaming.

Hayley's eyes fly open. Scrabbling to sit up, she scrapes her wrist against a stone.

The shrieks come again, shredding the air. They suddenly multiply, echoing terrifyingly above her. There's a flash of green. Hayley's racing heartbeat begins to slow. The feathery tips of the palm trees are heavy with birds, acid-green and scarlet plumage swirling in the sunshine, sharp cries louder than any birdsong she's ever heard.

Brian is sprawled in the sand, fast asleep. In the center of the group, a few charred sticks are still gently smoking in a circle of gray ash. The fire has been out for some time. May and Jessa are stirring sleepily, cardigans and sweaters tangled between them. Elliot, Jason, and Shannon are nowhere to be seen. With a nasty little surge of panic, Hayley wonders if Elliot ever came back last night.

The sun is already skimming over the sea's mirrored surface, the sky cloudless. It's hot but not uncomfortable yet, just humid enough to stick the hairs to the back of her neck. The sand is still again, the waves running smoothly up and down the beach.

Hayley runs her hands through her rich brown pixie cut, her fingertips discovering a smattering of little bumps on her scalp. Her whole body is dotted with raised bites, screaming to be rubbed and scratched until they bleed.

"Don't scratch it," her mom would tut. "You'll only make it worse."

She staggers to her feet, her muscles protesting sluggishly. Tentatively, she tests her ankle, putting a little weight on it and then a little more, pressing the ball of her foot into the sand. It groans a little, gives a grumpy burst of pain, but then subsides into grudging acceptance as she walks a few steps, deeply relieved to be mobile again.

Out in the distance, a solitary figure is standing in the shimmering water, her silhouette outlined against the amber flood of morning light. Hayley, squinting against the glare, thinks that there's something different about Shannon here on the island. She's more *still* somehow. Watchful. Another silhouette approaches, Jason's solid frame dwarfing Shannon's, her thin shadow almost rippling at the edges. Shannon seems to flinch, turning her head as Jason approaches. Are his hands flailing in the air, or is it just a reflection? The silhouettes seem to writhe, gesticulating as if they're arguing, but Hayley can't see properly. She can't hear anything above the shrieks of the birds and the endless white noise of the waves on the shore, and the sun drills into her retinas until she has to blink and look away.

May stirs and stretches like a cat, unfurling her slim frame and baring her neat, small teeth in a yawn. She sees the sleeping guard and grins, jumping lightly across the sand and landing almost on top of him with a loud bellow: "GOOD MORNING!"

Brian startles to attention, his body snapping rigid in alarm. "Christ's sake, May," he slurs, cradling the back of his head in both hands. "What are you, a goddamn ninja?"

"Oh, nice." May narrows her eyes and juts out her pointed chin. "Because I'm Japanese American I must be a ninja, right?"

"Jesus, that's not what I meant, and you know it." Brian looks uncomfortably at Jessa, who offers him no help. "My head is pounding, I just—"

May bursts out laughing. "Chill, man, I'm kidding." She runs down the beach, past the wreckage of the plane, and splashes straight into the sea with an exhilarated whoop. "Can you believe the others are missing this?" She shrieks and throws herself backward into the waves. "Flying back early lost them the chance of the best vacation they'll ever have!"

They all watch her silently as she begins to sing "Come Alive" at the top of her voice, splashing around. You can almost believe she's having the time of her life, except it feels forced, like she's performing for some inane sunscreen ad. "Let's go wild…" she sings, launching herself into the air and plunging under the water.

None of the others move to join her.

"Oh, come on!" She runs back up the beach, panting, her soaked white cotton skirt and pale pink blouse clinging. "Everybody's okay, Erickson's probably already been rescued, we'll be picked up in a couple of days, and in the meantime, we're on an all-expenses-paid desert-island getaway. This is paradise! We should stay forever! No adults, no rules—"

"No food, no medicine, no way to communicate or let anyone know where we are," Hayley breaks in.

"Don't be such a buzzkill." May waves dismissively at their paltry stockpile of food. Her excitement is too deliberate, her voice a bit too high, like she's trying to persuade herself as much as the others. It would be a little more convincing if the deep scratches from the plane crash weren't standing out like a dark red barcode stamped across her cheek.

As her now-transparent blouse rides up, revealing a flash of muscular, tan stomach, Brian puts his fingers in his mouth and whistles. She immediately responds with a middle finger of her own, so he forms his fingers into a shape and lasciviously begins to lick the space between them.

Hayley sees May's face crumple just a little before she wheels around. And she knows she should say something, knows she should call Brian out, but she hesitates. There's a fear in her that is so familiar it slips around her shoulders like a well-worn shawl. The fear of confrontation. Of ridicule. Of escalation. Of his anger. And she says nothing.

May grabs a towel from the pile of improvised bedding and stalks away down the beach, but the look she throws Brian over her shoulder is one of mingled distrust and real, cold hate.

Then, as if nothing has happened, she spreads the towel ostentatiously on the beach and stretches out in the sun, fanning her wet hair out on the sand to dry.

"So much for staying in the shade," Hayley whispers, but

nobody answers her, and she's not surprised. This new May is appealing, and joining in with her obvious state of denial is tempting. It would be so comforting to block out the crash, Erickson, the possibility of running out of water...to stop worrying.

By midday, Hayley's stomach is clenched tight with hunger, and the single bread roll she has been allotted for the whole day is already a distant memory. When her eyes slide toward the remaining food trays for the third time, she decides she needs to distract herself. There is still no sign of Elliot, which makes her uneasy. She feels untethered here, insecure. If a plane can fall out of the sky, suddenly there are no guarantees anymore. No safety. And as much as Elliot's dire warnings scared her, the idea of not being near him somehow scares her even more. He's the only one who seems to have any idea how to survive.

She sets off in the direction Elliot headed last night, passing Jessa, who's sitting in the shade examining the crusted wound on her arm and tentatively trying to rotate her shoulder, biting her lip in pain.

Hayley finds herself almost immediately tangled in the matted vines and creepers that cover the ground. She has to pick her way forward, stumbling occasionally when she forgets about her ankle and tries to move too quickly, grabbing on to tree trunks for leverage and ripping through patches of thorns that bite at her shins and leave gleaming pearls of blood on her forearms. Once, she freezes as a snake ripples liquidly across the path ahead, paying no attention to her. A few minutes later, she thinks she sees a scorpion glinting on a tree trunk, but it scuttles into the shadows before she can be sure. She shudders and spends the next few minutes swiping phantom insects from her arms and back. Each leaf that brushes her bare shoulder might be a two-inch spider, each weed tickling her ankle a millipede's myriad legs.

There's a smell among the thick plants, a kind of woody, vegetable wetness like the humid tang of her mom's greenhouse. There seems to be less air here than out on the breezy beach, the trees catching any movement in their net of stillness, bearing quiet, slow witness. Some of them are breath-taking, their ancient bark scarred and gnarled, brittle pieces peeling back to reveal softer flesh. They wear their curling necklaces of creepers lightly, the vines reaching effortlessly up to tangle with their branches in the dense canopy. Hayley wonders if another human being has ever been here, feels like she is intruding on something silent and precious. With every footstep she feels she is being somehow weighed, judged by the island.

Which Hayley does it see? The dogged student journalist who chases down leads, holding the school board accountable for failing to keep its promise to recycle waste from the cafeteria? Or the awkward girl on the edge of the crowd, wishing she could find the words to blend in?

She can see herself picking at her chicken burger in the corner of the red leatherette diner booth after their first tour game, wishing she had Jessa's easy laugh or May's quick wit. Watching while Jason ordered for Shannon without even having to ask her what she wanted to eat while May reduced everyone to fits of laughter with her impression of Erickson falling asleep on the bench in the last quarter. Jason dropping his Amex on the table to cover everyone's bill: "Someone else can get the next one. I'm looking at you, Brian, you freeloader." Brian grinning and scarfing his triple burger with chili fries while May pretended to vomit into her milkshake. Elliot claiming not to be hungry, counting out the change for his Diet Coke and putting it in a neat pile next to Jason's card. "But we should talk strategy. Am I the only one who's bothered that we lost that game by thirteen points?"

"Don't worry about it," Brian told him. "It's tour, it doesn't count for anything. It's about the free ride, so loosen up and enjoy it."

As Hayley thinks of this, wondering how it could only have been six days ago, she hears a raspy gnawing sound. There's a thud and a muffled curse from her left. She turns away from the incline where the trees start to rise, pushing farther through the bushes on the flatter terrain instead. Elliot is sitting on the ground, sucking the palm of his hand. It can't be called a clearing exactly—the vegetation is too dense for that. But next to him there's a sort of gap where two saplings have been roughly broken off at shoulder height, a third bent and splintered but still standing.

Elliot looks up and holds out a large stone with a sharp, narrow edge. "Got myself by mistake," he grunts. Hayley wordlessly takes the stone and starts to attack the tree trunk. It's a lot harder than she expects. The fibrous trunk is tough and sinewy, and hacking at it makes no progress whatsoever. "Like a saw," Elliot offers, and she starts to rub at it with the edge of the stone instead, feeling the fibers give way one by one like cutting through a thick rope. Her hands, already cut and sore, start to chafe against the stone, but she doesn't stop until she's panting and hot in the cheeks. She leans against the trunk for a minute, then starts again, painstakingly making a few inches of progress at a time. She wonders how long Elliot's been at it.

"Here." He takes the stone from her, his hand wrapped in a bandana from his pocket, and starts sawing away again.

Hayley watches his back, taut with the effort, his narrow shoulder blades lifting his thin gray T-shirt away from his smooth skin. He's different here too. Her eyes are drawn to the damp hair that curls at the base of his neck, the sinews of his hip tautening above the waistband of his scruffy khaki shorts.

She shakes her head and looks away. "What are we doing?" she asks.

"Trying to make a water collection station," he gasps without looking up. Hayley sees the drawstring bag lying on the ground and understands the plan, though she can't see how he intends to attach it to the tree stumps.

Experimentally, she picks at one of the thin green vines snaking across the ground. It's wiry, but when she wraps it around each hand and pulls hard, it snaps in two quite easily. "Going to braid them," Elliot pants, looking up. His eyes are golden brown, a metallic amber glint there that Hayley has never been close enough to notice before.

As he continues hacking at the sapling, Hayley starts to forage for vines, tracing them across the ground and around tree trunks, gathering the longest ones she can find. When she's collected three, she ties the ends in a firm knot, clamps it between her knees, and begins to braid.

They work in a silence that is broken only by Elliot's heavy breathing, the buzzing of insects, and the occasional shriek of a bird.

"So, why'd you wait until eleventh grade to try out for the team?" she asks.

Everyone was kind of surprised when Elliot signed up for the tour squad since he wasn't exactly jock material. But he turned out to be a natural shooting guard, his instinctive ball handling and ability to hit three-pointers causing something of a sensation at tryouts.

The steady rhythm of his stone grinding against the tree fibers pauses, stutters, resumes.

"Couldn't afford it before."

Hayley, expecting a different answer, feels stupid and embarrassed. Suddenly, the worn, almost threadbare clothes she'd always taken for a snobbish aesthetic choice, his absences when the team went to a diner after practice, even the out-of-control curls make more sense. She's glad he has his back to her as she composes her face, hiding her surprise.

But then he turns, shrugs like he's letting go of something, and looks her straight in the eye.

"I can only play in the off-season because I work a part-time job with the groundskeeper after school and on weekends. The past few years, tour team members have paid for their own flights, which ruled me out. But it was different this year when Jason's parents offered their firm's jets."

"I didn't know."

"Yeah, well, it's not exactly something you advertise at a school like ours."

Suddenly, Hayley pictures Elliot bent over a lawn mower in a pair of mud-covered boots, watching through his curls as the other kids start their cars or jump into their parents' SUVs at the end of the school day. Oak Ridge is one of the most prestigious private high schools in the state. It's close enough to Miami for the wealthy business owners and real estate magnates whose kids attend the school, near enough to the coast for the students to get a local reputation for lavish beachfront parties with occasionally scandalous outcomes.

"Hope nobody from that firm needs to fly anywhere anytime soon," Hayley jokes, trying to break the tension. "I wonder if they'll be liable for the crash…"

"I doubt it," says Elliot shortly, turning back to his task. "People like that tend to protect themselves."

"It would be pretty ironic," she concedes, "Jason's dad founding one of the most successful law firms in the country and then getting sued himself. I wonder how much you have to pay out for a plane crash?"

"Depends on whether anyone ever finds us alive or not," Elliot replies without turning around, and Hayley falls silent, seeing those blue lights again, Dad's hand clenched on Mom's shoulder.

By the time Elliot finally rips through the last stubborn piece of bark and punches the air in satisfaction, Hayley has braided two long, tough lengths of vine "rope." Elliot runs them through his hands and nods his approval. "We can use the drawstring from the bag for the third one."

He carefully removes the drawstring, spreads the plastic bag out flat, and then lashes it to the three tree stumps in a rough triangle, leaving enough slack for it to sag in the middle, creating an improvised basin suspended about two feet off the ground.

"Looks great."

"Sure," says Elliot, "if it actually rains." They both look up at the sky through the canopy of leaves. There's not a cloud in sight. Hayley can feel the thirst like dry clay cracking in the walls of her throat, sticking her tongue to the roof of her mouth.

Apparently she's not alone. Before they even get back to the beach, they can hear a cacophony of raised voices. They look at each other and start to move faster, stumbling over rocks and plants.

"—was supposed to be for everybody, you selfish asshole!" It's May's voice, sharp and fierce. She's leaning forward, fists clenched at her sides, screaming furiously into Brian's face.

"—not that big of a deal—" Brian is protesting, his hands raised defensively.

"—point is knowing we can trust each other—" comes Jessa's voice softly, half drowned out by the others.

"—time of the month?" Brian shoots churlishly at May, who looks like she's inches away from raining a hail of blows down on him.

"What's going on?" Hayley waves her hands above her head to grab their attention, and they all fall silent.

Shannon sighs like an embarrassed parent admitting to her child's misbehavior. "Brian drank a bottle of water while nobody was looking."

Hayley almost laughs. It sounds like something a kindergarten teacher might say, the punch line to a joke about a petty argument blown out of proportion. Except it isn't petty here. Here, a single bottle of water might be the difference between life and death. She looks at May's contorted face, Jessa's distress, Shannon's scowl.

"You can't just decide things unilaterally," she shoots at Brian, surprising herself.

"Uni-what?" Brian asks sarcastically. "Sorry, we're not all on the honor roll, Hayley."

"On your own," she snaps, feeling heat rising in her neck. "It's not fair. We're in this together."

"Jeez, stop being so melodramatic." Brian tosses the empty water bottle in the sand behind him. "I'm the one who was unconscious with a head injury, remember?" he adds sulkily. Though he has seemed much more like his usual, bullish self today, Hayley realizes with wry relief.

Elliot is looking at Brian like he's never seen him before. "How long is it going to take?" he asks, and his quiet fury is more alarming than May's explosive anger and Jessa's disappointment put together. "Before you all stop pretending and realize how serious our situation is? How long is it going to take until you start to listen?"

DAY 3

IT TAKES THREE DAYS.

By the morning of the third day, the food and snacks are long gone. The water has been administered in stricter rations under watchful eyes since the "incident." But even the careful single swallows, measured out three times a day, have emptied the bottles. And there isn't any sign of rain.

That morning, the last phone battery dies. They all sit around and watch it as it flicks down from 2 percent to 1 percent and finally goes black. Their last remaining connection to the outside world. Dead.

It's a thirst like nothing Hayley has ever experienced before. At first, she swallowed too much. Now her throat is too dry to let her swallow at all. Sometimes it pulses angrily in the back of her throat. Sometimes it blurs into hunger, her stomach gnawing desperately at itself and releasing only the painful warmth of bile. Mostly it makes all of them weak and irritable, sniping and arguing with each other endlessly. They spend a lot of time asleep, finding brief release in semiconscious snatches of rest, but Hayley is plagued by fitful dreams and cruel visions of cool lemonade splashing freely into a glass just out of reach.

She begins to get confused. She watches Shannon and Jason enter the gym together at the first tour game. The crowd goes wild, Jason jogging a lap and waving to the crowd, Shannon cartwheeling and backflipping behind him. They end with a lift, his hand up her skirt, her arms in a triumphant V, both basking in the applause. But that's not right. Hayley isn't in that gym, sitting awkwardly on the bench while the other girls flash megawatt smiles and jump up and down, loving the pageantry and hullaballoo. The roaring in her ears is the rush of water on sand and grit, not the shouts of the home crowd welcoming the touring side.

The island looks soft and gentle as it slowly squeezes the life out of her. The sand is like fine sugar, the heat radiating from it blurring her vision and throbbing in her head.

Elliot is trying to organize them, and Hayley knows she should listen, but it's so hot and she is so tired. She watches a mosquito crawl slowly up her leg, pausing at the prickly fuzz that has begun to regrow in the cleft next to her kneecap. She doesn't have the energy to care if it bites her or not.

"We have to split up," Elliot is saying wearily. "We should have been making survival plans from the moment we arrived. Now we're playing catch-up."

"All those who vote we survive by killing Elliot in his sleep and drinking his blood, raise your hands," croaks Jason. "What? Too soon?" Hayley shudders and wonders if it is really cold or if her body is just starting to shut down.

Elliot hesitates, but ignores Jason, turning to the others instead. Behind him, Hayley thinks Jason looks like a lion lounging in the heat, powerful but prone, lacking the energy to lift a paw and take a swipe at the...what kind of animal would Elliot be? Her brain is too frazzled to finish the thought.

"The most urgent thing is finding something to drink. We can't just keep waiting and hoping. We have to act now, before it's too late. The island's covered in palms: there could be coconuts somewhere. I've been looking, but there's too much ground for me to cover on my own. We should search through the denser vegetation for fruit trees or bushes and check for any sources of fresh water."

He pauses and looks around, frowning, as if he's waiting for the insults to begin. For the first time, nobody contradicts him or sneers. He looks a little surprised, then nods.

"After that," he says, standing up a little straighter, "we should focus on ways to signal to rescuers. We need to collect a huge pile of wood for the fire and make an SOS sign on the beach that's big enough to be seen from the air. And we should make some kind of shelter for sleeping in. We don't know what the weather's going to do, and we really need to be prepared."

Brian picks at the peeling skin on his sunburned forehead. "Maybe Elliot's got a point," he mumbles, looking down at the sand, his head turned slightly away from Jason. "I could really use some fruit juice right about now."

Hayley watches as Jason's face contorts in quick, betrayed fury, then flickers through a range of expressions, like he's choosing which one to wear. For the briefest moment, she wonders if he's going to cry.

"Nice idea, Brian, maybe you should visit the juice bar with the girls." Jason laughs, sweeping his golden hair out of his eyes. "You stay here and rest, babe," he says loudly to Shannon without looking at her. "I'll get the wood for the fire." And he turns and crashes noisily into the trees, jolting Hayley out of the heavy daze that has settled on her like a blanket.

"Brian, you and I should head to the opposite side of the island," Elliot says urgently as Jason retreats. "The coconut palms are more likely to be along the beach."

He turns to Hayley. "Can you guys look for fruit and make the SOS?"

She nods wearily, dragging herself to her feet.

"Jessa and I will look for fruit," May volunteers, and Hayley looks at Shannon, who hasn't moved since Jason left. She shrugs. "Hayley and I will do the SOS then, I guess."

"Look for any edible fruits or roots, any water source," Elliot tells Jessa and May. "But don't eat anything you don't recognize. Bring it back here first. Start with the trees and bushes to the south."

May looks at him expectantly.

"That way." He points, turning to the tree line and waving his hand to the left. "It's where the trees are thickest, and the part of the island we've explored the least."

Jessa stands next to May, putting a hand on her best friend's shoulder and gently pushing her to face the ocean.

"Look," she says, "this beach faces east—that's why we see the sun rise over the sea in the morning." She rotates 180 degrees to face the tree line, May swiveling with her. "Brian and Elliot are going straight across to see if there are coconuts on the beach on the other side of the island, the west side."

Elliot points to the right. "The land rises to the north, and there are fewer bushes or trees. That's where I climbed up on the first day to get a bird's-eye view."

Jessa turns May ninety degrees left. "So south is the jungly side, where the trees and bushes are thickest and there's the best chance of finding fruit or water."

"The SOS needs to be really eye-catching, as big as you can," Elliot tells Shannon and Hayley.

"Oh really?" Shannon's voice is biting, a shade of her usual sardonic sharpness returning through the exhaustion and thirst. "Because I was going to write 'NOTHING TO SEE HERE. PLEASE CONTINUE ON' in really tiny letters."

"Right." Elliot smiles awkwardly, caught somehow between his unexpected leadership role and his usual detached silence. "Well, good luck."

Jessa and May haul an empty backpack from the pile of

supplies still heaped on the beach and set off into the trees behind Brian and Elliot, soon peeling off to the left and disappearing into the bushes.

"OW!" May yelps, her surprised pain floating out loud and clear. "If Jason thinks this is the easy option, he did not account for thorns," she mutters furiously, her voice fading as she moves farther away.

Hayley turns awkwardly to Shannon. "Shall we?"

Time crawls. Hayley and Shannon slowly pile wood and rocks at the edge of the tree line, working in the shade for as long as they can. When they've collected a mound of materials, they drag it down the beach piled on a towel, Hayley tugging at the front corners and Shannon walking behind, holding the pile steady and collecting the sticks that tumble off.

They lug the heavy rocks painstakingly across the sand, then start tracing out the letters two yards tall, carefully keeping the SOS message above the high tide line so their efforts won't be swept away. The heat beats relentlessly against Hayley's shoulders, burning uncomfortably into her hair, finding every unprotected part of her and biting down hard. They only salvaged a single bottle of sunscreen from the plane, and she's wearing the faintest smear. While Brian slathered handfuls of the lotion onto his angry red skin, she knew hers could cope better with the sun, but now it feels like her whole body is screaming in protest.

Her tongue feels heavy, like a furred slug too big for her

mouth. Her breath comes in short rasps, uncomfortable and hot on her cracked lips.

The sea dances tantalizingly close, its cruel ripples calling to her parched throat. It sparkles innocently, taunting her. Her brain knows that drinking saltwater would be a death sentence, but her body leans magnetically toward the liquid. She forms the letters as quickly as she can, ignoring the splinters driving into her soft palms, exhaustedly heaving the stones into place. As soon as they can, she and Shannon turn their backs on the sea and take refuge in the shade. Closing her eyes, Hayley feels herself come untethered from the beach, like she's slipping out of her parched, dry, cracking body. Pictures float on her eyelids. She drifts backward and forward in time.

A huge white yacht lined with imposing sailors in shining uniforms, saluting as they approach the beach. An airplane improbably dangling seven long ropes like jellyfish tentacles, each one miraculously attaching to a castaway before they whoosh into the sky to safety.

The whistle blowing as the first game of the tour kicks off. A whirl of color and sound, violet pom-pom tassels rustling and spectators chattering and cheering. Erickson barking orders left and right. Hayley zooms in and out as if she's watching it from above.

She admires the deftness of the other girls as they leap in formation, muscles taut and quivering, their athleticism easily as impressive as the boys making free throws and streaking down the court. Squatting at the bottom of the pyramid or just high kicking to one side, Hayley is left out of the more complex routines she hasn't mastered the skills for, left to gasp along with the crowd as Shannon flips dizzyingly from six feet high to land on her feet, hands extended to receive the rapturous applause.

The cheer squad comes alive in front of a crowd in a way Hayley had never seen in practice, their individual talents coalescing into an almost liquid, golden thing, a single body that swirls and morphs in front of her as she tries, sluggishly, to keep up. A group of people she's always, somewhere deep down, felt herself superior to, pulling off moves she can't even begin to attempt.

She drifts forward again, suddenly, to arms reaching out to pull her into a fishing boat, the sweet relief of cool bottled water splashing over her face and bathing her fiery neck. Her parents, there in the boat with oars, rowing and rowing, but the boat sitting still in the water...

Hayley has drifted in and out of sleep so many times before Elliot and Brian return that she doesn't trust her eyes at first. But the familiar grumble of her ankle (the pain muted now but not gone completely) reassures her that she is awake as she scrambles to meet them. Coconuts. Four pale, milky-brown, slightly wrinkled, waxy-skinned coconuts clasped to their chests, and the widest smiles she has seen in days.

They let the coconuts thump heavily, miraculously, into the sand, and Hayley reaches out a wondering hand to touch their cool, smooth skin.

"How do we open them?"

"Here." Jason appears from nowhere, an armful of sticks and wood tumbling into the sand. He holds out a fist-size rock, gray on the outside and shiny black where it has been split down the middle, leaving a long, sharp edge. "I've been using it to cut wood."

Elliot holds out his hand for the rock, but Jason grabs one of the coconuts instead and starts hacking at it.

"Don't cut the sides—" Elliot's voice is drowned out by Jason's grunting. His ears slowly redden as his broad shoulders tense and release, tense and release.

"You don't want to—" There's a splintering crack as the stone finds the coconut's heart. Little white flecks spray up onto Jason's dimpled cheeks, and the milky water gushes quickly away into the sand.

"Jason!" Shannon screeches, flying at him, clawing at his back. "You idiot. You fucking asshole. We could have drunk that." She's almost sobbing, dried spit flying from the edges of her mouth, her long dark hair electrified into frizz by the humid weather, splaying wildly out around her face. Her mouth is like a red slash, her pale face consumed with rage.

"SHANNON!" Brian grabs her delicate shoulders, pulling her easily backward as Jason gapes in shock, staring at her as if he has never seen her before. "There are others. It's okay. There are others."

She turns on her heel and stalks off down the beach without looking back.

"Ooh-kay," Brian sings quietly. He turns to Jason. "Dude, you got beat by a girl." He sniggers, then stops when he sees Jason's thundercloud face.

Hayley can't remember ever seeing Shannon really lose her temper before. Biting sarcasm, yes. But there's usually a coolness about Shannon, a haughtiness that seems to radiate off her. Has this hot, furious temper always been there, hidden underneath? Or is the maddening thirst transforming them all into people she doesn't recognize?

Elliot is picking through the pile of branches. Choosing a piece of wood about three yards long and as thick as his forearm, he takes the cutting tool from Jason's hand. Jason, still looking dazedly in the direction where Shannon disappeared, doesn't protest. Elliot saws off the wood at an angle, then cuts the remaining edge into a sharpish point. He drives the blunt end of the stake as deep into the sand as he can.

Hayley cannot resist. "Please tell me that's not for a pig's head," she deadpans. She sees a flicker of recognition in Elliot's eyes, but everybody else looks nonplussed.

"There are pigs?" Brian asks excitedly.

Hayley rolls her eyes. "*Lord of the Flies*? Sixth-grade English lit?"

"Yeah, we made Arthur Windley do that assignment for us." Brian grins, punching an unresponsive Jason on the arm. Elliot selects a coconut and brings it crashing down onto the stake, splitting the brown skin, opening up a long crack down one side.

"Camping," he says again with a sheepish smile as the others look on helplessly. "None of you guys have ever taken a tent to the Keys?"

"I've stayed at the Waldorf Astoria there," Brian offers helpfully.

"Yeah, not quite the same thing," Elliot mutters. He smashes the coconut down on the stake again, then uses his hands to pry off a long strip of the outer husk, caramel-colored straw-like fibers ripping slowly away from the nut like Velcro. The others watch as the little round center emerges, a miraculous orb that calls to Hayley's dry throat like a siren.

When the husk lies in discarded sections at his feet, Elliot rests the coconut in the palm of his hand, testing its weight.

He looks at the three dark spots on top of the coconut carefully, turning it so they resemble two eyes and a mouth. He pulls a sharp sketching pencil from his pocket and carefully pierces the soft shell, right through one of the eyes.

"Hayley, can you hand me one of the empty water bottles?" He takes it and turns the coconut, sending a stream of slightly cloudy water trickling inside, until the bottle is about a quarter full. Hayley's tongue twitches involuntarily. Hawkishly, she watches as Elliot prepares the two remaining coconuts, adding their riches to the bottle.

They pass it around the circle like a holy cup, each taking a few precious sips before handing it on.

When it's Hayley's turn, she closes her eyes and lets the

warm, almost salty liquid gush into her mouth. Stopping herself from gulping down the rest takes more self-control than she knew she had.

When the bottle is drained, Elliot uses the sharp stone to split the coconuts down the middle, and they use their fingers to tear out the firm white flesh, hungrily devouring each piece until only the hollow shells remain. Hayley chews gratefully, enjoying the feel of the firm meat giving way between her teeth, the sensation of actually swallowing something solid at last.

"We should get more," Elliot says, looking at the smooth, empty bowls. His eyes flick toward the trees, and with a lurch of guilt, Hayley realizes they haven't saved anything for the other girls. It didn't even cross her mind.

"Let's all go," Jason says, and Hayley wonders if he's scared of what might happen when Shannon comes back. Elliot pockets the cutting stone, wrenching the stake out of the ground and resting it over his shoulder. Hayley wonders why, then realizes they'll be able to eat and drink some coconuts before they return, fueling them for the journey back and freeing their arms to carry more. Elliot has already thought of this.

Fear drives little tendrils into Hayley's brain every time she stops to let herself think. How long can they really last? The coconuts feel like a goldmine, and the thought of being able to drink her fill makes her feel almost dizzy with relief, but coconuts won't last forever. And what then? How much longer?

It is best, Hayley tells herself firmly, *not to think too far ahead.*

She concentrates on putting one foot in front of the other, weakly picking her way through the trees behind Elliot, trying to avoid scratching her legs as they stumble through dense bushes. She has given up on slapping at mosquitos, her skin so used to the constant, gnawing itchiness that she barely registers it anymore. She claws at her scalp periodically, sunburn and raw-scratched bites combining in a constant ebb of discomfort. Her usually soft hair is becoming stiff with sweat and sand.

Her hot feet feel swollen and angry in unwashed socks, her sneakers starting to rub red blisters on her sore ankle. "Try. Something. A. Little. Less. Academic," she mutters angrily as they push through the trees. "'Branch out,' Mr. Curtis said. 'It'll be fun,' he said. I swear, if anyone else ever asks me what's the worst that could happen…"

They head west, cutting a perpendicular line from the beach through the trees. There's no sign of May and Jessa. To the north, she can see the beginning of the rocky incline Elliot talked about. But they push forward, heading straight across the island to the other side. After about half an hour of heavy going, the trees begin to thin, and Hayley can see the sparkle of the sea in the distance. Their meager rations of coconut water are a distant memory, her exertions leaving her desperately thirsty again, light-headed and short of breath. The humid air sits heavy in her lungs. Sweat makes her sleeveless white shirt cling uncomfortably to her armpits, and her thighs chafe under the cheerleading skirt she pulled out of the salvage pile this morning in a pointless attempt to freshen up. She left off the cycling shorts she'd usually wear underneath because of the heat. Now she wishes she'd put them on.

To her right, Brian staggers to a stop, steadies himself with one hand against a tree trunk, and vomits weakly. Thin bile and spit dribbles down his front, plus a few small chunks of coconut. There's nothing else left in his stomach. He looks at Jason, eyes wide, all his usual clownish vulgarity stripped away. He seems like a scared little kid. Elliot and Jason support him from either side, wrapping their arms around his waist. "Nearly there," Elliot encourages him with surprising tenderness. "You can do this." Jason just grunts and heaves Brian forward.

They emerge onto a rockier, wilder beach than the one Hayley has become used to. The sea is rougher here, crashing onto large rocks that are scattered along the beach and jut out of the water. To Hayley's immense relief, palms grow thick along the shore, thick clusters of smooth green and yellow coconuts hanging beneath the leaves in large, pendulous bunches. At the bases of the trees are dozens of brown coconuts in different stages of decay, some rotting away or split, but many smooth and intact, just starting to wrinkle.

Nobody speaks. For the first time since they arrived on the island, it's like they are all on the same team. Elliot helps Brian to the foot of a tree, carefully lowering him down in the shade. He sits with him, rubbing his back, while Brian puts his head between his knees, breathing fast. Jason drives the stake firmly into the sand nearby, and Hayley roams the beach, selecting the most promising coconuts she can find, delighting in their weight and depositing them in a pile at Jason's feet. Together, using the stake, the cutting stone, and the pencil, he and Elliot work to open them.

When the first coconut is pierced, Elliot hands it wordlessly to Brian, and they all pause, standing motionless across the beach, watching as he suckles at it like a baby animal, eyes scrunched shut.

Elliot works quickly, handing the coconuts out until everybody is slurping at the sweet, nutty liquid. When they've finished, they open more and drink again, then claw at the flesh with their fingernails. For the first time in three days, Hayley feels sated. Now accustomed to gnawing need, her belly feels uncomfortably swollen, though in reality she's eaten only a little.

"Take it slowly," she warns the others. "It's going to take our stomachs a while to adjust."

They sit there on the beach, quietly feeling their bodies resettle, not saying much, but each, Hayley imagines, steeped in the same soft flood of relief. Only now that the clamor of thirst has abated does she realize how noisy it has been, crowding out other thoughts, her stomach and brain consumed with need and panic. She knows how serious their situation still is, but just for this moment she lets herself lie down and breathe, her shoulders sinking into the softly yielding sand, the breeze stroking her cheeks and the soothing splash and pause, splash and pause of the waves hypnotizing in its regularity.

It's late afternoon before they stagger back to the wreckage of the plane, their return journey slowed by the heavy coconuts. They carry nine between them. Brian, still staggering weakly along, is unable to manage any at all. Hayley waddles awkwardly with one tucked under each arm. Jason, shirtless, drags his yellow T-shirt like a makeshift bag with four coconuts stuffed inside, his muscular stomach gleaming with sweat. Elliot, whippet-like by comparison, balances three in a pyramid under his chin.

May greets them with an excited shriek, clamoring for coconut milk.

And the girls have their own bounty to share. Shannon is with them, picking over a pile of bright fruit, quiet and focused, not looking at Jason, who hovers, looming behind her, as if he isn't sure how to approach. "There are bushes and trees with more, farther inland, but this was all we could carry," Jessa gasps between gulps of coconut water. Hayley notices that she is only using one arm, her injured one hanging heavily by her side.

"Look what we found!" May is chirpy, boastful even, gesturing to the pile of fruit. Its plump sheen and delicate sweet scent make Hayley's stomach clench again, and she reaches out an eager hand to grab a small, bright green sphere like a little apple.

"STOP!"

Elliot leaps toward her, knocking it roughly out of her

hand. The fruit rolls across the sand, coming to rest innocently a few feet away.

"Ow!" Hayley looks down at her hand and sees a nasty red rash springing up on one side of her palm, angry red dots straining her skin. It itches and burns as if she had plunged her hand into scalding water. "What the hell?"

"It's a manchineel," Elliot gasps, breathing heavily. "A beach apple," he adds, looking around at the confusion on their faces. "Wow, you guys really never have been camping, have you?"

He walks over to the fruit and nudges it with his toe, turning it over. There's a thin cut in the skin, a little whitish juice oozing out. "The sap is poisonous," he mutters, nodding to Hayley's hand.

She gasps, feeling panic close her throat and fill her lungs. "It's okay," Elliot says, kindly, seeing her fear. "It's just a surface reaction. You didn't eat any; you'll be fine."

He turns to the other girls. "Were there any more of these?" Shannon looks shocked as she shakes her head, already rubbing her own hands in the sand. "No, we just brought one back to try, we thought the others looked more promising." She points toward the fruits, and Elliot stoops to examine them, sorting through the pile carefully.

Hot tears spring to Hayley's eyes. Tears of shock, fear, and relief. The horrible sensation of lurching from good news to deadly danger in a split second. Wondering if she'll ever feel truly safe again. Her hand throbs with pain, and she squeezes it angrily into a fist, letting the tears prickle her eyelids but brushing them quickly away before anyone else notices.

"I think they're okay," Elliot says. "I don't know the names of them all, but my dad taught me how to recognize anything poisonous when I was a kid. I don't see anything here to worry about."

So they fall on the pile of fruit greedily, ravenous hands tearing, lips sucking, tongues eagerly licking.

There are luscious mangoes, their honeyed flesh bursting through reddening skin, sticky juice running down fingers and arms. Round, firm guavas with pinkish hearts, their bitter skin yielding reluctantly to insistent teeth and offering a woolly, subtle sweetness within. There's an earth-brown fruit the size of a small avocado with a thin wrinkled skin like a baked potato, its flesh a soft yellow bleeding into crimson like a sunrise, its shining black seeds half the length of a thumb. The supple, pulpy flesh tastes sweet and malty. They quickly learn to eat only the softest of the crop after May bites into a firmer fruit but then sucks at her teeth, her mouth dried out by its sour shock. And, strangest of all, a squat green fruit like an overgrown tomato, its skin dark and bruised, a star-shaped circle of leaves standing up around its stalk. They pierce the skin, expecting a firm orange or green flesh, and recoil at the monstrous reality: a blackened, jellyfish-like fruit with seeds the shape of large shelled walnuts sticking out in a central circle like a sea monster's teeth, the flesh making an obscene sucking noise as it pulls apart. "Ugh, it's bad," Jessa grunts, discarding it in the sand, but each one they open is the same, so after Elliot has given it a cautious smell, they taste it and find it to be subtly sweet and silky smooth, like a heavy, slightly pumpkin-flavored pudding.

One of the coconuts has sprouted, its bright green shoot just developing leaves. When they open it, instead of water and flesh, it yields a spherical, spongy ball, wrinkled like a yellowish brain, filling the cavity of the shell. It is light and salty-sweet, the spongy texture giving way with a slight crunch.

They sit in a circle on the sand and eat their fill, scooping flesh from skins with plastic spoons left over from the airline meals, dragging teeth across fruit peels to strip the last scraps of flesh.

Suddenly, with a quiet rustling of leaves, a pair of shining eyes is watching them from the edge of the tree line. Hayley sees the creature first, scrambling to her feet with a sharp intake of breath, her mind whirling with images of tusks and claws and charging boars or pouncing wildcats. But as the others spin around in panic, it creeps forward, its pointed, triangular nose followed by a bushy, bulbous body and striped tail.

"A raccoon," Hayley breathes, collapsing back to the ground with relief. "Here, little guy. You hungry?" She holds out a husk of fruit, expecting the creature to be wary of her, but it darts eagerly forward and seizes the morsel straight from her fingers, sitting up on its back legs to nibble it, black button nose twitching enthusiastically.

They laugh in delight and continue to feed it, though

Shannon warns that they should save their supplies and if they encourage it now, it'll never leave them alone. But even she yields when the little creature darts over to pick up a piece of coconut flesh that's fallen on her knee, putting its handlike claw on her leg first and looking up at her as if to ask permission.

There's something deeply reassuring about it, somehow, a surprise that is pleasant instead of horrifying. It gives Hayley a welcome boost to realize that not every secret the island guards is potentially deadly.

After they've eaten their fill, there's an exuberant mood of excess and celebration, and even Elliot, glancing at the glassy, still sea, agrees that shelter construction can wait until tomorrow.

They keep the campfire burning and sit around it late into the evening. There is a camaraderie born of success that balloons almost into hysteria. Shannon and Jason, sitting on opposite sides of the campfire, both seem prepared to set aside what happened earlier—or at least to ignore it for the time being.

May teaches everyone a campfire game that involves dotting their foreheads with charcoal, and they shriek with laughter as their graffitied faces become increasingly distorted in the twilight.

That night, Hayley is back on the plane again. Everybody is unbearably relaxed. The boys are joking around, throwing Jason's signet ring back and forth between them, crowing and shouting as he stretches to catch it. May and Shannon are painting each other's toenails, legs extended over the empty seat between theirs. And Hayley is screaming at them, shrieking that the plane is about to fall out of the sky, begging them to listen, to do something, but nobody can hear her.

And they can't seem to see the choking smoke that starts to fill the cabin or smell the bitter reek of gasoline. She forces her face in front of Elliot's, shakes him by the shoulders, but he just smiles and carries on sketching, sketching. Only Jessa looks worried, frowning at her arm and mouthing something, but Hayley can't hear her. The plane shakes and shatters around them, the lights flashing and fizzing, and they plummet into darkness.

DAY 4

"*WHAT* ARE YOU DOING?" MAY TILTS HER HEAD TO ONE SIDE and squints at Jason and the uneven mess of branches precariously propped next to him in a vague pyramid shape.

"What does it look like?" he huffs, squatting down and stretching up as he attempts to heave a thick stick onto the top of the pile.

"Like a constipated chicken in an aerobics class," May answers without hesitation.

"Ha ha." Jason pants, then swears loudly as the whole structure collapses around him with a clatter. "Stupid piece of—" He kicks out, scattering wood everywhere. "Get over here, Brian, dammit!"

"Tepees are too complicated," Elliot says quietly from behind him. "It has to be more of a lean-to."

He waves the others over to a tree near the campfire, where he's propped a sturdy forked branch halfway up against the trunk so it makes a sloping triangle with its right angle at the base of the tree.

"Then prop thinner sticks against the central pole from both sides," he explains, demonstrating with a few supple branches, balancing them in a triangle shape.

"We can use palm leaves to make a kind of matting on top," Jessa suggests, seeing where Elliot's plan is going. "Nothing fancy, but it'll be big enough to keep one person dry if they lie down, and that's better than nothing, especially if it rains or the wind picks up."

"And we can upgrade to a longhouse once we've been here a few years and have had the chance to really hone our skills," May jokes, but it falls flat.

Elliot makes it look easy, but the others struggle. At first, the sticks slide repeatedly to the ground, but Jessa deftly starts weaving palm leaves together with her one good hand, clamping the thick, rubbery stalks between her knees, the tip of her tongue poking out between her teeth in concentration. By weaving the end of each leaf into the top of the next, she creates long mats, which they layer on top of each other until no sunlight penetrates the small space below.

"Ooh, pretty," Brian says, looking over from the shelter he and Jason have put together. "Glad you guys are focusing on aesthetics, because it's super important for your island survival base to look stylish."

He pats the hulking structure Jason is piling with leaves and vines, and it falls apart in a crashing tumble of foliage, leaving the others in fits of laughter.

"Hmm." Jessa takes hold of one end of the palm matting, giving it a firm shake. It bends springily, the structure sturdy beneath the intricate weaving. "You were saying?" She flashes her wide grin, tongue tip poking beneath the gap between her front teeth.

The inquisitive raccoon makes another appearance, scuttling boldly down the beach to sit near them, "Judging the heck out of the boys' construction attempts," May says. "He'd have that thing rigged up in no time, wouldn't you, Rocket?" she says affectionately, throwing him a strip of coconut.

"You've named the raccoon after the Marvel one?" Elliot asks, and May nods.

"Yup. Thought he might come in handy if we need a weapons expert who's good with a machine gun." He grins and shakes his head as the striped creature scampers eagerly at May's heels, hoping for more food.

Next they collect thinner sticks, stripped of their leaves, and lay them in parallel rows, trying to create a kind of floor matting to lift them above the sand with its flies and irritants. But the sticks roll in all directions when May climbs awkwardly into the first shelter to test it, and she complains that they dig uncomfortably into her ribs and thighs.

So Elliot shows them how to make strong, thin cord from long strands of dead sea grass, pulled in great crackling handfuls from a patch along the beach where the bushes peter out into scrubby grass. They soak the dead, sun-bleached grass in seawater, then take three strands, twisting and turning one at a time, over and over, until a fine rope begins to emerge. When they near the end of one strand, they twist another into the pattern, carrying on until the "rope" is almost three yards long before starting a new piece.

When they've got enough rope, Elliot uses it to tie the floor poles into a flexible mat, managing to only roll his eyes very slightly when Jessa exclaims that it looks exactly like a larger version of the one she uses at home to roll sushi.

"Speaking of sushi..." Brian grins. "Who's up for some spearfishing?"

Elliot looks doubtful but doesn't say anything; Hayley senses he knows there's only so much the other boys are willing to accept his authority and he's picking his battles. He shrugs. "It might work, but you'll need something really sharp."

"Yeah, *obviously*, dickweed." Brian rolls his eyes and pulls out a chunky stick from behind his back, one of the amateurishly sharpened branches they'd used for "protection" that first night. The patrols have not resumed since the failure of the first attempt, though everybody has tactfully avoided mentioning it.

Brian has split the tip of the stick and wedged a jagged piece of broken glass from the plane wreck firmly into the crack, making a brutal-looking primitive spear. Hayley isn't convinced he'll catch anything—the makeshift weapon looks heavy, and she doubts Brian has either the delicacy or the patience for spearfishing—but she hopes she's wrong. Fresh fish would make a welcome change.

After two meals, the novelty of an all-fruit diet is already beginning to wear off, the sweetness of the fruits becoming cloying and having an unwelcome effect on their bowels. ("Step away from those bushes," Jessa thundered when she spotted Brian slinking off toward the tree line the previous night, armed with a few sheets of paper torn out of Elliot's sketchbook. "New rule. Zero toilet activity within a five-hundred-yard radius of the camp," she'd ordered, sending a ripple of sniggers around the campfire. "AND BURY YOUR BUSINESS AFTERWARD," she shouted as he shuffled off down the beach.)

"Want to share one?"

Hayley stops braiding and looks up, half hidden by a clump of sea grass. Jason and Shannon are alone, standing by the nearest lean-to as Jason jerks his thumb toward it and grins at her. She tuts, turns her head away. Her hair falls over her face in a dark cloud, obscuring her expression.

"What's going on, Shan?" Jason asks, his tone softer than Hayley has ever heard it. "I love you, babe, you know I do. Why are you being like this?"

"Like scared and panicked and constantly anxious?" she retorts, still not looking at him. "Gee, I can't imagine."

"I'm here. You're my girl. You know I'll take care of you like I always do." Jason moves closer, his hand circling Shannon's waist and caressing her stomach, lifting the black strappy top she's wearing above a white tennis skirt.

"Jason." Shannon's voice is careful, softer now, but Hayley

sees her hand moving beneath his, gently pushing him away. He flinches, and Shannon quickly interlaces her fingers with his. She turns and leans into him briefly. "It's just a lot, okay? I'm trying not to break down and freak out, same as everyone else." She takes a tiny step back, away from him. "And those shelters are built for one and one only."

He steps closer. "We could squeeze in…" She holds up a hand, a fragile barrier between them. "C'mon, baby, we nearly died. Isn't that worth something?" Hayley squints at Shannon. She seems to be holding her breath.

"I know, I know you want to wait," Jason wheedles, "but there's…other stuff we can do. No parents, no curfews…"

She looks up at him. "Not things that can be done in a tiny leaf-covered beach shack without getting sand in some extremely uncomfortable places," she says lightly, quickly side-stepping him. "Trust me, the only thing worse than being stuck on a desert island would be being stuck on a desert island with a sand-filled vagina."

"I deserve better than this, Shan, you know I do," Jason calls after her, a low warning in his voice, as she walks lightly back down the beach toward the others.

And Hayley watches as Jason frowns and sets off to meet Brian, kicking up sand as he goes.

Elliot and the girls work steadily through the day, heaving the biggest branches into position, each propped as securely as possible against a sturdy tree. They learn as they go that the branches are most stable if driven into the ground, wet sand and mud swathing the bottom of each in the hope it'll shore them up against the wind. They work their way along the beach, a few yards between each shelter, building up the sides of each one with sticks and then covering them with braided leaves. There's a strange satisfaction in watching each one look a little straighter and sturdier than the one before, the sleeping mats neater and firmer.

Jessa and May soon fall into a rhythm, May placing the leaves Jessa has painstakingly braided, quietly humming as she works. It's the same smooth cooperation that makes them so effective on the team, Jessa providing a stable base as May catapults into a backflip from her shoulders, knowing exactly where her best friend's palms will be as her pointed feet plummet down to land on them. Their connection is so fluid they give the impression of a single body moving to the music. Not that anybody is going to be climbing on Jessa's shoulders anytime soon, Hayley realizes, watching the stiffness in her movements, the way she automatically twists her body to protect her damaged arm. May has noticed too, concern creasing her forehead as she watches her best friend wince again and again. Wordlessly she goes to rummage among the clothes they salvaged from the plane and returns with a neon-orange chiffon scarf she wore at the party on the last night of the tour. She ties it firmly around Jessa's neck, carefully easing the injured arm inside it to rest more comfortably.

Once the trunks are all in position, Elliot disappears to fetch more firewood, and so Hayley finds herself paired once more with Shannon, their awkward silence noticeable in contrast with the others' easy companionship. She glances at Shannon between the palm fronds, dark eyebrows drawn together in a sharp frown of concentration, black curls, greasier now, swept back in a ponytail. Hayley wants to ask her about Jason, check if she's okay, but she doesn't know how. It's not like she and Shannon have ever exactly been friends, even after all the weeks of practice and their time on tour.

In the distance behind her, Hayley can see Brian, still lumbering about in the shallows, stabbing excitably at the surf. He shouts something to Jason, who's bent double, examining something near his foot.

Hayley doesn't know what it is exactly that makes her feel sort of on edge around Shannon. Maybe it's that she sees more of a reflection of herself in the cheer captain than she'd like to admit. When she first joined the squad, Hayley had a pretty clear idea of what it would be like—or rather, what *they* would be like. And she definitely didn't expect to find that they'd have anything in common.

May, Jessa, and Shannon had been on the squad since their freshman year, and they weren't so much students who happened to cheer as cheerleaders who went to school. But if they were the headline-making A-listers of Oak Ridge, then Hayley wasn't even on the same page. In fact, she was usually the one who wrote about them, clutching her notebook on the sidelines while the three of them struck a pose for the camera. So it was a shock, actually spending time with them. Take Jessa, who seemed so achingly cool from a distance with her funky twists and designer sunglasses, perfect toe touches and crowd-pleasing splits. Hayley barely dared to breathe around her when she turned up at her first practice. But it was Jessa who'd approached her, sweeping her into a hug, all "call me Jessa" and "Don't worry, Shannon's bark is worse than her bite." Jessa, who only ever drank soda with lime when the others partied after the games on tour, who drove everyone safely home and quietly disappeared for two and a half hours on Sunday morning to find a local church while the others were still too hungover to get out of bed.

May was less accommodating. She frowned when Jessa took pity on Hayley at that first practice, and Hayley had found herself on the sharp end of May's tongue several times since. But who hadn't? It felt like you had to earn your way into May's good graces, and Hayley was about a decade behind the other girls.

But the biggest surprise was Shannon. It was hard to put her finger on what was so different from Hayley's expectations. Shannon was beautiful, popular, and talented up close, just like she seemed from afar. But it was as if she didn't enjoy it, like it was all a job. Shannon didn't just drill the team at practice; she turned up with pages and pages of detailed, complex notes. She'd call at nine o'clock on a Friday night to discuss your dismount. Her knowledge of other cheerleading squads and their routines was encyclopedic. On the first Saturday of the tour, when the team had no games scheduled, she insisted on dragging them all to a local competition, silencing May's loud objections with a single *look*, while the guys used their day off to head to a local arcade. Hayley didn't only admire Shannon's conscientious approach, she recognized it. Shannon was just as driven in her pursuit of cheerleading excellence as Hayley was in her quest for an Ivy League entry ticket.

She's never had any classes with Shannon, but she tried to interview her once, the year before she joined the squad, on assignment for the school paper. There had been a huge party at someone's parents' beach house, and it had ended badly; the police were called, and there were rumors that Chad Maxwell, the star quarterback from a private high school in Tampa, had been taken away in handcuffs. But apparently he was back at his school the next week, and nobody at Oak Ridge seemed to be talking much about what had happened. Or at least, when they did, they weren't talking about Chad. They were talking about some girl who'd been working at the party, a waitress. How she'd been drinking on the job and had caught Chad's eye and seen her chance. How she fancied bringing him down and getting a cut of the family fortune and five minutes of fame in the process. It hadn't worked, though, people said with satisfaction as they murmured about it in the oak-paneled hallways between classes. Police must've seen right through her.

Hayley pored over Instagram posts from the night until

she spotted a familiar figure; Shannon, framed by a doorway in a metallic silver halter top, Jason's hand draped around her hip. Hayley visited the yearbook committee room with a carefully practiced story about needing to surprise Shannon at home for a 'prom queen in waiting' feature and left with Shannon's address on a scrap of paper. She figured Shannon would be less likely to give her the brush-off if she turned up on her doorstep.

But Shannon wasn't home when Hayley arrived outside a small one-story house in an unassuming neighborhood in Carsons Park. Cheap peach paint peeled around the windows and a bucket stood beneath a leaking gutter. There was a beat-up old sedan in the driveway and a graying Rottweiler barking half-heartedly at the end of a heavy chain. It occurred to Hayley that she'd never seen Shannon's car, though she'd assumed she had one. She'd only ever seen her hopping lightly into the back of Jason's Jeep, waving to a crowd of friends as they sped off. And once, Jason reacting furiously as the metal buckle on Shannon's bag scraped the Jeep's paint job, shouting something that Hayley couldn't hear as he pulled away, Shannon's back rigid in the passenger seat.

Just as she raised her hand to knock, the door was opened by a quiet, mousy woman with round owl-eye glasses and an oversize cardigan clutched tightly around her. Hayley noticed her finger-nails were all bitten down to the quick. For a moment, something flickered across her face when Hayley said she was from Oak Ridge. Hayley thought it might be relief or pleasure, and she gave a little "oh," as if it was a surprise. She asked Hayley in to wait and led her into a modest sitting room with slightly faded pink wallpaper and a vase of plastic flowers in the empty fireplace. Hayley had just accepted a glass of iced tea when Shannon swept in, eyes flashing, refusing to comment on the party and insistent that she had no idea what Hayley was talking about.

"So, is that everything?" she asked pointedly, and Hayley found herself standing on the other side of the front door inside of three minutes, her drink left untouched.

She never got any further with the story—some other staffers on the paper poked around a little without turning anything up except a furiously worded letter from the Maxwells' lawyer threatening a libel suit—but Hayley was anxious the episode might count against her when she came to try out for the cheer squad.

She didn't have to worry, though. Shannon barked "Name?" when she entered the audition room and wrote it down without a flicker of recognition. Like she didn't even remember having met her at all.

And in spite of Shannon's spikiness, in spite of her sharp tongue and standoffishness, there's a part of Hayley that wishes she could break through that outer shell and just talk to her. Wishes she didn't feel so nervous and tongue-tied around her. Because deep down, she suspects they've got far more in common than Shannon knows.

They've almost finished seven shelters when Jason and Brian return disconsolately with only saltwater-soaked clothes, sun-singed shoulders, and a sore foot to show for their troubles. "Stood on a goddamn anemone," Brian gasps, wobbling on one leg and squeezing his big toe with both hands.

"Not as easy as it looks?" Hayley asks sympathetically, biting the inside of her cheek to keep from laughing.

Brian looks more and more aggrieved, his face contorting as he hops around. "That's it, sorry, guys, I've got to pee on it. Look away now or don't say I didn't warn you."

"Er, Brian?"

He hooks his thumbs into the swimming trunks he's been wearing for the past several days and bends over, pulling them down in one quick motion.

"BRIAN!" Shannon steps toward him, not exactly averting her eyes. "That's for jellyfish."

"Huh?"

"Jellyfish. You pee on jellyfish stings. Not anemones."

"Oh. Well, okay, then. Good. I'm gonna—" He pulls his pants up and hobbles off toward the campfire, arms swinging, neck glowing like a beacon.

Later, after picking unenthusiastically at her apportioned fruit and coconut, Hayley finds herself wandering along the beach, feeling the grainy resistance of the sand beneath her heels and listening to the soft swish of the waves. The sun is dipping behind the trees, sending long, waving shadows stretching toward the water's edge. For the first time in four days, she doesn't feel terrified or panicked. The reality of their situation is starting to sink in. This morning, for the first time, she awoke without a fluster of disorientation. And there is space to breathe, now that the immediate threat of dehydration and hunger has receded, loosening the cage of anxiety squeezing around her lungs.

Just for a moment, she lets herself follow May's example and tries to trick herself into believing this is a free vacation, a wild adventure she'll tell her grandchildren about someday. She walks down to the edge of the water, letting it whisper over her bare toes. If she stands very still with the warm breeze brushing her arms and the salt tang of the air on her tongue, she can almost imagine herself on a beach holiday, about to head back to the fluffy towels and crisp white sheets of an air-conditioned hotel room.

"Want to help?" Elliot has followed her down the beach, a battered backpack slung over one shoulder, a slender stick grasped in his left hand. He settles himself in the sand, pulling somebody's phone out of the backpack. For a moment, her heart jumps. Has he found a way to rig up the phone somehow, to send an emergency call? If anyone could, it would surely be Elliot. But the phone is dead, the screen dull and lifeless.

"E.T. phone home?" she asks lightly, trying to ignore the lurch of disappointment.

"Better." He grins, pulling the phone case open with his fingernails and starting to separate its internal components. "E.T. catch fish."

She watches closely as he peels apart the circuitry inside, the complex web of electronics that can power a thousand tasks in the palm of her hand at home and yet lies completely useless here. First, Elliot removes a mirror about the size of a credit card, which he turns over thoughtfully in his palm and then slips into his pocket. Next, he takes out a dark green circuit board criss-crossed with silver lines like a tiny map and littered with gold and silver dots.

"It's very soft," he explains, holding the thin wafer of metal delicately between his thumb and forefinger and gently scraping it back and forth against a hard stone. One corner quickly wears down, and then another, until a knife-sharp arrowhead rests lightly in his palm. He pulls a pair of white headphones from the backpack and splits open their plastic casing, separating the coppery wires inside. Taking a single, fragile strand, he binds the blade tightly to the long, thin stick.

"You really know your stuff, don't you?"

He shrugs. "I've really been on that many camping trips. But if you want to hear about shopping centers in Dubai or diving the Great Barrier Reef, you might want to ask one of the others." He checks himself, perhaps realizing how bitter he sounds. "Want to try your luck?" He smiles at Hayley and hands her the spear— she tries not to notice the brush of his fingers against hers—and together they wade into the shallow water.

The sea rests motionless in that long, lazy moment when late afternoon turns imperceptibly to early evening. The water is turquoise, so still that they can see the sun shining on the seabed like a silver net, irregular loops shifting and sliding across the sand. She watches their toes, sand seeping up between them to anchor their feet in position, sucking them into the fabric of the place. There's an exhilaration about feeling rooted in, a closeness to the natural world that Hayley has never experienced before.

A silver flash ripples beneath the surface, breaking her train of thought. It's gone before she can draw breath, but there's another, and another—a shoal of tinfoil scraps, darting and hesitating, pouring themselves between rocks and soaring upward again like liquid smoke. They move as a single body, iron filings drawn by the same magnet, moving so swiftly that it seems impossible she could ever catch one. But she crouches, grips the spear tightly in her right hand, jabs it through the water as suddenly and quickly as she can, aiming wildly not at an individual fish but at the middle of the shoal itself. A silver firework explodes in the water, her hand at its epicenter; she stands, frozen, as the fish vanish in all directions. She draws back her arm. Nothing. The spear is empty, the tip clean.

They try again and again, standing stock still in the water, waiting until the fish swarm confidently around them before pouncing, holding the tip of the arrow to the very surface of the water. Still nothing. The fish are too fast or the arrow too blunt. Elliot clicks his tongue.

"Why do you think nobody has found us yet?" Hayley asks, resting the spear in her hand as she waits for the fish to settle again.

Elliot sighs. "There could be a million reasons. It wasn't a big commercial flight with hundreds of passengers on board. Maybe there are fewer resources available to look for a private jet than when a big airliner goes down. Maybe they are looking, but there's bad weather somewhere affecting the search. My best guess is that whatever went wrong with the plane killed its communication systems, so they have no idea where to start. Maybe the pilot flew off course to try and correct the problem and we're not where we should have been."

"They could be looking in completely the wrong place," Hayley whispers, horrified. But part of her has grimly noted the passing days and is not so surprised.

"That's not the worst of it," Elliot says quietly, glancing back toward the shore, where the others are starting to build up the fire, adding extra sticks in anticipation of nightfall.

"What?" Hayley asks flatly.

"What if they've found the other part of the plane?" Elliot whispers, even though they are much too far away for anybody else to overhear. "What if they've found it and it's completely mangled, or floating in the middle of nowhere, and maybe Erickson and the pilot…you know…and they assume the rest of us must be dead too?"

"You mean they might have given up looking altogether?"

"I don't know," Elliot says, suddenly sounding weary and irritated. "I don't have all the answers, okay? It's just a thought I had, that's all. But there's no point in freaking everyone out."

"Mind if I try?"

It's Jessa, standing next to the abandoned backpack with the remaining strands of copper wire in her good hand. She wades in to meet them, uncurls the fist of her injured arm to reveal a safety pin, unclasped and bent into a rough shape.

"A fishhook." Hayley grins, impressed—and grateful for Jessa's interruption.

Elliot stumbles sideways, splashing awkwardly, water slopping up his front as Jessa approaches.

"I'll see you later," he mumbles, and Hayley watches him go. For a moment, she thinks she sees disappointment flicker over Jessa's face, but she's soon smiling again, instructing Hayley to twist the strands of copper wire together to make a single strong thread and teaching her how to attach it to the safety pin to make a basic fishing line.

"How do you—"

"My dad's taken me fishing every summer since I was seven. Elliot's not the only Scout in the group, you know," Jessa says quietly, pulling a handful of coconut scraps from her pocket and handing them to Hayley, nodding to indicate she should spear one on the sharp end of the hook. "One year I forgot my rod and he showed me this. I'd have thought of it sooner, but I was"—she glances down at her arm—"distracted."

Hayley drops the hook into the water and steadily feeds out the line, letting it trail deeper. Almost immediately, the wire goes taut, a rippling circle skidding over the surface of the water as something beneath pulls it from side to side. Hayley tugs sharply on the wire and the hook flies up to break the surface, glinting emptily, the coconut gone. "Greedy nibbler," Jessa murmurs, handing her another piece of coconut. "Not so suddenly this time." They watch the wire drift lazily with the sea's movements, feeling the cool silk of the water caressing their calves. The fierce heat of the day is gone, replaced by a soothing warmth. Nothing happens.

Jessa frowns, and Hayley sees her eyes flick down to her arm again. The swelling has subsided around her shoulder, the deep cuts bulkily swathed in a bandage Jason found in the single first aid kit to survive the crash. May's orange scarf is a little more tattered already, its edges fraying.

"Jessa," Hayley asks gently, "is your arm okay?"

"It's fine," she says quickly. "I'm fine."

Suddenly, there's another jerk on the fishing line, and this time Hayley releases her grip, feeding more out instead of yanking it in, patiently waiting as the surface of the water seethes and froths.

"Slowly, slowly," Jessa whispers. Hayley tentatively starts to wind the line in, wrapping it around her left hand like a bobbin. She can feel resistance, something pulling determinedly in the opposite direction. It reminds her of flying a kite on the beach with her dad, running into the wind, feeling the pressure of the string like a wild thing pulsing in her hands.

With a little splash, the end of the line emerges from the water, a glittering peacock-blue fish the length of her hand twisting and whirling on the end. Hayley gasps and Jessa lets out a loud yell of triumph.

"Beginner's luck." She smiles modestly as they splash back across the shallows to deposit the fish in the backpack.

"It's weird," Jessa says quietly, glancing up. "Everything's different somehow." She laughs. "I mean, obviously everything's different, we're stranded on a deserted island, but…"

"I know what you mean," Hayley says. "It's not just every-*thing* that's different, it's every*one*."

"Yeah," Jessa agrees thoughtfully. "I never thought I'd see the day that Shannon and Jason were anything less than rock- solid, but now…who knows?"

"They've never argued before?" Hayley asks.

"Oh sure, they've fought, but not like this. Jason would fill the locker room with flowers, or he'd write some cheesy poem about Shannon and read it over the loudspeakers while we were in the gym, or he'd come in and sweep her off her feet in the middle of practice in front of everyone, and it would always blow over, you know? She'd *have* to forgive him. But it's different here. She's different. And he is."

"Do you know what started it?" Hayley asks.

"I wonder," Jessa says, almost whispering, "if it has something to do with how Shannon was at the party on the last night—"

"I doubt it." May is suddenly there behind them, wading through the shallows, peering curiously at the makeshift fishing line. "It wasn't a big deal, and I don't think Jason even saw, anyway."

"Not a big deal?" Jessa sucks air through her teeth. "I've never seen Shannon like that. She was wild. I wonder what got into her?"

May looks briefly unnerved, or maybe it's just the coldness of the water, but at that moment the line jerks again, then again and again in quick succession. The conversation is quickly forgotten as they rush triumphantly back to the others with their treasures glittering in the old backpack.

While everyone argues about how to prepare the fish, May insisting they let them die "naturally" and Elliot begging her to let him bash their heads quickly on a rock, Hayley sits back, pleased to have been useful. For the first time, it feels like there is solid ground beneath them—food, water, and shelter—but she knows that something is still very wrong. And it's not just the pathetic number of tiny fish to share between seven people and the terrible fear of not being found. Maybe it's just the pressure of the situation, but she has a nagging feeling that there's more to it than that. There's something about the fabric of the whole group. Like a jigsaw puzzle where all the pieces have been slightly reshaped and none of them fit together anymore.

DAY 5

BY THE FIFTH DAY, HAYLEY'S SKIN HAS DARKENED TO A DEEP tan and her body is covered in bites, scratches, and scrapes.

It's suffocatingly humid inside her shelter, the armfuls of leaves she spread to soften her sleeping mat adding an unpleasantly musty scent to the already clogged air. Shifting her body weight, she's uncomfortably aware of the smell of her own sweat, the stale sweetness that returns no matter how often she washes in seawater. Not that everyone is so concerned with hygiene; Brian can now be smelled from six feet away, as May disgustedly pointed out to him at dinner last night. ("All I'm saying is, you either need to wash or sit downwind.")

When Hayley wriggles out onto the beach, it doesn't offer much relief; her lungs feel hot and thick even outside, like they're full of cotton wool.

Shading her eyes with her hand, she looks out toward the sea. Elliot cuts a lonely figure, standing knee-deep in the water, silhouetted like a statue as he patiently pursues more fish. In the distance, she can just see May's head bobbing along as she swims the length of the island, a morning ritual she claims is keeping her sane.

The fish they caught last night were a success of sorts, cooked over the fire on a sharp stick, eager fingertips singed as they scraped scales off soft white flakes and picked minute translucent bones from between their teeth. But there was barely a taste for each of them before the fish were gone, the heads and tails sizzling and spitting in the embers.

By midmorning, the bottles of coconut water and the shallow pit they've dug in the shade to keep a supply of fresh coconuts cool are empty. Hayley hasn't kept track of how many they've consumed, and she didn't take an exact count of how many were scattered at the foot of the trees on the western coast of the island. But the supply isn't infinite, and as one long, hot day stretches into another, they've been working through them fast.

"We're going on a coconut run," Brian calls to nobody in particular as Jason charges into the trees. "Going to try and get some of the green ones down. Elliot says they'll have more water inside." He cups his hands around his mouth, shouting through them like a bullhorn. "Yo, Elliot!" He gestures toward the other side of the island. "Come show us what we're looking for."

"But—" Shannon waves a hand dismissively as they disappear without waiting to hear what she has to say. "Your funeral," she mutters, going back to the damp grass she is carefully twisting into a new length of twine.

When she's finished, she ties one end to the top of the tall stake they've kept by the fire to split coconuts and the other end to one of the closest palm trees, creating a washing line to hang up some wet clothes she's rinsed in the sea.

"Any of the boys help with that?" May asks as she towels her hair with a dry T-shirt, rolling her eyes when Shannon quietly shakes her head and starts spreading the clothes out on the line.

The row of dangling shirts and pants creates a wall on the south side of the camp. To the west, the tree line is a few yards away, providing a natural windbreak and helping to keep the fire from being blown out. They've built up the fire pit with bigger stones and placed some tree stumps, rocks, and airplane seat cushions around it in a rough circle, providing a focal point where they can gather for food and sit in the evenings.

A pair of overhead bins that was thrown clear of the plane has been dragged nearer to the fire, providing a largely rainproof approximation of a cupboard. One side is filled with dry clothes and blankets, the other stacked with firewood.

When the tide is at its highest, the waves lap at the sand about twenty-five yards from the camp, and when it's low, the beach stretches out in a molten gold flood, the water so far away they almost can't see it at all. A little ways to the south, close to the tide line, the twisted wreck of the plane remains, but it has become almost normal to them. In less than a week, it has morphed from a shocking reminder of their situation to a familiar landmark that Hayley almost doesn't notice anymore.

The sleeping shelters stretch out in a line on either side of the camp, four for the girls on one side and three for the boys on the other, about ten yards between them, each leaning up against a sturdy palm trunk.

May and Jessa are sitting in the shade, both wearing black yoga pants and spaghetti-strap tops, using white shells and stones rubbed in black soot from the fire to play backgammon on a board scraped into the sand with sticks.

"Double six," May gloats, unfolding two scraps of paper she's picked out of the shoe that holds their makeshift dice.

"Oh, really? Again?" Jessa narrows her eyes suspiciously while May flashes her an angelic smile and skips two of her shells to safety.

"How many sixes are in there, exactly?" Jessa asks teasingly, and May quickly changes the subject.

"Does anyone else have their period? Mine's due soon, and I have literally nothing to use."

"Sorry," Shannon says. "I had tampons in my bag, but it hasn't turned up in the stuff from the crash." The others shake their heads too.

"I *cannot* deal with *that* here," May declares dramatically. "We are going to have to get rescued in the next"—she counts quickly on her fingers—"nine days or less. We just have to. It's nonnegotiable."

"Right," says Shannon drily. "Because Jessa's possibly infected arm can wait, but God forbid we should still be here when your period arrives."

"It's getting better, I think," Jessa interrupts with forced brightness. She flashes a smile that doesn't come close to her eyes. "I think it's much better than it was, actually." She turns to May, abruptly returning the focus to her best friend. "We'll manage something, sweetie. Rags or whatever. That's what they used to do in the old days."

"Oh, good. I'll look forward to it." May makes a face.

Jessa leans over to take the shoe and gasps, her face twisting in pain. May leaps to her side, shells and stones scattering beneath her feet.

"It's nothing, it's nothing." But Jessa's breathing is heavy and she's biting down hard on her lower lip.

"Show us," Shannon commands, and Jessa reluctantly loosens the scarf sling, groaning as her arm droops into her lap. Gingerly, she begins to unwrap the bandage, and as the layers peel back, it darkens with a wet, seeping liquid. Hayley's gut twists as Jessa lifts the last layer from her arm, revealing a slick, pulpy mess that reminds her sickeningly of the fruit she ate for breakfast.

"Jessa!" May gasps, and Jessa swallows hard.

"It's not as bad as it looks," she says shakily.

"Why didn't you say something sooner?" Shannon sounds almost irritated, but Hayley recognizes the tone; it's the same disguised panic that crept into her voice when Coach Robinson canceled a Saturday practice at the last minute because the gym roof was leaking. It's the tone that creeps in when something happens that is outside of Shannon's control.

"Hayley," she barks, "get the first aid kit."

There's not much left of in the battered red case that Jason dragged out from under the twisted metal remains of one of the plane seats. They've already used one of the bandages, but there's a tube of ointment, some gauze, and Band-Aids.

"Iodine, get the iodine," Shannon snaps, and Hayley rummages through the box until she finds a small shattered bottle at the bottom, shards of glass floating in a sticky pool of dark ochre.

"It's broken," she whispers helplessly.

"We need something else then," May says, smiling reassuringly at Jessa, her voice about two notes higher than usual. "Something else that's a disinfectant." She casts around wildly. "Alcohol!" she shouts. "How many cop shows have you seen where they pour vodka into a wound when they can't get to a hospital?"

"Can I just say that I am *not* reassured by how many of our survival instincts on this island have been guided by stuff people have seen on TV?" Jessa says with a weak smile, though her teeth are gritted against the pain.

"It's actually not a bad idea," Shannon says. "We need to clean out that wound." But they can't find any alcohol in the supplies Jason pulled out of the plane, supplies that have dwindled to some pieces of metal and plastic trays, a fire extinguisher, and random plastic eating utensils piled neatly next to the overhead bin cupboard.

"There has to be something they missed," Hayley says, cautiously approaching the metal carcass of the jet. "What kind of a plane doesn't have those miniature bottles of booze on board somewhere?"

She has to bend double to get inside, wriggling between jagged edges and deformed, unrecognizable shapes. She inches forward on her knees, passing a pile of smashed glass, long triangular shards sticking into the sand at odd angles like peanut brittle. And she has to stop for a moment to let the familiar clench of pain pass, to clear her head of the image of making peanut brittle with her mom in a cozy, steamed-up kitchen, laughing more and more hysterically as it completely failed to set and started bubbling uncontrollably over the stove top.

Unclench. Breathe. Don't remember.

Almost everything that was inside the plane has already been stripped out. The one remaining overhead bin yawns empty, its door hanging wildly off a single hinge. Hayley reaches the tail, where the food was stored. A metal rolling cart lies on its side, its drawers lolling out like dead tongues, emptied of food trays by Jason. But there's another drawer at the top, a locked drawer that doesn't look as if it's been touched. Hayley pulls at the metal handle; something rattles inside.

With some difficulty, unable to fully turn in the cramped space, she looks around until she finds a loose, thin piece of metal. She slides it into the narrow slit at the top of the drawer and begins to wiggle it back and forth, forcing the flimsy lock. The drawer slides open, revealing rows of shining glass bottles with brightly colored labels and metal caps. "Bingo," she calls, grabbing a handful.

Jessa screams when Shannon pours the vodka into her wound. She can't help it. Her lips curl back from her teeth and tears spring to her eyes as her fingernails dig deep into May's hand.

The liquid runs black, then brown, then yellow, then red, like a grotesque rainbow.

"That's cleaned some of it out at least," Shannon says apologetically. She pours another bottle over her own fingers to clean them, then dabs ointment into the wound, pausing each time Jessa flinches. Then she carefully dresses it with the remaining clean bandage.

"We need to get you a drink," Shannon says firmly. "The boys should be back with the coconuts by now. I'd say they've had long enough to attempt it on their own. Shall we?"

"Not you, sweetie," May says firmly as Jessa tries to get to her feet. She gently ties the orange sling back around her best friend's arm. "You stay here and try to rest."

"Don't tell the guys," Jessa whispers as they leave. "They're not strong enough to handle it. They think they are, but…" She sighs and closes her eyes.

When they reach the other side of the island, the boys are a sorry sight. Brian is sitting in the sand, panting, nursing what looks like a split fingernail. Jason is a few feet up, clinging to the trunk of a palm tree, sweat beading his forehead, cheeks puffed, desperately clamping his knees together and pushing himself up a few inches only to slide back down several inches more. And Elliot is stripped to the waist, trying unsuccessfully to use his T-shirt as a makeshift catapult, flinging rocks toward the green coconuts clustered twelve feet above him, his missiles going nowhere near his targets but landing dangerously close to the others.

"Knock it off," Brian shouts angrily as one of the stones whistles past his elbow. They're so wrapped up in their exertions that they don't even hear the girls emerging from the trees.

May takes in the scene and starts to laugh, a wicked, infectious cackle that shakes her whole body.

Hayley is starting to think that each person on the island has a like in a game of poker. Whenever anyone mentions how unlikely they are to be rescued, Jessa's fingers worry at the little crucifix around her neck without her even seeming to realize it. Jason goes quiet at first when he's worried, but then his panic builds up and builds up inside him until it bursts out in a fit of cursing, usually aimed at Elliot. Shannon becomes hypercritical, her sarcasm sailing off the charts. Elliot withdraws back into his familiar, silent shell. Brian seems to swell somehow, wrestling whole saplings out of the ground and pounding away at the coconut stake like he can smash his feelings away. And when May is scared, she becomes exuberant, a sparkling, bubbling stream of songs and giggles.

"It won't be so funny when you don't have anything to drink tonight," Jason says, his low voice angry.

"I'm sorry," May gasps, trying to catch her breath, "I'm sorry. But it's just…hasn't it occurred to any of you guys that you have a group of people here with the exact skill set you need?"

"What are you talking about?" Jason slides irritably down from the trunk, rubbing his grazed palms.

Shannon cracks her knuckles and takes a deep breath. She flicks up her head, smiles widely, and strikes a pose beneath the palm tree, one arm in the air, the other hand jauntily on her hip. "Go, go, Ridge Raptors, go!" she chants, and the boys look at her like she's got heatstroke, but Hayley suddenly sees what she's doing, and May is grinning too as she moves to stand behind her captain.

"Go, team, go! Get into formation!"

And as the guys watch, Hayley moves smoothly, lining herself up directly in front of Shannon, her feet planted shoulder width apart, knees slightly bent, hands firmly on her thighs. Ready and braced for the impact as Shannon leaps lightly up behind her, planting one bare foot in the crease at the back of her knee, the next in the small of her back, and then pushing herself deftly up, placing first one and then the other foot on Hayley's shoulders.

"Steady, now," Shannon whispers, and Hayley grips the tops of Shannon's calves as they both focus carefully on a spot in front of them, thinking of nothing but balance, as May scampers catlike up Hayley's back, clasping Shannon's hands, using Hayley's wrist as a stepping stone, and finally emerges on Shannon's shoulders. She straightens carefully, triumphantly, to her full height, her bare toes curled in a tight grip.

Hayley hears the wild applause of the crowd rushing in her ears, feels the tingling sense of elation she had when they pulled off this formation at the end of the last game of the tour. They'd finished out the trip at Duke Academy, a prestigious Texas private school packed with the children of elite oil oligarchs and banking bosses. It was a rush, that last game. They were five points behind coming into the last quarter, and Hayley saw the strained looks on the boys' faces as Erickson brought them in for a huddle. Sweat dripped from Elliot's face, Erickson was shouting something, his clenched fist smacking into his palm, Jason animated beside him. Shannon was vibrating in front of Hayley, her face alight with intense excitement, outlining their final routine, urging them to give it everything they had.

She felt the pressure ramp up as the whistle blew, forcing her high kick higher than she'd ever managed before, the roar of the crowd whirling her out of her handspring as Elliot made a basket, followed quickly by a free throw from Brian, closing the gap between the teams to just two points. And as she felt Shannon's toes dig into the back of her knee, as the last moments of the game ticked away on the clock, Jason took a long shot from outside the three-point line, the ball sailing past May as she straightened on top of Shannon's shoulders, the triumphant climax of the routine perfectly coinciding with the ball swishing lightly through the net and winning them the game.

A wide grin spread across her face as the crowd noise surrounded her like a wave; she was aware of the tension in her every muscle as she strained to keep perfectly still. She felt better than she ever could have imagined this could make her feel. And as May and Shannon backflipped smoothly down to land, as they were enveloped in a chaotic, elated sea of hugs and backslapping and sweaty necks, she was, for a moment, one of the squad.

That was when one of the Duke cheerleaders, a tall, pretty girl with curly red hair, had come over to congratulate them and invite them to a party at her house. "To celebrate your last night on tour," she'd said with a wink, "we can be gracious winners!" And Brian laughed, saying something gross about how much action he could fit into one night, and one of the Duke players shrieked that it would be wild, and Shannon laughed, Jason suddenly there with his arm around her shoulders, his lips on her mouth. Meanwhile, Hayley's feeling of lightness and excitement quickly hardened into the usual foreboding that preceded any major social gathering—especially a house party with strangers—and she mentally flicked through underwhelming outfit combinations, already planning her excuses for slipping away early.

May lurches suddenly to the left, wrenching Hayley back to the present.

"OW! Careful!" Shannon shouts crossly from above.

"Sorry, mosquito!" May prods experimentally at the bunch of coconuts now immediately in front of her and frowns. "Well, are you all just going to stand there *staring*, or is somebody going to pass me something to cut them down with?"

Elliot hands the cutting stone over wordlessly. Hayley passes it without looking to Shannon, who reaches up to May, who bends slowly down to get it, one arm out wide for balance.

"Well, we did not think of that," Brian mutters sheepishly as May begins to cut delicately through the stalk of the first coconut.

"Catch!" She tosses it in Elliot's direction, and he jumps forward, arms outstretched.

The young coconuts are different; their husks are shinier and tougher, and opening them is harder work. It takes Brian almost half an hour of carving and swearing at one before he finally reaches the hairy brown shell inside. But it's worth the effort. The meat of these coconuts is less developed, a jelly-like layer almost like underboiled egg whites that clings to the tongue with a rubbery wobble.

"It's like vomit-flavored pudding," Brian protests, letting it drip out of his mouth into the sand. But there's at least twice as much water inside these nuts, its taste far sweeter and fresher than what they've become used to. They won't need to worry about thirst again, at least not for a few days.

It's ironic, really, that the rain clouds don't begin to gather until they arrive back at camp with the fresh coconuts. Elliot is already working on the shelters, adding extra layers of leaves and even tucking in pieces of plastic and metal from the plane here and there in an effort to make them waterproof.

The sky is swollen. Gray clouds quickly deepen to heavy, hanging purples and angry browns, reminding Hayley unpleasantly of the wound in Jessa's arm.

But the rain doesn't come. They busy themselves finding extra clothes for warmth, moving their supply of fresh fruit and remaining equipment into the shell of the plane to keep it dry. They move quickly, not talking much. There's something in the air, a kind of electric tension, that makes Hayley feel on edge, like she's holding her breath, waiting for something awful to happen.

Brian and Shannon disappear into the tree line, hurrying to find as much wood as they can, planning to stash some in the shell of the plane. Jason returns a few minutes later with more palm leaves for the shelters, his eyes darting around, calculating, counting.

"Where's Shannon?" he barks, and when Hayley tells him she has gone to fetch wood with Brian, Jason disappears after them at a loping run. They reemerge shortly afterwards, Brian's arms piled with wood, Jason's hand viselike around Shannon's.

"Doesn't want her to be alone even for a moment in this place," Jessa whispers to Hayley with an admiring sigh, as if this only confirms Jason's perfect boyfriend credentials. But Hayley, studying the white tips of Shannon's fingers, is not so sure.

When there's nothing left to do, Hayley sits in the sand at the mouth of her shelter, scooping up handfuls and letting the grains trickle through her fingers. The methodical, repetitive movement helps her to feel anchored, slowing her racing heartbeat and brain. May is humming the same few notes over and over under her breath, a little ditty that makes the hairs on Hayley's arms stand on end. Not because there's anything particularly eerie about the tune, but because she's heard it before. An innocent trill of notes that might sound absent-minded coming from someone else but that means something completely different when it's May.

It was about half an hour after that last triumphant game had ended, and the visitors' locker room was cloudy with steam as some of the girls finished up their showers. Shannon was dressed already and standing at the mirror, putting on cherry-red lip liner with a perfectly steady hand. Behind her, May's wet hair swept almost to the floor as she toweled it, head hanging down between her legs.

Hayley was tying her shoelace when Shannon blotted her lips and said, "I asked Coach Robinson to film us during the last quarter so we can do a quick play-by-play pinpoint our mistakes and look at where we can tighten up that finale routine. I'll see you all in my hotel room in thirty minutes."

May snorted, still rubbing vigorously with her towel. "Good one, Shannon," she laughed, slightly muffled. "Like you're going to drill us on the last night of the tour."

Shannon's gaze was icy in the mirror. "We need to look at it now while it's fresh in our minds. This is about putting us in the strongest possible position going into next semester's competitions."

"Hmm," May mused, a sarcastic edge to her voice. "What's going to put a team in the strongest position to win—a chance to let their hair down and relax with a well-earned night off, or a ridiculously intense captain who never gives anyone the chance to recharge?" She snapped upright, tousled damp hair falling around her flushed cheeks.

"Don't worry, May, you'll still make it to your precious party on time."

"Well, I'd like time to get ready as well. And you'll need"— May glanced at the clock, pretending to do a calculation in her head—"I'd say a good two hours at least to remove the stick from your ass."

"C'mon, May." Jessa's voice was soothing, ever the peace-maker, as she appeared between them. "We've got plenty of time to do both. It won't take more than half an hour to go through the tape, right, Shannon?"

"I guess we can do it quickly," Shannon assented, smiling gratefully at Jessa. And Hayley watched irritation flash across May's face as she bit her lip and said nothing, wondering if it was really the half hour that bothered her or the fact that Jessa had taken Shannon's side instead of hers. May started yanking a comb through the tangles in her wet hair, humming a trio of notes over and over again.

They're still waiting for the storm when they hear the engine. At first, Hayley thinks it's the thunder arriving, a distant, stutter-ing purr that comes and goes. Or the sea, the sound of the waves crashing more wildly as the wind starts to whip them higher. But it gets louder until it's unmistakable. A plane or a helicopter, perhaps very close, perhaps quite far away—it's impossible to tell between the rising wind and the thick, gray clouds.

"It's a plane! It's a fucking plane!" Jason laughs maniacally, screaming, "I fucking told you! I fucking told you so!" at no one in particular.

Jessa's face is flooded with relief, tears pooling quietly in the corners of her eyes. But Elliot looks worried.

"I think it's coming from the northwest," he says in a low voice, his eyes on Jessa.

"What does that mean?" Hayley asks him quietly.

"They might not see the SOS. And the fire's almost out."

Hayley looks at the fire. Nobody has fed it for hours. It's only the white powder of scattered ashes, not a single wisp of smoke rising up into the pregnant air.

"Can we stoke it up?"

"Not fast enough."

Jason has overheard; the elation on his face quickly turns to consternation, then to anger.

"Build it. Build the fire up NOW. Get it smoking," he yells, assuming the same commanding tone he uses to bark out plays on the court, a tone nobody argues with.

But Elliot spreads his hands. "I can't. There isn't time."

"You idiot. You fucking idiot." Jason is face-to-face with Elliot, his chest puffed out, his whole body bristling with rage.

"You think you're such a smart little Boy Scout with your clever water bottle tricks and your little fishing lines. But when we actually need a fire, where the fuck are you?"

"There's a storm coming!" Elliot protests. "I didn't see the point in wasting wood building the fire up again when it was about to be doused anyway."

The engine is getting louder, throbbing like a physical presence in the air around them.

"What good are you?" Jason's eyes are aflame, spit flying into Elliot's stricken face. "You think you're such a big man, taking over, seizing control, huh? But you can't even keep your stupid campfire burning, you asshole."

"We have to do something," Jessa says desperately.

They stand there, frozen, staring up at the sky. Hayley is caught by a frenzied desire to start throwing things in the air, as if she could possibly throw anything high enough to catch the attention of a pilot, even in a low-flying plane.

Elliot is patting his pockets, frantically searching for something. He pulls out the mirror he extricated from the phone yesterday.

"We can signal them!" he yells, setting off at a run, crashing into the trees. "If we can get to high enough ground, we can signal them."

And after a split second, the others throw themselves after him.

Elliot runs without looking back. He turns sharply to the right, pushing through the trees, and for the first time Hayley approaches the steep incline where the ground rises up into a hill, the trees becoming slightly sparser. They are halfway up when the rain starts, fat drops that penetrate Hayley's clothes and soak her hair, somehow wetter than any rain she has felt before. The noise of the plane is louder at the top of the hill, a motorized roar that sounds as if it must be directly above them, but all Hayley can see are rolling black clouds, the raindrops whizzing down faster now, stinging her eyes when she tries to spot the plane.

Elliot has the mirror in his palm, tilting it this way and that, but Hayley can see that it's useless—there's no sun left to reflect, no glinting beam to force whoever is flying above to take notice of them. The clouds are so thick, hanging so close she would be surprised if the pilot even realized there was an island below at all. What was left of the sunset has been swallowed up completely, darkness strangling the island faster and more completely than it ever has before.

Still Elliot strains his arm up, holding the useless mirror above his head like a shield. And even though the others can see it's useless too, they crowd around him, the ground in front of their feet falling away in a sharp twenty-foot drop. They screech and wave their arms shamelessly, voices grating hoarse in desperation, hands stretched up toward what little moonlight penetrates the clouds. They are drowning, screaming their fear at the dark, bruised sky.

Nobody could say later exactly how it happened, or even at what moment, except that one minute they were all there, suspended in the clammy hot-and-cold air, their eyes raking the sky as the rain sliced down in sheets around them, their own harsh voices filling each other's ears. And the next moment, Elliot was falling, his body U-shaped as his arms and legs floated up toward them, plummeting in slow motion into the welcoming jaws of the bushes and rocks below.

DAY 6

IT'S NOT ACTUALLY AS EASY TO CARRY A BODY AS YOU might expect. Just disentangling Elliot from the greedy claws of the bushes that ensnared him and yanking him back up the rocks takes what feels like hours. Hayley shudders at the unwelcome thought that the island seems glad to have claimed him, that it doesn't want to give him up without a fight. Like it has demanded a blood sacrifice for their trespass there, a price to pay for the vines they've trampled and trees they've torn, the unwanted footprints they've left in the sand.

The battered face of Elliot's wristwatch, now hanging above his limp fingers, shows that it's after midnight before they begin the dejected journey back to the camp.

First, they try carrying him slung between them like a sack of potatoes, four of them taking a limb each, bumping him roughly along the ground when their grip slips. But it's awkward and impractical to move that way. The thick undergrowth and narrow spaces between bushes and trees make it hard to travel two abreast, let alone with an extra person hanging immobile in between. So Brian and Jason take turns heaving Elliot over their shoulders, clutching tightly to the backs of his thighs, his head hanging limply down behind. The group spreads listlessly out in a scattered, dejected procession: Shannon silent and tense; Jason spitting out swearwords like he's releasing pressure from a gasket; May singing again, a perky, flippant pop song about embracing your booty, starting again from the beginning every time she runs out of notes, as if she's scared to stop. Brian has gone very quiet, his head hanging low, his breath coming in short, jagged gasps. Nobody speaks about the plane. Hayley moves close to Jessa and realizes she is repeating a prayer over and over under her breath, saying the words so fast Hayley can't even make them out.

"Shut up, Jessa. That's not going to make any difference," May snaps at her irritably, and Hayley sees Jessa flinch and recoil, hurt painted across her face.

"Well, Meghan Trainor's not about to swoop in and save us either," she replies with uncharacteristic anger. "But I don't see you keeping your mouth shut."

"That can't be good for him," Hayley frets, watching Elliot's cheek bashing unceremoniously against Jason's back. Following closely behind, she can hear Jason's heavy, rasping breathing. Elliot's face looks serene and somehow innocent, mouth slightly open so she can see the glistening shell pink of his inside lip.

"He's lucky to be alive," Jason replies curtly, pushing his

soaked hair out of his face. "I don't think he's going to be too worried about a bruise here or there when he wakes up."

"If he wakes up," says Shannon, sounding terrified. She's worrying at the edges of her nails with her teeth, more openly panicked than Hayley has ever seen her.

There's a stark, eerie flash, and the trees around them are suddenly illuminated in bright white, the cracks and twists of their bark standing out in sharp contrast, before the cold, gunmetal-gray night sweeps in again. It's darker than before, making it harder than ever to see where they're going. The air tastes of metal too, a bloody tang that coats the sides of Hayley's tongue, setting her even more on edge. A few moments pass between the lightning and the angry drumroll of thunder that follows. The thick blanket of leaves above holds off the worst of the rain, but now and then they step into the path of a mini deluge where the water pours like a waterfall through a gap in the canopy. The air smells like earth and electricity. Hayley watches Elliot flopping around like a doll.

"I'm tired," May complains petulantly, flopping down and crossing her arms as if they're not in the middle of a midnight thunderstorm.

Jason stops and unceremoniously deposits Elliot in a heap. "Oh, *you're* tired? I'm so sorry, you poor thing. Can I interest you in taking a turn with this hundred-and-fifty-pound weight so you can see what actual tiredness feels like?"

May scowls.

"Maybe we should just leave him here," Jason mutters angrily.

"Are we sure we should all be going back to camp?" Brian's voice is flat, subdued. "Shouldn't somebody stay up there in case the plane comes back?"

"It's not coming back," May whines. "They don't know we're here."

"Which probably means they'll cross this area off the map and never come back," Jason adds darkly.

"Is he definitely breathing?" Hayley bends over Elliot, relieved to feel his warm breath flutter against her cheek.

May gives an exaggerated sigh and Brian turns on her. "I don't know what you're complaining about. If you all hadn't left the camp this afternoon, the fire would have still been burning and they would have seen the smoke."

"Oh, come on," cries May. "If it had occurred to you that the girls might actually be good at something physical, or maybe even—shock horror—*better* than you guys, then we could have finished collecting the coconuts hours ago and gotten back in time to get the fire going again."

"It's my fault," Jessa says, her voice tight. "I was resting in the shade, my arm..." She sighs heavily. "I should have kept the fire going. I'm so sorry."

"There's no point infighting about it now," Hayley says, feeling a cold jolt as a stream of water unexpectedly finds its way down the back of her neck. With Elliot out of commission and the plane gone, she feels utterly defeated. Thoughts about being stuck here forever, about starving here, about never seeing her parents again—all the thoughts she's been trying so hard to block out since the day they arrived—are crowding back into her head. Thoughts so heavy she feels like Jason isn't the only one lugging around a dead weight.

"It's my mom's birthday tomorrow," Jessa whispers, and begins to cry.

"Maybe they did see the island," Hayley says, though she doesn't really believe her own words. "Maybe they saw us, and they've gone to get help, and they're going to come back when the storm has passed."

"Yeah, right," mutters May.

Shannon is sitting quietly, her legs crossed, staring fixedly into the dark forest.

"We're never getting off this island, are we?" Jessa's voice is beginning to rise, half sobbing. "If they were going to find us, they'd have done it by now. They're going to decide that we're dead, and then they'll stop looking…and they'll hold our funerals and bury empty caskets…and everyone will forget about us…" She is talking faster and faster, her voice increasingly shrill as the words start running into one another.

"Jessa, we're not going to die of old age here," Brian says, and she looks up hopefully, sniffing. "We'll die way sooner of starvation or thirst or, like, a tick bite. Or something stupid like a cut that gets infected when we don't have the basic antibiotics to treat it."

Jessa looks up in horror, and Hayley's isn't the only voice that rises in a scream of "SHUT UP, BRIAN."

"Jeez, touchy much?" Brian takes his turn hoisting Elliot up around his neck like a bizarre scarf, head and arms hanging down over one shoulder, legs over the other. "C'mon," he grunts, starting to head back toward the camp, and the others have little choice but to heave themselves to their feet and trail after him. May and Shannon wordlessly lace their arms around Jessa's back while Hayley follows alone.

On the beach, the wind is much wilder, whipping their hair across their faces and flinging the gritty sand into their eyes. The rain is torrential, drumming hard on their scalps without pause and streaming down their faces. It is too dark to see the sea, but they can hear it, like some hideous monster tethered nearby, snarling in its throat, threatening to break its shackles, to leap up and devour them. And each lightning strike illuminates the crests of the waves surging forward, foaming and boiling toward the sky. Jessa has already taken refuge in her sleeping shelter, and the others scramble to do the same, Jason first shoveling Elliot unceremoniously into his own, his head propped sideways on a folded jacket. Shannon promises to check on him regularly.

It's at least a little bit drier inside her makeshift tent, Hayley thinks, realizing with a tightening feeling in her chest that she might not get the chance to tell Elliot how well his shelters worked in the storm. But it's harder to control her imagination in here, lying on her own in the dark. There's just the wet-dog smell of the rain on the sand, the crashing of the waves, and the incessant drumbeat on the plastic meal tray that Elliot wedged into the branches above her to keep her dry.

She closes her eyes and tries to control her breathing, a trick her mom taught her years ago to calm her nerves before exams.

She can hear her mom's voice, soothing and cool. "Breathe in for one. Hold for one. Breathe out for one."

Her thoughts flit wildly, like grains of sand caught in the storm. "Breathe in for two. Hold for two. Breathe out for two."

"You'll be valedictorian one day, you know that?" Grandma once said, neat hands curled around the tortoiseshell handle of her walking stick, smelling of lipstick and soap. "But don't work too hard, my sweet girl. Save something for you."

"Breathe in for three. Hold for three. Breathe out for three." The sea fizzes and hisses. As if the seawater is boiling.

Elliot lying unconscious. Jason's face, angry and taut. Jessa's arm, heavy and useless, hanging from her body. The sticky remains of the iodine sparkling with slivers of glass.

"Breathe in for four. Hold for four. Breathe out for four."

"*C'mon*, Hayley, come *out*." Nella, the girl who used to live next door, shaking her tight blond curls, clutching a pair of walkie-talkies and perched astride her red bike with the training wheels. Pouting. "You never come *play* anymore." Going back to her spelling homework, turning up the volume on her headphones.

"In for five."

Standing quietly in the entrance at the South Florida Science Center on the fifth-grade aquarium trip. Trying to blend into the glass tank behind her. Watching the others easily obey the teacher's command to get into pairs. Knowing she would be the odd one out.

"And six."

Smoothing out the *Oak Ridge Tribune* and staring, staring at her first ever front-page byline. Smelling the fresh, crisp paper, the cheap ink transferring to her palms. Stroking it over and over.

"Now seven."

"Come on, Mom. Do you think Woodward and Bernstein had time to go to their eighth-grade Spring Fling? Believe me, I'm missing *nothing*."

"Breathe in for eight. Hold for eight. Breathe out for eight." Ninth-grade prize day. Kids shuffling up to the stage to collect their awards. Most Improved. Best Effort. Then the list.

An unbearable seven subjects. "Math, English, history, biology, chemistry, French, geography…outstanding academic achievement in every single one goes to…" The longest pause in the world. "Hayley Larkin." The snickers. Pride and shame. Biting the inside of her cheek. Walking up, shaking hands, looking straight ahead. Trying not to listen.

She never could get past eight.

The wind howls and a few sticks shift, leaving a gap above Hayley's head. The sky is a deep, menacing gray. She can just make out the leaves of the palm tree whose trunk her shelter leans against, thrashing and writhing like wild things, trying to take off into the storm.

A squall buffets the side of her shelter, and a cold spray of rain stings the side of her face.

Her eye smarts and burns. Hayley blinks, trying to dislodge a grain of sand, feeling it scratch painfully against her eyelid. She wishes she had some fresh water to wash it out.

Fresh water!

Without thinking, without pausing, she is out of the shelter and running full speed into the trees. The storm is still howling in the distance, but it's getting quieter here, muted, and the clouds have lifted enough for a little moonlight to leak through. Her sneakers slop and slap against wet mud, its stickiness seeping inside, her feet squelching.

The stumps crouch like squat sentinels in the gloom. She can see the plastic slung low between them, bulging now, stretching closer to the ground.

She plunges her hands into the icy water. Three inches, maybe. Cool and silky on her skin. She cups her hands and brings a scoop to her lips; it tastes somehow sharper and cleaner than she remembers. She gulps another mouthful, feeling the chill race into her chest while the rainwater drips from her nose and earlobes, like she's being cleansed inside and out at the same time.

When she gets back to the beach, the wind has dropped and

it isn't raining anymore. She can see the pinpricks of stars piercing the velvet. There's enough moonlight to make out the shape of Elliot's shelter, his sneakered feet just visible at the entrance.

"It worked, Elliot! It worked!" She pats his ankles awkwardly, wanting him to wake up, needing him to share this, to feel the same rush she does now that something positive has finally happened.

"Okay, okay, you don't need to shout," comes a grumpy voice.

"You're awake!" She shrieks it so loudly that heads poke out of other shelters. The others gather around, grinning, as Elliot shuffles out like an ungainly caterpillar. They all look as bedraggled and soggy as Hayley feels.

"It worked, it worked! Elliot built a rain reservoir in the trees to catch water and it worked—there's a few gallons in there at least!" Hayley babbles excitedly.

"I'm glad," Elliot says slowly. "But it's not our first priority." He is carefully scanning the faces around him.

"What are you talking about? What else is more important than water?"

Elliot looks at her.

"Finding out who pushed me."

They can't get the fire going on the wet sand, so there's no warmth, and there aren't enough dry clothes to go around. They sit in a shivering circle, lit weakly by the gray beams of the moon, apart from May, who returns immediately to her bed after saying they're all being ridiculous and nothing will change before morning so they might as well get some sleep.

"Tell us again, Elliot," Shannon says, with the tone of a skeptical but patient teacher trying to get to the bottom of what she suspects might be a tall tale. "What happened, exactly?"

Elliot sighs, frustrated, and rubs a hand through his unruly curls, leaving them even wilder than before. "We were at the top of the hill. I was looking up, trying to spot the plane, doing everything I could to signal the pilot with the mirror. It was loud and windy and it all happened really fast, but I felt a pair of hands shove me, hard, in the small of my back, then I was falling. The next thing I remember is hearing Hayley's voice and waking up here."

"Elliot." Jessa speaks slowly and quietly, like she doesn't want to upset him. Hayley notices that she's cradling her arm, sitting very still, trying to avoid any sudden movements. "Isn't it possible that you just slipped? If everything happened so fast?"

"Yeah, it was super chaotic up there." Jason latches eagerly on to this explanation. "I couldn't hear myself think, everyone was shouting at once, and the storm was wild—"

"No. No." Elliot shakes his head irritably. "I felt it. I felt somebody push me."

"Okay, but we were all looking up, all trying to get the plane's attention," Brian chimes in. "Maybe someone did push you, but by accident? Like they sort of banged into you or shoved you by mistake?"

Elliot starts to shake his head, but Brian is in full flow. "I mean, most of us had never been up there, we didn't know the lay of the land. I totally didn't realize that drop was so steep."

Elliot gets to his feet and turns around. "I felt two hands, here and here." He balls his fists and places them on either side of his spine, just above his shorts. "It was hard and quick, *definitely* deliberate."

He sits heavily back down.

"That's silly," Jessa says eventually. "Why would anyone want to hurt you?"

"I don't know," Elliot admits.

"I mean, totally apart from anything else, you've basically been saving our asses since the day we got here," Brian chimes in with surprising warmth. "It's not like we'd even have survived this long without you."

Jason gives a tiny snort.

Suddenly, something else occurs to Hayley. "Could it have been about the mirror?"

Elliot frowns at her. "What do you mean?"

"What if they weren't trying to hurt you, but they wanted to stop you from signaling the plane? Someone who doesn't want us to get off the island?"

"This *is* ridiculous." Jessa sighs impatiently. "Why are we talking about this as if it's an unsolvable mystery? If one of us shoved Elliot, they should admit it."

There is a long, uninterrupted silence. Hayley feels goose bumps rising on her forearms that have nothing to do with the cold.

"So..." Brian raises his eyebrows and jerks his thumb toward May's shelter. "Then I guess..."

"Oh, shut up, Brian," snaps Jessa. "May would never do something like that."

"Well, someone did," Brian says. "Apparently," he adds, looking at Elliot a little skeptically. "Sorry, man, but you did bang your head hard enough to pass out. Maybe you're just imagining it."

"Or maybe someone was so angry with me that they wanted to punish me," Elliot says quietly, and everybody turns to look at Jason.

"Oh, sure, just because I pointed out his idiocy with the fire, I must have tried to murder him," Jason says bullishly. "Yeah, that makes lots of sense. I'm definitely guilty."

Hayley recalls the fury that passed over Jason's face, the spit in Elliot's eyebrows, and doesn't know what to think. Could Jason really have been so pissed at Elliot, so devastated that the plane wasn't seeing them, that he'd lashed out? Surely not. Jason was all charm and bluster. He wouldn't actually hurt somebody...would he?

They talk in circles, Elliot continuing to stick stubbornly to his story, the others trapped between his certainty and their own unwillingness to believe that one of them could have done what he described, Jason angrily maintaining his innocence.

"I've had enough of this," he finally explodes, stumbling to his feet. "It doesn't even matter whether you believe me or not, does it? It's not going to change the fact that we're never getting off this goddamn island."

The silence he leaves behind is heavy, loaded with each of their fears and unspoken anxieties. Hayley runs her fingers over and over the deep cut on the back of her wrist, sealed over now with a thick scab. What if Jason's right? What if that plane was their one real chance of rescue? She picks at the edge and feels the wetness seeping out.

One by one, tiredness catches up with them and they traipse off to try and sleep. And as Jessa settles in for the night, it is the first evening that Hayley doesn't hear a soft, rhythmic murmuring of prayer coming from inside her shelter. Only silence.

The last thing Brian says before they leave the campfire does nothing to raise anyone's spirits.

"Guys. I've been thinking about it every which way. My man Elliot says he was pushed." Elliot raises his eyebrows, looking like he doesn't know whether to be amused or grateful that his accident has suddenly made him far more popular with his teammate.

"Okay, so he was pushed. And each of us says we didn't push him, right?" There's a pause, some nodding. "Well, there's another possibility, isn't there?"

Hayley watches the others' baffled faces. She thinks she knows what is coming; she's been trying not to think it ever since Elliot's bombshell.

"There might be someone else on the island."

DAY 7

THE MORNING DOESN'T BEGIN WELL. HAYLEY MAKES AN EARLY pilgrimage through the trees, enjoying the rich, earthy smell that rises up from the wet ground after last night's deluge. The birds are noisier than ever, shrieking exuberantly as if to celebrate their victory over the storm. A beautiful golden-yellow blur flutters to a stop on a branch just yards away from Hayley, its shining black eye fixed on her with bright curiosity. She holds her breath, amazed at the glossiness of its feathers, drenched in color, the buttercup hue gleaming against its delicate black-and-white wings.

For one ridiculous moment, she entertains the fantasy that it has come to tell her something: to warn her, perhaps, or to help her. There is such intelligence in that fierce little eye. "Who did it?" she almost asks out loud. Then it tilts its head to the other side, as if to chide her for hers silliness, and is gone as quickly as it came.

She walks on eagerly, a backpack full of empty water bottles slung over her shoulder, glad to have a purpose to distract her from the murky fears and questions hanging over the camp. The memory of the clear, cool water she gulped down last night dances tantalizingly on her tongue, pushing her forward, making her stumble in her eagerness.

But when she reaches the shady clearing, she stops dead.

Rocket the raccoon is floating on his back in the water, his body horribly bloated, his eyes milky and unseeing. Hayley cannot bring herself to touch him, although she knows she should remove the carcass and discard the contaminated water. She trudges dejectedly back to the camp.

"Not Rocket," May wails, while Jason smashes his fist into a tree trunk in frustration when Hayley breaks the news.

"We'll try again," Elliot says quietly. "At least it worked."

Brian has decided they have to check the island. He's calling it a search party, which May says is stupid, because how can you search for something if you don't even know what you're looking for? Elliot says it's stupid too, but for different reasons. He doesn't think someone could have slipped out of the trees and shoved him and then melted away again without anybody noticing, even in the chaos of the storm.

Jason says looking will give them an answer once and for all.

Hayley can't decide what's worse—the threat that there might be someone else hiding on the island, waiting to launch another attack, or the idea that one of them could hurt Elliot so badly and then lie about it. She looks over at him, a purple bruise protruding from his temple. It could have been so much worse. But he looks different somehow, more alert, his eyes darting here and there, and he jumps a little when someone bumps into him from behind. It's like he can't relax because he doesn't know who to trust. And Hayley can't blame him. She's starting to feel the same way herself.

She takes in each of the others, one by one, as they pull on shoes and drag random items of clothing out of the overhead bins, getting ready to head out on what they all know is probably a wild goose chase.

May sniffs cautiously at the armpits of a yellow T-shirt before wrinkling her nose and throwing it to one side in disgust, choosing to pull one of the boys' jerseys over her head instead. It swamps her, but that seems preferable to wearing clothing that's stiff with someone else's encrusted sweat.

Brian is thumping the bottle of sunscreen, trying to get it to spit the last dregs out into his palm. His nose has started to peel so violently it looks like he's permanently shedding scraps of white confetti. Shannon is readjusting Jessa's sling, tying the orange scarf tighter and trying to find a more comfortable position for her arm. Jessa's face is rigid with concentration; she's staring down at the sand as if she can't actually see it.

Jason is sketching something in the sand with a sharp stick, pointing to different areas and murmuring to himself. Elliot is hunched at the edge of the trees, his features set in a stubborn frown, draining the water out of the last of the brown coconuts into small bottles he's scratched their initials into, making sure they each get an equal share. He's shaking his head and muttering about not getting dehydrated on a pointless mission.

Nobody looks like they're hiding anything. Hayley feels a stab of annoyance at herself. She ought to be able to figure out what's going on. She's an investigative journalist, for goodness' sake, or at least one in training. But nothing's jumping out at her like it should. Someone ought to be looking guilty, making excuses, trying to avoid detection. But there's nothing. Absolutely no clues at all. She watches them bustling around the camp, clearing away their breakfast things, fetching fresh wood to build up the fire. She watches Jason the longest. He's the only one with something approaching a motive. But he does nothing to give himself away.

Could there really be someone else on the island after all?

"Okay, guys, huddle up." Jason waves them all over, wiping his hands on his bright red jersey.

"I've divided the island into quarters." He points with the stick, a rough circle drawn in the sand in front of him. "This is the crash site and the camp, along the beach here. We've spent the most time in this area and the trees immediately adjacent to the beach, collecting wood. And we haven't seen anybody. So we can assume this area is clear. But here…" He stabs to the left with the stick, indicating the southernmost quadrant. "This is the most densely wooded area, where the girls found the fruit trees. We haven't searched that whole area yet, and it's possible someone could be hiding among the trees. Jessa, you can show us the way. Hayley, you're with us. And you, babe." Jason slides an arm around Shannon's shoulders and pulls her tightly to him. "I'm not leaving my girl alone with some lunatic running around the island trying to kill people."

"Jeez, overexaggerate much?" mutters May under her breath.

Jason pretends not to hear and slides the stick over to the opposite side of his map. "Meanwhile, Elliot, Brian, and May should go sort out the water tarp, then head back to the north, to the hilltop, and search the area around there. Elliot can try to pinpoint exactly where he was when he felt the push. See if you can figure out where someone might have taken cover." Elliot rolls his eyes but seems to have decided that there's no point in arguing.

"Then head to the beach where the coconut trees are," Jason continues, "and search for any sign of a shelter or someone hiding out."

Hayley grabs one of the water bottles Elliot has prepared from their makeshift "fridge" pit. She takes a sip. The liquid is unpleasantly warm with an overpowering sweet aftertaste, a little like a compost heap.

"I know," Elliot says, seeing her grimace. "Sorry, it's quite strong. I think it's because the coconuts were left out in the sun. We'll get some more green ones tomorrow."

Hayley follows Jason as he strides off to the south, Jessa and Shannon close behind her.

"I swear, if we ever get out of here, I'll never moan about my little brother again," Jessa pants as they start picking their way through the undergrowth. "He'd love all this. Deserted island...jungle adventure...it's like his idea of heaven. I can't stop thinking about him."

"We're going to get out of here." Jason says it firmly, like his word is the final say on the subject. Hayley wonders if he's ever experienced what it's like not to get his own way. It's an open secret that at the end of junior year, Jason told his guidance counselor he wanted to take AP Latin after the Princeton Review recommended it as a good way for law school applicants to boost their admissions prospects.

The trouble was, Oak Ridge offered only eight AP courses, and Latin wasn't one of them. But a week later, a Latin tutor miraculously joined the staff, and two weeks later, it was announced that a generous endowment had been made for a new classics wing in the school library. The *Angel* Wing. As in Jason Angel.

In fact, she suddenly realizes, even their current situation is partly due to Jason always getting what he wants. Hayley heard a rumor that the off-season basketball tour might be canceled this year because of funding issues before Jason's parents stepped in with their offer of private jets and free accommodations. None of them would even be here if it wasn't for Jason Angel and his charmed life.

"Have you guys thought about what our families must be going through?" Jessa asks, breathing heavily as, climbing over a particularly knotty vine, she uses her one good arm to grab a tree trunk.

"I've been trying not to," Shannon admits. "It's easier that way. We can't do anything about it, so it's best not to think about it."

"I know it's stupid," Jessa says softly, "but I have this idea, this hope, I suppose, that somehow my mom just knows…" She sniffs. "That she knows I'm okay. Because we're so close that she'd have some kind of sixth sense if I were dead. It's dumb, I know."

"It's not dumb," Shannon says quietly.

"I got my brother one of those stupid touristy cowboy hats at the airport," Jessa whispers. "I was gonna write 'My sister went to Texas and all I got was this stupid cowboy hat' on the back in magic marker."

Hayley swallows hard. She really, really doesn't want to think about how her mom and dad must be feeling. Partly because it hurts too much. Partly because on a good day, she can almost trick herself into thinking that things aren't so desperate…that they're on a wild adventure rather than trapped in an incredibly dangerous situation they might actually not survive.

She needs to think about something else. *Anything* else. So, as she automatically scans the ground ahead for tangles of vines and treacherous rocks, her brain is scanning too, going back over everything that has happened, trying to make sense of Elliot's fall, of his certainty that he was pushed.

If he's right, if someone pushed him, they must have had a reason. They'd have been acting differently, maybe, not seeming themselves. Hayley sighs. That could describe all of them.

Nobody has been themselves for a week, and who could blame them? But then Hayley thinks back further. It isn't just being on the island that's changing people, is it? Not entirely. She remembers that stupid cowboy hat. Suddenly, an image pops into her head: Jessa snapping at May when she knocked it onto the floor as they waited to board the plane. She thought it was weird at the time. People have been behaving oddly since *before* the island— ever since the morning of the crash. The night after the party.

The group assembled at the airport terminal that morning was uncharacteristically quiet. Brian sat on his own, excusing himself repeatedly to go to the bathroom. Elliot was hidden behind his sketchbook, Jason leafing through the same few pages of a sports magazine over and over again without seeming to take in a word. Hayley tripped and spilled a coffee over May's white sneakers, but she barely looked up, preoccupied and biting her lip, none of her usual spiky attitude on display. Jessa seemed on edge somehow too, drumming her fingers annoyingly on the arm of the uncomfortable terminal chair. Shannon arrived at the last minute, her face hidden behind a huge pair of sunglasses, and swept onto the plane without a word to anyone.

Then there were the little moments on the plane, things that seemed meaningless on their own but looked like something more substantial now. Shannon and Jason sitting apart. May and Jessa's whispered conversation. The way people reacted when Erickson mentioned the party—right before the plane went down. Had something happened that night?

They are deeper into the trees than Hayley has ever been. The sunlight filters down in long, glittering bars. It feels still here, like the island is trapped in this single moment. The golden light is like amber, preserving everything for eternity, as though they've somehow slipped outside time. Hayley wants to be able to examine other moments, frozen, like this one, to turn them over in her fingertips and look at them from every possible angle.

"What did you guys think of the end-of-tour party?" she asks Shannon and Jessa casually, walking a little faster to catch up with them. Jason is still ahead, out of sight, though the occasional rustle of a bush or crack of a stick makes him easy enough to follow.

"Why?" Jessa asks immediately, shooting Hayley a suspicious look. "Has someone said something about it?"

"No, no. I was just wondering, that's all. I didn't stay to the end," she says. She'd escaped back to the hotel just before she was drunk enough to make a fool of herself.

She tries to think back to that night. It was only a week ago, but it feels like a lifetime.

It was stuffy in the living room. The windows were open, but it was a warm evening and there were bodies crowded in. Thighs pressed against each other, elbows knocked, the loud, throbbing beat of the music pressing in close. And laughter, crashing over her like a wave as she came in from the kitchen, her red plastic cup of stronger-than-she-really-wanted vodka orange clutched tight like a talisman against her insecurity. Hayley couldn't have said how it compared with other parties, because she didn't really know. Did everyone usually just sit around like this? Sandwiched together and chatting, trying to look casual while sweat dripped in slow, uncomfortable paths between their shoulder blades? Laughing too loudly at the loudest person's jokes? Was that what you did to show you were part of it all, in the loop, one of the crowd? She remembers wondering whether everyone else at the party was spending as much time as she was thinking about whether she looked like she was enjoying herself.

"It was pretty standard." Jessa shrugs. "Not much happened, right, Shan?"

"Mm-hmm." Shannon nods, focusing on her feet.

"There was a lot of alcohol, right?" Hayley asks, thinking back. "There was that keg the Duke guys set up, and the cheerleader, the redhead...her name was Sasha, right? She put out all her parents' liquor bottles in the kitchen with mixers and things."

"I wouldn't know," Jessa says dismissively. "I don't drink. May was acting a little weird, though, now that you mention it. Like, halfway through the evening, she suddenly seemed all jittery and nervous. I don't know why. Then she started acting pretty *wild*, even by May standards. Dancing on the tables and everything. Like she was trying too hard to have fun."

"Elliot could tell you how much liquor there was." Shannon smirked. "I found him in the bathroom toward the end of the night, getting pretty cozy with the toilet bowl, if you know what I mean."

"That wasn't his fault," Jessa protests. "Did you *see* the concoction they made him drink during Truth or Dare? It was gross."

The game had come later. The atmosphere was different by then, the living room smudged somehow by the blur of alcohol and sweat and awkward excitement. Hayley should have been terrified of Truth or Dare, but it actually came as a relief. There were obvious pitfalls—dares that could expose her inexperience or questions that could reveal gaping holes in her pop culture knowledge—but at least it was organized. It had rules, structure, a pattern she could follow.

Brian had already stolen a gnome from the next-door garden, one of the Duke cheerleaders had TP'd a mailbox, and Shannon had begun to perform a pretty explicit act with a banana and a can of whipped cream, at least until Jason had yanked her down from the table she was standing on, shouting, "Show's over, folks." Elliot, who'd been hovering awkwardly on the edges of the party, had downed a disgusting concoction of every drink in the house mixed together with a squeeze of toothpaste stirred in. Hayley didn't know whether to be relieved or disappointed that her turn never seemed to come.

"Right, how close are we to the fruit?" Jason asks from up ahead, crashing out of the trees and interrupting Hayley's train of thought.

"It's over this way." Jessa moves forward confidently, pointing at some nearby tree trunks. "I tore bark and branches off trees on the way last time so we'd be able to find our way back." Now that she knows what she is looking for, Hayley can see the snapped-off, splintered ends and scratched sections on several of the trees they walk past, their green muscles bristling through the torn skin. She remembers what Jessa said about Elliot not being the only Scout in the group.

"So what are we supposed to be looking for, exactly?" Hayley asks.

Now that they're actually in the trees, Jason seems a little less confident than he was with his simplistic sand diagram on the beach. The tree trunks are choked with vines so thick they've solidified like bones, the ground uneven and cluttered with small plants and bushes underfoot. The visibility is limited because the vegetation is so dense. Hayley finds it pretty hard to believe that anyone could be living in all this, but if they were, she's not convinced they'd be able to find them anyway. It wouldn't be difficult to stay hidden, dodging behind trees, hiding in bushes, cutting back behind the group once they'd passed—especially given the amount of noise their search party is making as they crash and stumble along.

"We're looking for any evidence of someone living here," Jason hisses. "A shelter of some kind...probably a camp setup."

"Nobody else picked up the coconuts," Hayley says suddenly, stopping so abruptly that Shannon bumps into her from behind. "The ones we found on the other side of the island. If someone else was living here before we arrived, then all those brown coconuts wouldn't just have been left lying there on the ground, would they?"

Shannon is frowning. "That's a good point. It's a small island—they'd have covered it within a week. If they'd been here any time at all, they'd have needed those coconuts. So can we just agree this is completely absurd?" she asks, hands on her hips. "It's a huge waste of our time and energy combing a clearly deserted island looking for a phantom pusher when the *obvious* explanation is that Elliot had an accident."

"Maybe he doesn't want to admit that he slipped," Shannon continues. "He's certainly enjoyed playing the hero these last few days. And falling down a steep drop and knocking himself out doesn't exactly fit with the skilled hunter-gatherer image, does it?"

Jason grunts approvingly.

Hayley doesn't know what to think. It does seem unlikely that anyone else could have survived for a long time on this island—and even if they had, why wouldn't they have made contact with the new arrivals after the plane crash? Why would they want to hurt Elliot?

After another hour of searching through the untouched undergrowth, they've seen nothing suspicious or strange at all. Until they get back to the camp.

At first, Hayley thinks May is just joking around.

"We found...NOTHING!" She shouts it loudly as she comes crashing back through the trees with the rest of her group, attempting a drum roll on a tree trunk and missing. "Nothing like a dasted way, hey?" She frowns, chews the words in her mouth, tries again: "Wasted day! Way hey!"

She does what Hayley thinks is supposed to be a sarcastic celebration dance, but it looks like her arms and legs are getting messages from completely different brains. As she whirls wildly, she sings at the top of her voice, something about mixed messages and a wild-goose chase, but the notes don't seem to be coming out in the right order, and the words are all garbled and slurred. Eventually she becomes tangled up in her own limbs, lurching to the ground and subsiding into silence.

"She's been like this half the journey back," Elliot says uneasily.

Hayley takes a step toward May, watching her closely.

"S'all right Sh…shayley?" May attempts to stand up and give Hayley a hug but almost misses and ends up sort of hanging around Hayley's waist, her face level with Hayley's belly button. May dissolves into helpless giggles and slides back to the ground.

"Ow," she says thickly, trying to sit up and falling over again.

Jason is laughing, clapping her on the back and whistling. But Hayley feels sick. Something is very wrong.

May has never voluntarily hugged her in her life. The more Hayley stares at her, the more she notices the slack jaw, the slightly glazed, unfocused eyes.

"What's going on?" Shannon crouches down next to May, looking uneasy. "May, can you look at me?"

May spins around, her gaze landing on a spot somewhere over Hayley's right shoulder.

"May. Focus."

"Hmmm?" May's starting to look less confident now. Hayley can see her eyes starting to flit quickly from side to side. A look of panic is creeping in.

Jessa comes back from a bathroom trip and takes in the scene, her eyes widening in horror.

"Jessa, whaddami…" May takes a breath, shakes her head heavily like a dog, and tries again: "Wasssa…" Her speech slurs, and her eyes lock onto Jessa's, shining with fear. A tear escapes and slides slowly down May's cheek.

"It's okay, May." Hayley tries to keep her voice steadier than her jangling nerves. "I think…have you guys eaten anything? Berries or roots? Or drunk something?"

Elliot shakes his head.

"Brian, have you guys been drinking without me?" Jason snaps the words out accusingly, sounding more team coach than team captain.

Brian looks surprised. "No, I swear!" He holds up his hands like he's trying to prove his innocence. "Honestly—we've been trawling the beach on the other side of the island, looking for a hut or signs of a fire or something. The only thing we've drunk is that disgusting coconut water." He holds up his half-full bottle. "We really need to get some more green ones," he adds.

"Where's May's bottle?" Hayley asks. They look around. There's an almost-empty bottle lying on the ground by the campfire, the initial just visible, scratched into the side. "Is this it?" She takes off the lid and cautiously sniffs the contents, then takes a small sip. "That doesn't taste the same as mine," Hayley says, sipping from her own bottle to compare. "I think there's something in it."

May is limp now, her head resting on her knees. Without warning, she lurches forward, vomiting into the sand.

Shannon snaps into action. "Is there any fresh water left?"

"There's half a bottle. That's all we've got until it rains again." Elliot hands it over and Shannon crouches next to May, rubbing her back reassuringly. She helps her sip from the rainwater bottle while Jessa looks on, helpless and aghast.

"Guys." Elliot has been poking around in the overhead bins. He holds out his cupped hands. He's holding seven of the vodka miniatures they'd found in the back of the plane.

They're all empty.

"May!" Jessa shrieks, whirling to face her. "What were you thinking? What, you just felt like a party? All by yourself?" May lets out a muffled groan and waves her off weakly.

"You could've shared at least," Brian chimes in resentfully.

"Yes, because getting drunk and dehydrated is a fantastic idea in a survival situation with very little drinking water." Elliot frowns.

"I DIDNNN," May drawls angrily, sweat beading along her hairline. "Didnknow. Didn't know." It takes her a supreme effort to separate the words, frowning as she forms them carefully and deliberately with her lips. She points vaguely in the direction of Elliot's hands before slumping over again, cradling her head and groaning.

"Is she saying what I think she's saying?" Jessa asks. The bottles clatter together noisily as Elliot hurries to put them down, like he doesn't want to be the one left holding them. "Did someone spike May's drink?"

"Uh, yeah. *May* spiked May's drink." Jason shakes his head. "Can't believe I didn't think of it myself—those bottles were just lying there for the taking."

"Yeah," Brian says, but Hayley can see he's uneasy. "She is kind of a party girl. Look how wild she was the other night..." He trails off sheepishly. "You can't exactly blame her for wanting to forget"—he waves his hand around vaguely—"all this, can you? She probably just overdid it."

"What, overdid it by seven bottles?" Jessa sounds skeptical. "Drinking fourteen shots of vodka isn't exactly something you do by mistake, Brian."

"Well, what other explanation is there?" Brian asks. And his question hangs heavy in the air, because everybody knows the answer, but nobody wants to be the one to say it. Except Elliot.

"Maybe it was the same person who pushed me." He looks around at the circle of faces, slowly and uncompromisingly making eye contact with each of them in turn. "That coconut water was strong and sweet—the taste was so overpowering May wouldn't have realized it was spiked until it was too late."

"And everyone's bottles are labeled with our initials," Shannon says slowly, running her finger over the rough scratched into the plastic.

Rain starts to fall again, big fat droplets splashing onto Hayley's face. But she can't enjoy it, can't let herself bask in the relief of the waterbag filling again (after having been thoroughly washed out by Elliot in the sea), not while the creeping idea of sabotage is slowly seeping into the camp like poison. Elliot takes a deep breath with the expression of somebody who is about to take a dive off the highest diving board and knows there is no going back. "Someone is hurting people.

And since we've searched the whole island and found no sign of anybody else…"

Hayley finishes his sentence for him. "It has to be one of us."

DAY 8

OF COURSE, NOBODY ADMITS TO ANYTHING, EVEN WHEN May wakes up with a horrible hangover the next morning and swears blind she had no idea there was vodka in her drink. "Yes, I knew it tasted weird," she snaps at Brian when he questions her. "But that damn coconut stuff always tastes disgusting. I just thought it was grosser than normal."

They look at each other, the accusation hanging heavily over the camp.

"Was it you, Brian?" Jessa blurts out directly.

"What?" His voice is squeaky with indignation. "Why are you accusing me?"

Jessa squirms. "I'm sorry, it's just…it seems like the kind of prank you might play. You did put dish soap in half the team's water bottles during the second tour game…"

"Yeah, for a *joke*!" Brian sputters. "And don't pretend you weren't laughing when Tom Allen started spitting bubbles, Jessa."

"So was this just another joke?" she persists. "We won't be mad if you tell us. It'd be much better to own it."

"No. Jesus. I wasn't even the one who filled up the bottles. That was Elliot."

"And why would I want to get May drunk?" Elliot asks. "Besides, if whoever did this was also the person who pushed me, then that puts me in the clear, doesn't it? I wouldn't exactly give myself a serious head injury on purpose." Hayley watches him closely, the tense drawing together of his full, dark eyebrows, the cut on his cheek that has all but completely faded now, the bruise on his temple that's now a faint yellow, trying to sense whether or not he is lying.

"But you *were* the one who filled the bottles," Shannon says slowly, narrowing her eyes at Elliot. "How did the vodka get in there if you didn't put it in?"

"We were all rushing around getting stuff ready," Elliot protests. "I left the bottles under the trees to keep cool, so anyone could have slipped something in while we were getting wood or going to the bathroom. We all had the opportunity."

"But who wanted to?" May whines furiously. "If you've got a problem with me, say it to my face!" she shouts defiantly.

But nobody says a word. And eventually they fall into a dissatisfied silence.

Hayley can't stop thinking about the party on the last night of the tour. The more she tries to connect the dots between what happened to Elliot and May, the more convinced she becomes that the party is the key to unraveling it all. And though she wouldn't admit it, there's a part of her that feels energized, almost buoyed, by finally feeling that there's a role for her on the island. So she wasn't cool under pressure in the first days. And she doesn't have any particularly useful survival skills. But uncovering the truth? Getting people to reveal more than they intended? This is Hayley Larkin's wheelhouse. If anyone can figure out what is going on, she can. Ideally before anyone else gets hurt. The only problem is, none of it adds up. The only person with a clear motive to hurt Elliot is Jason. It doesn't take a crack journalist to see he's jealous of Elliot's new leadership role in the group. But why would Jason want to hurt May? Why would *anyone* want to hurt May? One thing is certain: Hayley can cross Jessa off the list of suspects. Elliot says he was pushed with two hands, and Jessa's injured arm is practically immobile. And there's no way Jessa would ever do anything to hurt her best friend.

There is always something that needs doing. It's all laborious, repetitive work, but it distracts them from arguing about whether Elliot's attacker was real or imagined, whether May was deliberately poisoned with alcohol or stole the vodka herself and lied about it.

The main jobs are collecting and boiling rainwater, catching fish, picking fruit and coconuts, and keeping the fire burning from dawn to dusk. If another search party comes close, they'll be ready.

They've decided not to worry about keeping the fire burning after dark, since rescuers are less likely to be out looking at night anyway, plus they're all completely exhausted by the end of each day and, though nobody mentions it directly, the last attempt at a night watch was such a total disaster. Elliot is convinced the island is too small to support any predators, so there doesn't seem to be much need for guard duty anyway. (Or at least, as Elliot darkly adds, they don't need guarding from anything *outside* the camp.)

But keeping the fire burning means collecting firewood. Lots of firewood. Hayley, whose family has one of those neat little electric fires behind glass for the rare winter night that's cold enough to turn it on, had no idea that wood fires gobbled up so much fuel. Within the first week, they've gathered and burned every piece of driftwood and most of the larger sticks in the trees that line the beach. Which is why Hayley finds herself deep in the dense, wooded central part of the island with Elliot on the afternoon of the eighth day, her back and thighs aching, her forearms ribboned with livid scratches, painstakingly adding piece after piece of wood to the backpack she has slung across one shoulder.

"I think my splinters have splinters," she grumbles, inspecting her reddened palms. The cuts and bruises left by the crash have almost all healed, but they've been replaced by other sore spots, souvenirs of more than a week on the island. There's a half-healed cut where she accidentally gouged herself with a fishhook while trying to bait it. A scrape down the side of her shin from tripping over a vine on a fruit-gathering expedition. A nasty bruise on her left thumb from taking aim at a coconut with the cutting stone and accidentally bringing the blunt side smashing down on her hand instead. And a smooth blister on her right index fingertip from a cooking accident.

They have started to attempt slightly more sophisticated "cooking," of a sort. Elliot showed them how to make a mini stove with a Coke can. He cut a hole in the side of the can to allow hot stones and tinder to be pushed inside, and the top provided a stable base for a cooking container made of half another tin can to stand on. They've boiled sea snails plucked from rough rocks at low tide and steamed pieces of white fish (more of them caught with Jessa's hook than Elliot's spear) wrapped in supple green leaves.

Everything is an effort. They don't eat, drink, or rest without working for it. It can take an hour or more to catch a single fish. Once they've scraped off the scales and pulled out the hundreds of bones, each one is barely a mouthful. And there are seven hungry mouths to feed. By the time they've prepared the fish, collected wood, made the fire, eaten, and cleaned up again, it's time to start scavenging for the next meal.

Hayley sighs and adds another stick to her bulging pack. "Can you believe we've been here over a week already?"

Elliot has his back to her, bent over a dead tree trunk, trying to break off some pieces of dry wood. But she can hear the care in his voice, like he's trying not to scare her. "It's not a very good sign," he says slowly. "If they had the means to find us easily—like if our radar had been working until the last minute or we didn't stray very far from the planned flight path—then we should have been found in the first couple of days, tops."

"So not being found quickly means we might not be found at all?"

Elliot nods apologetically.

"No." Hayley is embarrassed by the hot prickling behind her eyeballs. She can handle this. Just because Elliot's been camping a lot, that doesn't make him the final authority on all things island. He's guessing just as much as anyone else.

"They'll keep looking until they find us," she says firmly, trying to keep a wobble out of her voice. "It doesn't matter how long it takes. Our parents aren't going to stop. And you can bet Jason's parents will pay for a private search even if the authorities give up. May's too, come to think of it." In fact, the combined wealth of the families of the kids on the island could probably finance a round-the-clock rescue operation for months.

"Yeah, I can believe there aren't many of those booster club parents who'll take no for an answer," Elliot says drily. "I guess we should consider ourselves lucky it works in our favor this time around."

"This time?"

"As opposed to, say, when we're applying for college and our recommendation letters are being written by the school, but we're in competition with classmates whose parents can afford to fund a new library."

Elliot wrenches at the dead wood, twisting great clumps of it off and piling them beside him.

"Or competing for basketball scholarships with kids whose parents have been paying for them to fly around the country and play in the off-season for years, sending them to pricey summer camps since they were in elementary school. Kids who basically bought their ball skills instead of spending a thousand hours late into the night shooting at a single rusty hoop in their backyard because they can't afford to go out anywhere anyway."

He breathes heavily, concentrating on the stump, not meeting Hayley's eyes. She has no idea what to say. She feels a strange mixture of embarrassment and irritation that Elliot so often manages to make her feel like a naïve child. She likes to think of Oak Ridge as her beat, prides herself on knowing it inside and out. But she's never heard a story like Elliot's before. Partly because she's never spoken to a scholarship kid. Not because she's avoided them…just because, she suddenly realizes, she's never known who any of them were. And she's beginning to understand why.

Hayley's parents aren't off-the-scale wealthy, not by the standards of a lot of her classmates, but they live comfortably, managing the school tuition with enough left over to take a nice vacation every few years if they budget carefully. Somehow, she's always just assumed her peers' lives were all pretty similar, apart from the significant handful whose gold-plated existence revolves more around private pools, skiing in Aspen, and buying whatever luxe thing is trending on TikTok, that is. And, she is slowly beginning to realize, being around those kids has always made her think of herself, by comparison, as...normal. But talking to Elliot, she's beginning to realize just how lucky she is. And just how little she's ever really stopped to appreciate it.

"Elliot," Hayley begins hesitantly, "do you really, honestly think someone pushed you off those rocks?"

He sighs and turns to look her directly in the eye, wiping his hands on the same scruffy khaki shorts and thin gray T-shirt he's been wearing pretty much constantly since the day they arrived.

"Here," he says, walking over to her until they're so close that she can see a slight dusting of freckles across the bridge of his nose. Elliot takes her shoulders and gently spins her around so she's facing away from him. Then, suddenly, before she has time to realize what he's about to do, he shoves her hard in the back with both fists, sending her crashing to the ground.

"OW!" Hayley protests, rubbing her elbow and picking leaves out of her hair. "What did you do that for?"

"Do you think you could have imagined that?" Elliot asks. "Is it possible you just tripped? Could you be confused?"

McCOMB PUBLIC LIBRARY
McCOMB, OHIO

"Okay, okay, I get your point," Hayley mutters grumpily, brushing herself off.

She looks at him for a moment. Out of everyone on the island, he's the person she probably knew the least before they crashed. But somehow, now he feels like the one she's most willing to trust.

"I think maybe something happened at the party and that's why someone pushed you, and maybe why they spiked May's drink as well." She lets it all come out in a rush before she changes her mind about confiding in him.

Elliot looks troubled. "At the party? Why do you think that?"

"Think about it. Everyone's been acting weird ever since the morning after—we just didn't really notice because the crash happened. Shannon and Jason haven't been the same, Jessa says May was acting strange that night, nobody seems to want to talk about it…" She runs her hands through her greasy hair, frustrated. "I can't explain it, exactly. I just feel sure that whatever happened that night holds the key to what's going on here."

Elliot thinks for a while. "I guess you could be right," he says thoughtfully. "It was kind of a rowdy party. But it was Shannon who was acting the weirdest, if you ask me."

"What do you mean?"

"It was like she was high or something, the way she threw herself into that game of Truth or Dare, the way she was dancing with that Duke player later, them grinding up against each other like that…"

Hayley remembers the sweaty, heaving, swaying mass of bodies, arms coiling and necks arched, hands twisting and finding flesh, colors whirling and legs rubbing and hair sticking to the sides of their necks. By that point, Hayley had been comfortably numbed by the vodka, sliding into that sweet spot where her knees tingled and a cloak of somebody else's confidence was softly draped over her shoulders. Not yet at the point when her tongue started to grow rubbery and floppy so she had to concentrate hard on her words in order to avoid tripping over them. Surrounded by an invisible force field of protection from her own constant inner monologue of self-consciousness. The whispering voice in her head—*you don't know what you're doing, you're totally out of your depth, everyone's looking at you*—finally stopped. And it hadn't hurt that really, nobody was looking at her at all. Brian was huddled in the corner in a sweaty, pulsing ecosystem of his own with two of the Duke cheerleaders. Jason seemed to have disappeared. Shannon, head thrown back and nostrils flaring, was dancing like her life depended on it with the tall, muscular Duke basketball captain, his light blond hair elaborately gelled into place. May was dancing alone, her long limbs making beautiful, angular, unpredictable moves and somehow completely pulling them off as only May could. Hayley couldn't remember seeing Jessa. And Elliot was on the table, feet splayed and propped on one arm, his top ripped off, humping the air, his hips plunging and arching to the music. Surrounded by a chanting crowd of faces, a buzzing muddle of admiration and mockery.

And without saying a word to anyone, Hayley slipped out, shutting the door gratefully on the wall of noise and damp heat, writhing bodies, and pulsing music. She walked slowly back to the hotel in the moonlight, going over the night the way Shannon would analyze her performance in a complicated routine. It had been a solid non-disaster as far as Hayley was concerned. Which, for her, was a big success. And as she snuggled down between the crisp hotel room sheets, she'd whispered quietly to herself, "You went to a party. An actual party. And you didn't totally suck."

"So what about you?" She looks sideways at Elliot to gauge his reaction as she continues picking at the wood on the stump. "Shannon wasn't the only one who let her hair down that night, was she?"

Elliot blushes. "If by letting your hair down you mean being forced to drink the most disgusting cocktail known to man, then I suppose you could say that. I don't remember very much after that, if I'm totally honest."

"Shannon said she found you on the bathroom floor."

"Oh God." He cringes. "That was much later, I think. She sort of flew into the bathroom and collapsed over the sink, spitting into it and rinsing her face. That was when she spotted me. But then she disappeared again. I don't know, I think I passed out."

"You guys need any help?" Jason appears behind Elliot, flicking a bug off the sleeve of his grubby white T-shirt.

"Yeah, thanks," Hayley answers quickly, wondering how

much of their conversation Jason overheard. "We're trying to break down this stump for firewood."

It occurs to Hayley, absurdly, that this might be one of the only times Jason Angel has addressed her directly. Unless you count him making her feel extremely uncomfortable at her first-ever cheer practice, which she doesn't, since he didn't even bother to find out her name. Not that he deliberately ignores her, exactly. It's more that he just never seems to notice her. On tour, he'd talk to Jessa and May in front of her, and he was always with Shannon, of course, turning up to collect her from practice, shepherding her from their locker rooms onto the court. ("So everybody knows you're my girl. Don't want any of those opposing fans getting ideas.") But it's like he's never really *seen* Hayley. It's the way she imagines famous people just don't notice the aides who buzz around them, getting things done every day. Jason's not the sort of person who needs to notice everybody around him. Everybody else takes notice of him instead.

He took notice of Shannon, though. The day she arrived as a transfer student halfway through ninth grade, Jason picked her out. People were a little surprised, actually, back then. Jason could have chosen almost anybody, and Shannon wasn't the most obvious pick. She had a regal poise and pale, dramatic looks. But she wasn't the stereotypical prom queen type, not like May with her exuberant, social-butterfly popularity or Jessa with her dimples and her massive brown eyes and eyelashes that went on forever. But there was something about Shannon. And on Jason's arm, she walked into the world of cheerleading royalty with every door swinging open in front of her. That was a long time ago, though. Now Shannon is cheer captain, calling extra practice sessions and running drills like military exercises. It's hard to remember the coltish, shy girl who turned up in second-period math and slid quietly into a seat next to Jason.

Jason gets his nails into a crack in the stump and starts to heave, ripping off a substantial strip and sidestepping as a stream of tiny bugs with shiny black shells swarms out from underneath it. He's just starting to pull at a second piece when he stops suddenly.

"What was that?" Jason sounds uneasy. They all stop and listen.

The noise comes again: a cascade of descending notes like tinkling laughter. The skin on the back of Hayley's neck start to crawl. She tries to slow her breathing, standing frozen, straining in the direction the noise seemed to come from.

It comes again like a silvery waterfall of noise, so quick and light that it seems to slip through her fingers. But this time there's a pause and then a dry rustling noise, which sounds like it's coming from the trees behind Elliot.

Jason looks absolutely terrified. He quickly takes a few steps toward Hayley, putting Elliot between him and the noise.

"I think it's a bird," Elliot whispers, breathing heavily.

A flurry of dry leaves puffs into the air and a bird the size of a rooster struts confidently out of a bush just yards away from them.

Hayley's hand flies to her mouth, the shock of its unexpected appearance making her heart leap.

The bird is beautiful. At first, Hayley thinks it's a peacock, with its powder-blue head and long, decorative feathers, darker at the back but shining all over with a gasoline sheen. It has a little red comb on the top of its head and a red ring around each eye, with small decorative lumps like red and yellow baubles clinging to its face. Its pink scaly legs end in sharp claws that scratch and scrabble surefootedly through the debris on the forest floor. A moment later, it sees them and stops, looking more curious than afraid. It cocks its wrinkled face to one side and fixes them with its little currant eye.

"We have to kill it," Elliot breathes, barely even moving his lips.

"What?!"

"We need the food," Elliot replies immediately, his eyes darting around the clearing, already making calculations for a hunt.

"It's stunning," Hayley hisses, "and defenseless…and it's probably never seen humans. It won't even know to run away. It's not fair!" And what she wants to say, but doesn't, is that she feels, somehow, that the island will never forgive them if they kill this beautiful, majestic bird. It's bad enough that it has been forced to accept their rough intrusion without them spilling blood as well.

"All the better." Jason grins, moving quietly into a crouched position, his arms outstretched.

The bird flicks its head to the other side, staring unblinkingly at Jason. With a quiet whoosh, it fans out its tail feathers, a gorgeous array of intricate black-and-white patterns, each feather tipped in blue and gold as if it has been dipped in a shimmering inkpot.

"It's like some kind of turkey," Elliot whispers as the bird puffs out its green wing feathers, glinting mermaid-like, and extends its neck. It gives that beautiful call again, the pure notes scattering carelessly through the trees.

Elliot is cautiously moving to his right, blocking off a gap between the trees. "Jason, block its escape that way. Hayley, see if you can get around behind it so it can't go back the way it came."

"Uh-uh. No way. I am not involved in this."

"Hayley," Elliot whispers out of the corner of his mouth, never taking his eyes off the bird. "Do you and your family celebrate Thanksgiving?"

"Well, the holiday is problematic, but—"

Elliot cuts her off. "Do. You. Eat. A. Turkey? Yes or no?"

Hayley sighs. She can see where this is going. "Yes."

"Okay, then. This is no different from that. Actually, it's a lot more honest. We are killing this bird for survival. It is absolutely necessary. It's not a cranberry-filled, sentimental celebration of American ego and colonialist brutality. It's not cruel. It's biology. It's life and death. Survival of the fittest. It's nature."

Hayley crosses her arms and tries not to look the turkey in the eye.

"Do you want to eat something other than fruit and fish bones in the next month? Or is going to the bathroom five times a day a hobby you're happy to continue?"

She grimaces reluctantly. "Okay, okay. Fine. But I'm not participating. I'm conscientiously objecting."

"You're not going to eat any of the meat, then? The juicy, tender white breast meat, barbecued over a smoky fire? Or the tasty dark leg meat that slips off the bone?"

She feels her mouth start to water in spite of herself.

"You don't get to eat it if you aren't prepared to help catch it. It's dishonest. It does the animal a disservice. Those sterile, bloodless packages we pick up in the supermarket distance us from the reality of our food chain. They separate us from respecting and acknowledging the animals we sacrifice for our survival—"

"Dude, can we please just get on with it?" Jason hisses, as the turkey starts to move again. "Rock on with your natural-world philosophizing and all that, but it's going to get away if we don't shut up and catch it."

"Fine. I'll do it." Hayley starts inching to her right, trying to creep around behind the turkey. But it's too clever for her, or she's too unskilled a hunter. As soon as she moves toward it, it starts to panic, kicking up the leaves and scrambling to run, letting out a horrible, screaming gobble, lurching toward the gap between Elliot and Jason.

Jason and Elliot both dive toward the bird like linebackers, Jason half crushing it beneath his body, its feet clawing helplessly in midair, its body writhing as it continues to make that awful squalling screech, so different from the melody of its earlier call.

"Kill it," Jason squeals, panting, twisting his face to the side just in time as the bird arches its neck backward, trying to peck him with its sharp, curved beak. It rears, and its beak dives again, scalpel-like, finding its target this time and sinking into Jason's forearm.

He screams and rolls to the side, and the bird half rises, scrambling straight toward Elliot now, blind with panic, its shining feathers dirty and stuck with leaves, some broken and twisted, sticking out horribly at the wrong angles.

"It's suffering!" Hayley screams, and she finds herself lurching forward, her hands reaching out for the bird's neck, thicker and firmer than she'd anticipated, muscular beneath her fingers. And without really knowing what she is doing, without letting herself think too clearly, she twists with all her might, wrenching the gleaming blue softness to the side with a sickeningly muffled crack.

There's quiet. Its body lies grotesquely spread and broken, legs sticking comically up in the air, robbed of its grace and elegance. Its beady eye, it seems to Hayley, is trained on her still, reproaching her.

"Come on," Jason mutters, and there's a kind of shame on his face as he grabs it up by the neck so its heavy body dangles limply next to his leg.

"Oh man," Elliot groans, pulling a single blue-green feather from his hair. "May is *not* going to like this."

Her tirade begins the moment they trudge back into camp with the dead bird. "What gives you the right to take away its life? You're murderers, you know that? Murderers. I just hope you can live with yourselves after you've picked its greasy carcass clean."

"May." Elliot takes the bird, sits down, and calmly starts to rip out great handfuls of its jeweled feathers, twisting and bracing against its body as he wrenches them out of the skin. "We have to eat. Okay? You literally wouldn't be here if your ancestors hadn't killed animals to survive. Humans are carnivores. Get over it."

"Humans also used to live in caves and walk around naked," May retorts. "Are you suggesting we do that too?"

Brian raises a hand. "I would just like to say for the record that I for one have no objection to that."

It turns out plucking the bird is the easy part. Disemboweling it and removing the wings, feet and head are far more of a challenge with only sharp stones to help them. Hayley has to turn away as Elliot hacks at the bird's neck, flecks of blood and chunks of raw flesh spattering out in wet bursts. When it's finally done, he pulls out the slick, shining mess of its innards, saving them carefully in a plastic bag to use as fish bait.

But when it is finally prepared, threaded onto a long spit over the fire and resting on two forked sticks, the rich, smoky smell of meat and sizzling golden skin calls irresistibly to her tastebuds. Hayley's stomach growls and clenches like a wild thing as drops of translucent fat drip down to crackle in the embers.

"For the first time ever," Brian says, watching hungrily as

Elliot turns the stick to roast the bird's pale belly, "I can honestly say this is the kind of spit roast I am most excited about."

Jason guffaws while Jessa and Hayley exchange embarrassed looks but say nothing. Suddenly, Hayley is powerfully reminded of an afternoon in seventh grade when she'd sat uncomfortably in her plastic chair while the boys in her science class excitedly passed a novelty pen round, taking turns to turn it upside down and watch while the skimpy bikini slowly disappeared to reveal a nude, busty model grinning blankly back at them. She wishes she knew what to say now just like she wished it then, but somehow the words to describe how gross it makes her feel just won't come. And she knows, like she did then, that she'll be called a prude or accused of being uptight if she tries to object. So she says nothing at all.

They eat the bird the moment it's cooked, crouching in the sand around the fire, tearing off pieces of meat with their fingers and stuffing it into their mouths, the crispy skin melting away. The meat is deliciously, satisfyingly chewy after a week of sinking their teeth into soft, yielding fruit. May watches them from a safe distance, throwing them the occasional accusing glare while she chews sourly on some strips of coconut they've experimentally dried in the sun.

Hayley's brain plays tricks on her. There are moments when she feels almost normal, as if this life is something she knows, something expected. Her body cannot sustain the sensation of shock and fear, not for days on end. So there are times, even whole

DAY 9

AT FIRST, HAYLEY THINKS IT'S JUST THE BIRDS AGAIN.

The screeching of their morning calls, so shocking that first time, has become almost as expected as the morning light filtering through the leaves, tickling her eyelids open.

But this is something different. It's a male voice, urgent and angry, the words coming so fast she can't make them out. Hayley scrambles out of her makeshift bed, scattering sand everywhere in her haste, and waits impatiently for her eyes to adjust to the usual shocking brightness.

The boys are gathered around the campfire, where Elliot is attempting to reuse yesterday's spit to cook some fish for breakfast. Not very successfully, if his frustrated expression and the number of blackened fins charring in the fire are anything to go by. Shannon and May emerge from the trees with yet more firewood, and Brian is standing in front of Jason, frowning like he's trying to make sense of what he's shouting. Hayley hurries over, still half asleep, Jessa stumbling after her, drawn by the noise.

"I'm telling you, there's a fucking psycho on this island!"

Jason is apoplectic, his usually placid face red with panic, a vein pulsating in his neck as he gesticulates wildly at the sand around his feet.

"Huge shards of glass sticking up all around my bed like knives coming out of the beach," he shouts. "I almost cut myself to pieces when I woke up! I only just saw them in time. It's a threat, some kind of sick game someone's playing." He breaks off, chest heaving, looking accusingly around the circle as if he expects somebody to apologize.

"Sorry, you're saying someone surrounded you with pieces of broken glass during the night?" May stifles a yawn, not bothering to hide her unconvinced expression. "Broken glass from where, exactly?"

"From the plane crash," Jason yells, a ball of spit flying from his lips. "They must have taken it from the wreckage—huge, sharp, jagged pieces—"

"Could they have blown in there or something?" Jessa looks as confused as Brian.

"They didn't *blow* there!" Jason looks like he's about to have an aneurysm. "They were planted! It was like waking up in the jaws of a glass crocodile. Oh, for Christ's sake, look, I'll show you." And he grabs Jessa by her uninjured arm and drags her along the beach with the others trailing behind in various stages of wakefulness, their expressions ranging from perplexed to politely skeptical.

The sand around Jason's makeshift tent is smooth and soft,

unblemished by glass—or any other debris for that matter. He stops dead, staring at it in disbelief.

"It...it was there." He looks around, taking in May's smirk and Jessa's sympathetic smile. "It was all *right* here, I swear." He gestures helplessly at the empty beach. "Glass everywhere, sharp pieces—"

"Maybe you had a bad dream, J." Shannon puts a supportive hand on his back, rubbing it soothingly. "It wouldn't be surprising after everything we've been through, to have a vivid nightmare like that, to get confused..."

"I'm feeling pretty compos fucking mentis, actually," he roars, and her hand drops like a stone.

"COME ON, YOU GUYS!" Jason's eyes swivel wildly from one face to the next. "Are you seriously telling me this doesn't fit in with all the other weird shit that's been going on? Elliot gets pushed off a cliff—"

"Kind of an exaggeration, it was more of a small hill." May holds up her hands as Jason eyes her as if he's about to explode. "Sorry, sorry, go on."

"Then someone practically gives May alcohol poisoning..."

"Oh, so now you believe me?" May cuts in, sounding aggrieved. "The other day it was all, May's a drunk, May can't hold her liquor, but *now* you think I was telling the truth, do you?"

"Well, I didn't know it was a pattern then," Jason protests. "But add in blades of broken glass surrounding my bed, and you've got a pretty obvious string of attacks."

"Nobody actually did anything to you, though, right?" Jessa asks. "I mean, they didn't cut you or attack you with the glass?"

"They could have," Jason splutters. "It's a threat, don't you see? They're letting me know they could stab me to death in my sleep if they want to."

"Who would want you to know that? Who would have any reason to threaten you?"

"I don't know. But I did *not* imagine it. It was *not* a dream. Someone was trying to scare me, or threaten me, or cut me," Jason hisses between clenched teeth. "Not that I am scared," he adds quickly. "I'm just angry. This is getting stupid and dangerous, and it needs to stop."

Privately, Hayley thinks that Jason's rage-fueled outburst sounds exactly like fear. A particular male kind of fear. But this doesn't seem like the best moment to mention it, so she keeps her mouth shut.

"This is getting pretty damn weird, bro," Brian says, uneasily. "What the hell is going on?"

Hayley thinks about it all day. She mulls over everything that has happened while she stands knee-deep in seawater, her arms aching as she scrubs the few pieces of clothing she's worn in rotation for the past week. She takes herself back to the moment Elliot fell, the confusion and shouting, the feeling of the wind whipping her hair into her eyes, the straining, desperate hope for a miracle from the sky. She tries to make herself step into the memory, to look around for signs of anything unusual—to recall a shadow or a figure that might have slipped into their midst quietly, at the edge of her vision. But there's nothing except her imagination. Sometimes it shows her a masked figure hovering in the trees. Sometimes it's one or more of the others—Shannon, furtively looking around before her fists shoot out to shove Elliot in the back, or Brian and Jason nodding silently to each other and pushing him over in unison. Sometimes her feverish brain even shows her own scarred hands reaching out, forcing Elliot over the edge. Could she have done something like that in the trauma and shock of the storm and forgotten it? Her mind feels like it's spinning out of control, trying to find something real to grip on to.

She picks at the problem while she stands for hours on fishing duty through the afternoon, her feet slurping into the wet sand, the hot sun beating down unforgivingly on her shoulders, the limp line trailing off into the water, catching almost nothing.

She wonders about the others, trying to identify possible suspects and motives, none of them convincing. Could it be Elliot finding ways to hurt the classmates he's clearly had hostile feelings toward for years, taking revenge for their lives of luxury and the advantages it gave them? But he was the first one to be attacked. Could he have faked his own accident to divert suspicion away from himself? It doesn't seem very likely, considering how badly he could have been hurt. None of it makes any sense.

"Any luck?" May splashes out toward her wearing just a black sports bra and a pair of shorts, on her way to the daily swim she swears is keeping her sane. ("And fit, because you *know* the press is going to want to talk to us when we get out of here," she airily informed everyone on the third day, when she started the regime.)

"Not much." Hayley shows her the backpack she has slung over one shoulder, containing just one small gray fish. "Hey, May, this might seem like an odd question, but…" She shields her eyes, observing May's features. "Do you remember anything strange happening at the end-of-tour party?"

"Strange?" May freezes, her neck muscles tightening. "No, definitely not. It was just a normal party."

"Did anyone seem to be acting weird?" Hayley presses, and May's eyes dart from side to side as if she's trying to figure out what to say.

"Well, I guess everyone was relieved the tour was over and happy to celebrate our win, right?" she replies cautiously.

"Shannon was certainly in a celebratory mood," Hayley says, watching May closely. May takes a step back and loses her footing, splashing down into the sea and swallowing a mouthful of saltwater. She gets to her feet, coughing as water streams out of her nose.

"Sure, but Shannon deserved to have a good night. So what if she decided to have a few drinks? And doesn't she have every right to have a little bit of fun once in a while, like the rest of us? It's not easy being head cheerleader, you know."

May runs a hand over her face, wiping saltwater out of her eyes. "Anyway, why is it always all about the girls at parties? Brian was all over those Duke cheerleaders all night, but I don't see anybody giving him a hard time about it. Not that I necessarily respect their judgment," she mutters, "considering what he was up to earlier."

"What do you mean?"

"Oh, you know, those stupid running jokes he had going with those guys from Duke."

Hayley frowns and takes herself back to the party again, the crush of people and the hot, uncomfortably humid living room. She was perched on the edge of an armchair, trying to look like she was part of the conversation of a bunch of Duke girls standing near her. A great splash of laughter erupted from the sofa where Jason and Brian were sitting swigging beers and rippled out around the room. She remembers the half smile on her lips, like she could catch the wave and ride it, using the shared appreciation of a joke to unite her with the other partygoers. But she never heard the actual joke, or the ones that followed as the laughter swelled and crashed. They were lost in the din.

"Let's just say he wasn't exactly being complimentary to women," May says, tight-lipped. "Quite how he managed to attract several of them at once is a total mystery to me."

"What did he say?"

"I'm not repeating it, Hayley, it was disgusting." And before

Hayley can ask her anything else, she splashes off into the deeper water, launching into a rhythmic crawl.

After a few more minutes, Hayley decides to give up and wades in from the shallows. Any fish that might have been tempted by her bait have probably been scared off by May's splashing anyway. Farther up the beach, she can see Jason lying in the shade, still glowering. She stops next to his sleeping shelter and crouches down, running her hand over the warm, smooth sand.

Hayley gasps and cries out as a sharp, clean pain flashes through her finger. She sucks it, tasting metallic blood, and examines the fresh cut, bright and wet alongside the scabs of the scratches she got in the crash. Cautiously, she sifts through the sand with the end of her fishing stick and uncovers a long, razor-sharp sliver of glass. Hayley picks it up between her fingertips and examines it, then eyes the distance to the rest of the plane debris. There's no other glass nearby, nothing to suggest this piece was thrown from the wreck during the crash.

She digs out a Band-Aid from the first aid box and, finding the "fridge" empty, fills the skirt of her pale blue sundress with empty water bottles and sets off through the trees to fill them from the fresh water supply. There should be enough water left for another round of bottles at least.

When she steps into the shaded clearing, someone's already there: Shannon, standing over the water, staring at her own reflection, quietly sobbing.

She's suspended there in her own private world, and Hayley feels like she's intruding. As if the island has somehow accepted Shannon and is holding her in its embrace. Hayley has crashed unwittingly into this tender scene where she isn't wanted or needed. She's about to turn and leave when Shannon looks up and sees her, quickly wiping her eyes.

"Sorry," Hayley whispers.

"Don't be. Sometimes you forget for a few hours, you know? And then..."

"Yeah. I know."

And they stand side by side and push the empty bottles into the still water.

Later, after she has forced down yet another meal of dry, bony white fish, Hayley is pushing through the bushes to find a quiet spot to relieve herself when she overhears hushed voices whispering in the trees ahead. She pauses behind a tree, every nerve ending tingling, every muscle clenched, on high alert.

"—didn't want everyone to know—" a voice hisses furiously. And Hayley's stomach drops as she realizes it is Elliot standing next to a tree a few yards away with his back to her, fists clenched with frustration.

"I didn't say that," comes the other voice, and Hayley leans out very slowly from behind the tree and sees Jessa, hurt and anger playing across her face, standing opposite Elliot.

"I can see how it might tarnish your perfect image," he spits bitterly, and Jessa snaps at him.

"Oh, shut up. It's got nothing to do with that and you know it."

"Then why haven't you told your friends? Because you know exactly what they'd say if they found out."

Hayley leans farther, trying to see Elliot's face, and curses herself as a twig snaps under her foot with a loud crack. Jessa jumps and turns toward her as Hayley crashes through the bushes toward them, pretending she has just come from the beach.

"Oh, hi, guys." She beams as the sweat pools in the small of her back. "Nature calls!" And she strides cheerily on, pretending that nothing is wrong, that she didn't hear anything, that the two people she thought were the least suspicious on the whole island haven't just jumped right to the top of her suspect list.

nodding along to the beat, but Hayley sees how her eyes dart sideways toward Elliot every now and then. Could Jessa and Elliot be working together? What did Jessa do that Elliot knows she is keeping secret? Could it really have been Jessa who spiked May's drink? But why?

Hayley is still mulling it over when the girls set off on yet another a fruit-picking expedition, leaving the boys rattling around the camp like aimless marbles. She considers just coming straight out and confronting Jessa, telling her what she overheard and asking what it was about. But something holds her back. Even though the crash has obliterated some of their social hierarchy, there are still deep-seated boundaries, unwritten rules she doesn't feel able to break. Jessa, May, and Shannon are still *those* girls, still somehow distant and unreachable from Hayley's vantage point even though she's a member of their squad. Things are shifting slowly, but she still can't bring herself to accuse Jessa of something outright. Not yet, anyway. And she doesn't want to scare people off, alert them to the fact that she's listening and watching, probing into the cracks, trying to put it all together. Her confidence is returning as she tries to solve this mystery, but for now, she's still more comfortable gathering pieces of the picture and weaving them together from her place in the shadows.

The weather is mercifully cooler today, with thick, low bands of gray clouds blocking out the worst of the sun's direct heat. But the air feels muggy and full, pressing in around them and making it harder to breathe. Everything feels quiet and mysterious. The light among the trees is dappled and dark green, the thick air muffling noise as if they are swimming in a deep lake. Even the birdsong is absent today, and Hayley wonders if they know another storm is coming, if they're holed up in their nests and crannies, waiting in safety for it to pass. Wonders what's coming next.

Suddenly, May shrieks, her piercing voice ripping through the cotton-wool air, and Hayley's head snaps in her direction, her chest pounding. But it's just a bug, scuttling over May's hand as she steadies herself against a tree trunk.

"Ugh, ugh, ugh, get it *off* me." She shudders, shaking her hand frantically and spinning around.

"Aren't you supposed to be an animal-loving vegan, May?" Shannon can't resist asking with a sly smile.

"Vegan. Does. Not. Equal. Bug. Lover," May gasps disjointedly, jerking around as if she can feel its scratchy legs clinging to her skin.

They walk on, the forest grasping at Hayley's feet every few paces like an insistent child who will not be denied, clinging and encumbering her every step. In the quiet, close stillness, she notices the beauty in the trees around her for the first time. One trunk is enrobed in a fine mesh of thin red vines, the color so deep and lustrous it looks like a network of pulsating capillaries. A bush she has always avoided because of the vicious spikes that protrude from its waxy green leaves is sprinkled, on closer inspection, with the tiniest powder puff–pink flowers.

"I have the weirdest feeling we're being followed," May says under her breath, breaking the silence. "Like someone is watching us."

"Someone is watching us," Shannon says almost dreamily.

"What are you talking about?" Jessa looks alarmed, spinning around to peer through the trees that press close on every side.

"The island is watching us. I've felt it since the first night we arrived. We're not supposed to be here."

"I've felt that too," Hayley says, aware of the vibrancy of the trees, alive and listening, the vines and plants crushed beneath their feet.

"It's judging us," Shannon says, looking up into the canopy.

May laughs uncertainly. "I don't know about that. But I do feel very free here." She sighs, picking her way carefully between two bushes, one crawling with shiny, black-lacquered ants.

"Free? We're trapped!" Jessa speaks lightly, but Hayley recognizes the note of fear, never far from the surface.

"I know. I know it's a strange thing to say. I'm worried about getting off the island, obviously. But in those moments when you let yourself focus on the present, it just feels so different from home." May looks like she's trying to find the words to explain. "There's such freedom in being able to explore a forest like this... or walk down the beach alone in the middle of the night..."

"I know what you mean." Jessa nods. "I thought about it that first night, when the boys were so preoccupied with wild animals and protection. And I was thinking, this is the safest I will ever feel camping out, knowing for sure that my body isn't going to be found in some ditch in the morning."

"It's funny, isn't it?" Shannon sounds pensive. "The things that scare us are so very different from the things that scare them."

"Well, until now, anyway." May's voice is low and serious. "Now I'm not sure how safe any of us are anymore."

"Do you guys really think there's someone going around deliberately hurting people?"

"I think the boys have vivid imaginations." Shannon is curt and to the point. "Like May says, feeling exposed and threatened is a new experience for them. It's not for us."

"I don't know what to think," Hayley admits. "That whole thing with the glass… It'd be such a weird thing for someone to do, but on the other hand, it would also be really odd for Jason to make it up. Do we seriously think he could have had a nightmare that vivid?"

"Don't look at me," Shannon says as the others automatically turn to her. "My sleeping shelter isn't even next to Jason's. I have no idea what he is or isn't dreaming about."

"What's going on with you guys, Shan?" Jessa asks gently, curiously.

Shannon sighs. "I don't know," she says in a small voice. "Everything just feels different somehow."

"Did something happen?" May asks with characteristic bluntness.

Shannon shakes her head. "It's hard to explain."

"But you're Jason and Shannon." Jessa smiles. "You're the real deal! My world wouldn't make sense without you guys together." She's speaking lightly, but Hayley senses a real, child-like fear underneath.

"Did something happen at the party?" Jessa asks, and May stops in her tracks, staring at Shannon as if she already knows the answer.

"He got mad at you for dancing with that Duke guy," Jessa says sympathetically. "Was that it?"

"No," Shannon murmurs vaguely, shaking her head. "No, no, that was nothing. Jason had a headache. He'd already left before the dancing started."

"Where did you guys go?" May asks, looking uneasily between Shannon and Jessa. "When the party moved out into the backyard, I didn't see either of you. I ended up getting a cab to the hotel because I thought I must have missed you, but when I knocked on your room doors, you weren't there. And your phone was off, as *always*," she shoots reproachfully in Jessa's direction.

"I was there," Jessa replies, quickly glancing away. "I went back to the hotel early. The whole party scene gets a lot less fun really fast when you're the only sober one left. I must have already been asleep when you knocked." Hayley notices that Jessa doesn't meet May's eyes.

"I was with one of the Duke girls," Shannon says. "I went up to use the bathroom and found her in there sobbing. I stayed with her for about an hour. We went into one of the bedrooms to talk."

"About what?"

"She'd had a…bad experience," Shannon says, lowering her voice as if she thinks they might be overheard.

"What do you mean?" May asks.

"Well…" Shannon pauses as if she's not sure whether to continue. "She'd been…I think…" She stops and then says uncertainly, "I think maybe she'd been raped?"

"You think?"

Shannon shrugs. "She said she'd been making out in a bedroom with some guy, and it was all moving really fast, and she thought it was what she wanted, but then at some point she panicked and changed her mind."

"So she had sex with him and then regretted it?" Jessa asks.

"No, she changed her mind before the sex started, but he just carried on and did it anyway."

"That's awful," Jessa gasps. "Did she go to the police?"

Shannon shakes her head. "She said she had a boyfriend and she didn't want him to find out what had happened."

"She had a boyfriend, and she was making out in a bedroom with some other guy?" Jessa holds up a hand. "Was it because she was worried about what the boyfriend would say that she called it rape?"

Hayley feels as if Jessa has reached out and squeezed her stomach with an ice-cold hand, but Jessa continues with sincerity, "You know they call it buyer's remorse, right? When a girl has sex but then regrets it, so she says she was raped?"

"Jessa!" May shoots her a shocked look.

"I don't think that's an actual thing, Jessa," Shannon says. "And she seemed pretty upset."

"Well, did she actually tell him no?"

"I don't think so. She said she just kind of froze. She said he was heavy, that his body was pinning her down. But he must have been able to tell she wasn't into it, right?"

"Maybe," Jessa says slowly. "But isn't there a difference between rape and having sex with someone who's not that into it?"

"Not really," May says firmly. "It depends what you mean by 'not that into it,' I guess. If he didn't know whether she consented or not, I'd say that was rape. You need an enthusiastic yes, or you stop."

"What, like you have to get the other person to stop and sign a contract before you begin? Sounds sexy."

"What would you know about what's sexy, Jessa?" Shannon asks sharply. Jessa stops in her tracks, as startled as if Shannon has actually slapped her across the face.

"Nothing, I guess," she says slowly, cheeks flaming.

"Actually," Hayley interrupts, and it's as if the other girls have totally forgotten she was even with them, "it depends where you are when it happens."

"What? What are you even talking about?!"

"The laws about rape. They vary by state—I looked into it when I was writing an article about that guy who got arrested at the house party, Chad Maxwell." She glances quickly at

Shannon, but there's no flicker of recognition on her face when Hayley mentions the case. "We were in Texas the night before the plane crash, right? Texas is one of the ones I remember, because it really shocked me. In Texas, it's legally rape only if the rapist uses force or violence or threatens it. Or if the person is unconscious or unable to fight back. In other words…"

"She'd have had to try to push him off her," Jessa finishes.

"Yeah," Hayley admits. "It's completely messed up."

"But in the guy's defense, how did he know she thought he was raping her? She was kissing him," Jessa protests again.

"You'd never say that about anything else," Shannon says. "You'd never say, well, how was he supposed to know she didn't want him to take her phone? It was right there in her pocket, he might have thought she wanted to give it to him—that's why he robbed her. Why are we so willing to give a guy the benefit of the doubt when it's rape?"

"And why couldn't he take the time to damn well check?" May adds hotly. "If you're not sure, it should be on you to make sure. The onus is on him to know for certain she wants it, not on her to find a way to fucking protest."

"Amen," Hayley says, and Jessa rolls her eyes but doesn't say any more.

They walk on, the silence awkward at first. But at some point, May announces that this road trip needs a soundtrack and starts belting one out with gusto, flipping between Kesha, vintage Dolly Parton, and Beyoncé with wild abandon,

Shannon and Jessa occasionally joining in on backing vocals. Their singing is harsh against the silent undergrowth, and Hayley feels like they are desecrating something sacred, like they should apologize and lower their voices. But she doesn't know how to ask them to without sounding mad, so she says nothing and follows quietly in their wake.

Picking the fruit is harder work than Hayley imagined. The guavas are the easiest to harvest, their smooth, slightly textured skin turning from green to yellow as they ripen. She targets those the color of tennis balls, twisting the stems delicately until they pop off into her palm, trying not to wonder whether she'll ever feel a real tennis ball in her hand again.

She stubbornly blocks out the memories that come flooding in: summers at the court with her mom, Dad arriving to pick them up and honking from the parking lot, stopping for ice cream on the way home. When she told her parents about the tour, her mom pointed out that it'd take up half of summer break. "It's my last chance to beat you at tennis, kiddo," she said lightly, ruffling Hayley's hair, trying to keep the catch out of her voice. "You'll be heading off to college next summer, far too busy to hit the ball around with your old mom."

And Hayley dismissed her. Or at least she was impatient, focused on her Ivy League dreams and getting the cheer squad on her applications. "We'll play when I get back, Mom, I promise," she said carelessly. Not "I love you, I'll always have time for you." Not "Mom, I'll never be too busy to come back for a game, wherever I go to college." Just "We'll play when I get back." And now...

No. She isn't letting herself do this. Hayley Larkin is in control. She can't control the weather, or the island, or the bugs, or whichever one of the others is playing stupid, dangerous pranks, but she can and will control her own brain. And she is not going to break down now. On the flight home, Hayley has promised herself, she'll let herself break. Let herself acknowledge for the first time how terrifying and lonely this ordeal has been. Not. Yet.

The low-hanging fruit isn't difficult to reach, but they soon run out of easy pickings. Hayley stands, legs apart, knees shaking as May sits on her shoulders, reaching for ripe guavas and complaining that Hayley isn't steady enough.

"I'm doing my best," she fires back through gritted teeth. "You're not exactly the Sugar Plum Fairy okay?"

May leaps down, landing light on her feet, catlike. She grins. "It's taken a month of practice, a two-week tour, and more than a week stranded on an island for you to stand up to me, Hayley Larkin. I like it."

And Hayley's smile might be a little uncertain, but it definitely reaches her eyes.

The brownish fruits that Hayley thought looked like avocados are firmer on the tree than the wrinkled specimens she has eaten so far, tapering to points like overgrown, slightly squashed kiwis. These are harder to reach than the guavas, the tree trunks slender and tall, their leaves and fruit only appearing several yards off the ground. But May wriggles up the trees like a monkey, her skinned shins more than worth it for the abundant bunches of fruit she finds, clinging together like clusters of dark golden eggs. She picks them one at a time and drops them carefully into Shannon's waiting hands.

"Did you ever think about becoming a baseball catcher?" May asks with a low whistle of appreciation as Shannon dives for a stray fruit and catches it in the outstretched fingertips of her left hand.

"I'll keep it in mind as a backup." Shannon grins.

They eat as they go along, digging their teeth into any fruit that splits or bruises as they pick it, letting the juice run down their chins and congeal stickily on their arms. Hayley is just piling the last mango neatly on the heap they've collected when she hears the faintest noise, something at once strange and deeply familiar.

"Can anyone else hear that?"

"Hear what?" Jessa panics, shrinking closer to the others.

"It's not a person or an animal or anything." Hayley cocks her head. "Keep still a second." They all stand frozen, ears straining. Hayley hears the noises of the forest—a tree creaking slightly, a scuttling in the undergrowth, the rustle of leaves overhead. Then, in a moment of stillness, she catches it again: the faintest trickling noise, like somebody has left a tap on in another room.

"Have you heard that before?" The others shake their heads.

"It's always been windy when we've been here before," Jessa explains. "There was a lot more noise from the leaves."

Concentrating hard, Hayley tries to follow the sound. Every few steps, she has to stop and listen again, creeping forward painstakingly, the noise almost out of reach, her ears clinging to the very edge of the sound.

Even when she's standing right on top of it, she doesn't see it at first. The forest floor is so overgrown, and there are so many vines and dead leaves sprawling over one another. But she can hear it, a soft trickle, and when they scrape away moss and mud with their hands, they find it: a little spring, bubbling up among some rocks and flowing for a few yards in a shallow stream before trickling away between some bushes.

"It must run down from the top of the hill and under the ground." Shannon traces the path with her finger. "But it only comes up here in this one spot—it's so quiet and small, it's no wonder we never spotted it before."

"Well, I'm glad we found it." Jessa grins, pulling off her shoes and socks and sighing in pleasure as she dips her hot, sandy feet in the cool water.

"Never mind washing our feet, we've got water!" Hayley feels elated and buoyant, like a huge weight she didn't even realize she's been carrying has lifted from her shoulders. "We won't have to rely on rain and coconuts anymore. We can collect water from here and boil it to clean it." She's surprised that nobody else seems to be as excited as she is. Don't they realize how precarious their situation is?

"Ew, ew, ew, ew!" Jessa jumps up, scrambling to put her shoes and socks back on, physically recoiling from the stream.

"What, what?" May scans the water for some horrifying predator.

"Sorry, nothing major, but there are leeches in there." Jessa points and they all lean forward, spotting the slug-like brown creatures glistening in the water.

"Just when you thought this island couldn't get any creepier." After her morning brush with bugs, May looks like she is taking the leeches personally. But her outraged face is so funny Hayley can't suppress a giggle, and before she knows it, she is crying with laughter, infecting them all with it, giddy with the relief of that tight, tight knot in her stomach unwinding just a little.

That afternoon, the girls lie on their backs in the shade of the fruit trees. The clouds have lifted and a light breeze has swept away the thickness of the morning air, leaving Hayley feeling fresher, less constrained. She watches as the dappled sunlight plays across her forearm, highlighting the soft dark hairs.

At home, she'd have been worried about them. For years she's fought a pitched battle with her mom, who doesn't believe in arm waxes and calls her body hair "a beautiful part of my beautiful daughter." A beautiful part she's been teased about since grade school, leaving her self-conscious and always pulling her sleeves down over her wrists. "Just because you've never seen them before doesn't mean they're not normal," Grandma used to say, stroking her hands with long, papery fingers. "You just haven't seen them because all we see are white models with blond, invisible hair." She ran a translucent palm down Hayley's arm. "It doesn't mean this is any less beautiful, just because they choose not to show it to us."

"I know that, Grandma," she moaned, cutting her off quickly before she launched into the tirade about who "they" are. "The problem is, nobody else does." The breeze strokes her arms, and she closes her eyes, yearning for her grandmother's touch. The hair doesn't seem to matter so much here.

She has almost drifted off to sleep when Jessa speaks in that small, almost childish voice. "Is it any of you? Honestly? Look, no judgment, I swear, and I won't tell the guys, but I'm scared, and I just want to know what's going on. So…is it? Any of you?"

Hayley glances around. Jessa is looking determinedly straight up at the clumps of green mangoes huddled among the leaves above her head. There's liquid pooled at the corner of her eye. She and May are curled around each other like squirrels, May's arm slipped loosely over Jessa's hips, Jessa cradling her bad arm with her good one. They're breathing slowly, as if they're using each other's heartbeats to tether themselves.

Shannon is like something out of a classical painting, her dark waves of hair spread out across the ground, her slightly hollow cheeks still, tiny veins visible in her translucent eyelids. It looks like she's already asleep.

Nobody answers.

When Hayley wakes, disorientated and warm, the sun is

much lower and the forest is striped with slanting shadows. She gingerly rotates her cricked neck, propping herself up stiffly on her elbows. Her eyes are still heavy with sleep, her scalp damp and hot.

The others are stirring too, Jessa yawning and blinking and Shannon sitting up, pulling her hair back into a ponytail. It's Hayley who sees them first, but the shock hits her so hard she can't even speak. She sits there frozen, feeling ice rush through her veins. But something in her face makes Shannon look down, and her scream is enough to send the others leaping to their feet.

"What, what is it, where?"

"Our legs," Hayley manages in a strained whisper. They all look down.

"Get them off, get them off NOW!" May is high kicking, thrashing her leg around like a cancan dancer. But it doesn't make any difference. The leeches are stuck fast.

Four or five fat, globular bodies cling to each of them, dotted from their thighs to their calves, pulsating and swollen like balloons, suggesting that they have been feeding for some time.

Jessa is doubled over with what Hayley thinks are silent tears until she draws a trembling breath and lets out a shriek of laughter. "I'm sorry, I'm sorry," she wheezes, her shoulders shaking. "You just look so funny. It's like you're trying to make your own foot fall off." And she dissolves into tears of helpless laughter again.

"I'm. So. Glad. This. Is. Entertaining. To. You." May speaks through gritted teeth, each word punctuated with another wild flail of her legs. When the leeches remain stubbornly in place, she squeezes her eyes shut and reaches down to try and pull one off. "Grossgrossgrossgrossgrossgrossgross…"

"Wait," Jessa shouts, grabbing May's hand to stop her. "I had a leech bite once when I was fishing in a river; you can't just pull them off. They can regurgitate bacteria into your bloodstream or leave their mouth parts behind in the wound and infect it."

"*MOUTH PARTS?*" Shannon looks utterly disgusted. And something about her outrage, about the way she says "mouth parts," tips Jessa back over the edge until she's wheezing with laughter.

When she finally gets herself under control, she says, "You just have to use your fingernail—slide it under the mouth to break the suction, and then you can flick it off." Jessa demonstrates, her fingernail nudging under the thin end of one of the leeches that is gorging on her thigh. It subsides reluctantly, leaving a horrible little wound that immediately starts to trickle blood.

"It'll bleed for a while," Jessa says matter-of-factly. "When leeches start feeding, they release something into your blood to stop it from clotting so they can get full quicker."

"I think I'm gonna be sick." May gingerly starts to prize off her leeches, copying Jessa's technique.

Hayley looks down at her own unwanted passengers and almost gags. "Don't think about it, don't think about it, don't think about it," she whispers to herself as she slides her fingernail under the end of one, feeling the slight release as the suction breaks and flinging it as far away from her as she possibly can. She shudders and wipes her hand on her dress. A few minutes later, they stand, panting among the shadowy trees, their legs striped with long, narrow trickles of blood.

"Remind me *never, ever* to fall asleep near a stream again." May shudders, trying to stop the wound on her thigh from bleeding using the edge of her tattered violet cheerleading skirt. "I still feel dirty."

Jessa has stopped laughing. She's standing very still. "I don't think the leeches made it from the stream on their own," she says suddenly.

"What do you mean?"

"The last time I got bitten by a leech, it was because I was wading thigh-deep in a river for two hours trying to catch a fish. They aren't exactly speedy creatures. Look where we are. The water is at least fifteen feet away. I find it very hard to believe that two dozen leeches somehow made it out of the spring and across all these leaves and rocks and vines and then evenly divided themselves up between us."

Hayley's stomach feels cold. "What are you saying?"

Jessa looks angry. "Someone did this. No way it just happened by coincidence."

Shannon looks from the stream to the clearing and back again. She slowly starts to nod. "I think you're right. I didn't believe it before, but I'm starting to think something really creepy is happening on this island."

"Well, who was it?" May sounds furious, like she's reached the absolute end of her tether. "Which one of you bitches put a bloodsucker on my leg?"

They're all staring at each other. Hayley feels her cheeks getting hot, feels a prickle of shame and fear, as if they might see guilt written on her face even though it wasn't her. The others look just as panicked as she does.

"It wasn't necessarily one of us," she points out. "We all woke up at the same time. What if it was one of the boys?"

"Yeah, we *think* we woke up at the same time." May narrows her eyes suspiciously. "But how do we know one of us didn't sneak up, get the leeches, then lie back down and pretend to be asleep again until we all woke up?"

"What, and cover her own legs in leeches too?" Jessa has a point.

"Well, yes, obviously," May storms. "To cover her tracks."

"We don't have any way of knowing, do we?" Shannon automatically takes control. "So let's get back to the camp. If someone is really trying to sabotage us, it's better if we're all together."

Hayley likes the idea of safety in numbers. But it isn't lost on her that they might also just be running right back to the person who attacked them in the first place. Everything is so uncertain. It's like trying to find her way through fog. Suddenly, something else occurs to her.

"What if something happened to the boys while we were away?"

They crash back through the forest, ignoring the thorns and branches that tear at their hair and skin, jostling the fruits they're carrying in haphazard armfuls.

But the camp is quiet, the boys subdued. There's fresh fish cooking over the flames and a huge pile of firewood nearby.

Jason freaks when he sees Shannon's legs.

"You're not just messing with me now," he shouts at nobody in particular. "You're messing with my girl, and I will destroy you. Whoever you are, you don't mess with me or what's mine, you hear me?"

"Were you guys together all day?" Jessa asks seriously.

"No," Elliot answers at once. "We were fishing and fetching firewood and stuff. Between that and, you know, bathroom breaks, we all went off into the trees at some point. It could have been any of us."

Jessa raises an eyebrow.

"Not that I'm saying it was me!" he stutters. "It wasn't me, I swear. But it could've been. I mean, except that it wasn't, obviously. We all had the opportunity, is all I'm saying. On the upside, really great news about the spring, though." He trails off nervously and turns to tend the fish.

Hayley and the others race to the sea, scooping up handfuls of water and rinsing their legs over and over again. But somehow, no matter how much water she douses her skin with, no matter how much she welcomes the sharp tingle of salt in the wounds,

Hayley still feels gross, as if the leeches have left behind slimy trails that won't wash clean.

She visits the plane in her dreams again that night. But everything is happening in slow motion. She's floating like an astronaut in a cloud of fruit cups, loose pages, and pom-poms, the others drifting past her with wide, unseeing eyes, terror frozen on their contorted faces. She knows the plane is going down, knows there is nothing she can do about it, but still she tries to struggle, fighting against the heavy sluggishness of her limbs, wanting to make them move faster, wanting to run to the front of the plane, to help the pilot or grab the controls...something, *anything*. But instead it's happening tortuously slowly, and she can't speed it up, can't speed herself up. There's nothing she can do but wait for the inevitable impact.

She's outside the plane now, watching it plummet toward the sparkling surface of the water inch by inch. She tries to scream but her voice doesn't come out. She sees the island, and she's falling toward it alone, so close now she can see every individual grain of sand, so close she feels her whole body tense in terrified anticipation...

And then it's gone, and there's just her mom's face, strained and fearful, her eyes boring into Hayley's, her fingers gripping Hayley's shoulders so hard it hurts. "Hayley." She's trying to tell her something, trying to warn her, but Hayley can't hear her properly; the wind is howling in her ears and her mom's voice is distorted. "You're not looking hard enough." Her mom is fading, her fingers are slipping away, she's being pulled in the opposite direction, they're back in the plane and the force is too strong, smashing them into the sides of the cabin. "You're missing something, Hayley..." Hayley strains toward her, trying to reach her with every fiber of her being, but she's being pulled backward, can't see or hear her anymore, and she wakes in the dark with tears in her eyelashes and her mom's name on her lips.

DAY 11

IT'S BRIAN WHO FIRST SUGGESTS THEY TRY DIVING FOR conch. He's the strongest swimmer in the group, a member of the water polo team before he switched to basketball. He's been joining May on her daily swims, and he says he's spotted some shells deep in the clear water off the island.

"It sounds dangerous," Jessa warns, chewing her bottom lip. She's sitting on the beach, tipping a little spring water at a time into her hand from a plastic bottle, then delicately working it into her hair, massaging her twists, patting down the frizz that has started to grow at the roots.

"I've got this." Brian swaggers, pulling on the tattered pair of old shorts he always uses for swimming. "Want to guess how long I can hold my breath?"

"Why don't you show us?" May teases. "Give us all a few minutes of peace and quiet." She shakes her head. "Those conch might look close because the water's so clear here, but I'd guess they're at least twenty feet down. No way you can get down to them and bring one back up all in one breath."

"Watch me." Brian strides confidently off toward the water, his swagger slightly undermined by the peeling patches of red sunburn on his back.

"That sunscreen run out, did it?" May calls after him, laughing. He pretends not to hear her.

"Just you wait," he calls over his shoulder. "You'll be thanking me when you're eating fresh conch for dinner!"

"Ugh," May mutters. "Do I need to remind you that I'm a vegan?"

"NO!" everybody shouts in unison, and Hayley cracks up at the affronted look on May's face.

"I'll come with you a little ways," Hayley shouts, hurrying after Brian. "I could use a dip."

Hayley's been waiting for a chance to get Brian on his own to ask him about the party, but this is the first time he hasn't been shadowing Jason. Now that they're almost completely reliant on Elliot's fish to eat and his fire to cook it, Hayley feels like she's watching Jason's grip on the group get looser every day. And he isn't taking it well. He's surly and withdrawn, snapping at anyone and everyone, making fewer attempts to approach even Shannon. And he relies on Brian more and more to be by his side, like still having his right-hand man to slap on the back and share dirty jokes helps to mask the vulnerability of losing his authority. But today Jason's out of sight, crossing the island to collect fresh coconuts, finally leaving Brian alone. And Brian is the only person left whom she hasn't asked directly about the party, Hayley realizes, apart from Jason himself.

"Want to know my secret?" Brian asks as they walk down the beach side by side, leaving parallel paths of footprints, his nearly double the size of Hayley's.

"Huh?"

"I practice holding my breath every morning. Nearly doubled my lung capacity that way," he says proudly, patting his chest. "And I've read a lot online that says it increases your sperm count too. And makes you last longer, if you know what I mean." He glances sideways at Hayley. "Something to do with physical control, I guess."

"Oh." It suddenly occurs to Hayley that there is nobody within earshot. She glances casually over her shoulder, back toward the camp, but the others must have gone looking for firewood or fruit, because there's nobody in sight. She suddenly feels very exposed. Very aware of how close to her Brian is, how few clothes they are both wearing. She hears May's words again as if she's whispering them in her ear: "*Let's just say he wasn't exactly being complimentary to women... It was disgusting.*"

Almost imperceptibly, she shifts her shoulders, angling her body away from him. She lengthens her strides just a little, extending the distance between them. *Don't be stupid*, she tells herself sternly, trying to calm her swiftly accelerating pulse. *Nothing's going to happen.*

"So, Brian," she says casually as their soles slap the wet sand. "Did you have a good time at the party? The night before the crash?"

He stops dead and looks her straight in the eye. "Why, what did you hear? You talk to one of the Duke girls?"

She stumbles backward, then starts walking again.

"No. I was just making conversation. What did you think I heard?"

"Nothing. Nothing." He seems relieved, falling back into step beside her. "I was just wondering what you meant."

"So you didn't see anything out of the ordinary that night?" Brian glances immediately back up the beach, toward the camp, before his eyes flick back to Hayley.

"Why are you asking now?"

"I'm just…testing a theory. Humor me."

"Well…" He looks conflicted. "There was one thing, but I don't know if I should say."

"I won't tell anyone." Hayley speaks in her most soothing, reassuring reporter voice, usually reserved for reluctant sources in the school administrators' office. "It'll stay between us, I swear."

He looks to the beach again. "It was after Truth or Dare finished. I went up to the bathroom and as I walked past one of the bedrooms, I saw the door was ajar. I wasn't peeping, I swear." He looks panicked, like he's regretting the conversation already.

"Of course not." Hayley smiles, nodding encouragingly.

"Well, I saw Jason and Shannon through the door, having a major fight."

Hayley is careful not to act surprised. She says nothing, letting the silence stretch until he feels compelled to fill it with more details.

"I dunno what they were arguing about, but he had her hotel key card; he pulled it out of his pocket and kind of flicked it at her hard so it clipped her right in the face." He looks guiltily at Hayley. "He must have had good reason to be so pissed."

"Sure." Hayley nods. "Sure. Did he say anything?"

Brian scrunches up his face like he's trying to remember. "He sort of hissed, 'Walk yourself home, then,' and then he stormed out so fast he didn't even seem to see me, and he charged downstairs and slammed the front door behind him." He shrugs as if it's all beyond him. "Okay, well, those conch aren't gonna collect themselves. See you later, Hayley."

And she feels her whole body relax as he splashes through the shallow waves, leaving her alone.

Out of everyone she's spoken to, Brian is definitely the worst liar. But if he was willing to break his best friend's confidence to tell her about the fight, then what else is he still hiding? And what exactly was he joking about that night?

Hayley watches as he begins to swim, his head little more than a bobbing dot against the glimmer of the sea.

She does a few hundred yards of breaststroke. The water soothes and caresses her tired limbs. Hayley is more active here than she has ever been in her life. The constant fetching and carrying, crossing the island, and climbing trees has produced muscles where she never had any before. By the time she falls asleep each night, she is thoroughly, achingly exhausted.

Eventually, she drags herself out of the water and heads up the beach, toweling herself off with somebody's spare hoodie and pulling on a newly rinsed tank top and a pair of shorts.

They've dried in the sun and their salty stiffness chafes against her skin, but at least they don't smell, which is more than she can say for the boys recently.

There's work to be done, as always. Hayley starts trying to cover a hole in one side of her shelter, where some of the sticks have shifted and the wind has started blowing in. She swears in frustration as the sticks she tries to shove in slip through her fingers and fall to the floor. She needs more of the narrow palm leaves to braid together and make a kind of base.

It occurs to her that she could borrow some leaves from a pile Jessa keeps near her sleeping shelter, weighted down by a few large rocks. But as she reaches the leaves, everything happens at once. May emerges at the edge of the trees, not seeing Hayley where she kneels, stooped, half hidden behind Jessa's lean-to. She looks both furious and terrified, a strange sort of panic on her face that Hayley has never seen before. And she is speaking in a low voice trembling with emotion to somebody in the trees behind her.

"You could have killed me, I hope you realize that. I easily could have slipped and hit my head on a rock with that much alcohol in me. I could've gone for a drunk swim and drowned! I know it was you. And I know why you did it. I'm sorry, okay? I shouldn't have done what I did, and I'm really, really sorry. I don't

even know what got into me. But two wrongs don't make a right."
She pauses like she's listening to somebody speaking too quietly
for Hayley to hear. "You know perfectly well I can't tell everyone
what you did without them finding out what I did, too. But if
you're the one who's behind all the other things as well, you have
to stop, okay? You have to stop before someone gets really hurt."

And Hayley half rises, ready to sprint toward her, ready to
crash into the trees and unmask whoever May is talking to, when
a cold, thin, horrifying scream slices the moment in two. She
turns instinctively and stumbles toward the noise, and suddenly
they are all there, in a jumble of people that gathers so fast she
doesn't know where everyone comes from—May and Jessa and
Elliot and Jason and Shannon, all wearing the same expression of
sheer panic, all fumbling to count heads, all turning in unison to
the sea and realizing at the same moment that the awful noise is
coming from Brian.

Hayley squints, trying to see among the flashes of light
that bounce up off the water. The sea swells and shifts restlessly,
distorting her perspective.

"Is that him?" She sees a bobbing smudge that might be a
head and next to it a hand flicking upward, jerking, writhing,
almost. There's no further sound except the soft shushing of the
water, no more screams or cries for help, yet there is something
frantic and desperate about the movement of that figure in
the water. Suddenly, the head jerks, then snap backward, and,
for a horrifying, endless moment, it slips under the water and

disappears. Then it surfaces again, barely moving, a floating speck, and Hayley knows, looking at it, that something is terribly, terribly wrong. Elliot has already started pulling off his shirt as he runs toward the water, and Hayley follows him, not thinking, not asking questions, just gripped by a terrible sense of dread.

Dimly, she hears the others racing behind them, hears a voice she thinks might be Shannon's rise in a question, but there isn't time to stop; she is running, her feet pounding across the hot, soft sand, her legs splashing into the shock of the cold waves, wading out as quickly as she can, pushing against the firm resistance of the water.

They're closer now, though still at least twenty yards away, and she can make Brian out, starting to swim toward the shore, toward Elliot, who is a few yards ahead of her. Brian's face is awash with terror, his eyes skating across the surface of the water, his head jerking frantically as he scans the waves around him.

"Elliot, move!" Brian's voice cracks with urgency as he glances over his shoulder. "Get to the shore, NOW."

Elliot doesn't listen, his arms driving through the water like pistons until he reaches Brian, who throws his arms around Elliot's neck, his face drained of all color, coughing through the spray. "Hayley, get back to the beach, get back as fast as you can."

May has reached Brian too, supporting him from the other side, helping him swim faster, murmuring something reassuring that does nothing to ease the stricken look on Brian's face. So

Hayley turns and pounds back toward the beach, salt stinging her eyes. Half expecting at any moment to feel something grab her legs, tear at her skin, or pull her under the surface.

Elliot and May stagger out of the water, half dragging Brian between them. And it's only as they tear him from the clutches of the innocent, feathery surf that they see the trail of blood staining the sand a horribly vibrant red.

"Shark," Brian gasps, his mouth opening and closing, his arms twitching as his face creases in pain. "My leg."

Shannon is white with shock, frozen next to him like a statue. It is the first time Hayley has ever seen her look truly helpless.

"Towels!" May screams. "Fetch anything, any clothing, anything." And Hayley is running, stumbling across the hot sand, feeling a searing pain as a sharp rock cuts into her foot, racing on, scrabbling frantically in the overhead bin for every item of clothing she can find and racing back across the beach, faintly wondering where the quiet whimpering sound is coming from before she realizes it's in her own throat.

"It must've been at least four or five feet. Came straight for me." Brian is gasping for breath, grimacing every time he shifts his weight. He braces himself, clenching his fists and gritting his teeth, before he lets himself look down and inspect what's left of his calf.

The leg is still there. It's attached, his foot unharmed, but there's a hideous groove of missing flesh, a cruel, gaping crescent like somebody has taken a giant knife from his ankle to his knee and carved at it. The blood is coming faster, gushing out into the sand and trickling down to mingle with the sea, spurting in time with his heartbeat.

"We have to stop the bleeding," Shannon pants, still rooted to the spot.

Hayley and May crouch in the wet, bloody sand, swathing Brian's leg as fast as they can in T-shirts, towels, everything they have.

"Pressure, put pressure on it," Elliot urges, kneeling beside them and placing his warm, calloused palms beside Hayley's, forcing the sides of the gash together beneath the cloth, pinning the wound shut as Brian screams in pain and jerks away. Elliot's breath is warm on Hayley's neck; he smells of sea salt and coconut and something else she can't place.

"You'll have to hold him down," Elliot tells Jason grimly, and for the first time, Jason nods and obeys, all his bravado stripped away as he kneels beside his stricken best friend, his face slack and uncomprehending.

"It's okay, Brian, you're going to be okay," he chokes as he grasps him by his meaty wrists, forcing them down into the sand. And as Elliot rips a strip off a T-shirt and ties a tight knot above Brian's knee to cut off the blood flow, as more blood seeps out into the pool surrounding them, as Brian heaves and strains again and tries to move away, Jason falls across him, using his whole body to force him still, and sobs, "I'm sorry, man. I'm so, so sorry. This is for your own good. It's for your own good."

The blood seems to slow. Brian lies still, his face ashen, tears trickling out of the corners of his eyes to mingle with the blood and sand. The tourniquet is working. When Elliot discards the sopping layers of clothing saturated with blood and replaces them with a new white T-shirt, the bleeding is slower, visible but under control.

"Thank God," Jessa repeats over and over again. "Thank God."

Hayley doesn't know how long they sit there, keeping silent watch as Brian drifts in and out of sleep, sometimes waking with a great shuddering, keening cry of pain, only to fade into merciful oblivion again moments later. Once he calls out for his mother, pleading for her like a baby until Shannon eases his head onto her lap, tears in her eyes, and strokes his hair. "Shh, shh," she whispers, her voice breaking. "I'm here now. I'm here." And he sighs a little and sleeps again.

It's a subdued group that gathers around the fire for a dinner of fruit, fish, and no conch. Brian is asleep in the sand a little distance away, his head still on Shannon's lap. She won't leave him or swap with anyone else, refusing to take a break even to eat. She reluctantly accepts a bottle of water, which she drinks with one hand, careful not to disrupt for a moment the gentle rhythm of her fingers stroking Brian's hairline. His absence hangs over the others like a heavy cloud though the evening is calm and warm, the golden pre-sunset light lazily licking across the sand. The sea glitters close, mischievous and taunting. Hayley can't look at it. She doesn't think she'll ever be able to look at the sea again without seeing blood. Even now, she can't get it off her cuticles, from under her fingernails.

Long after the meal has ended, Hayley sits listlessly against the trunk of one of the palm trees, watching the fire die slowly down to a red glow, matching the first tendrils of crimson starting to leak into the sky from the edge of the horizon. She tries again and again to mentally reconstruct the scene near the camp earlier that day, trying to figure out who might have come out of the trees behind May, whom she might have been accusing. But it's hopeless. It's all just a blur. May seems subdued, building a pile of broken shells in the sand, the usual cloud of music that surrounds her noticeably absent. She's not even humming. Whatever the reason, she doesn't want everyone else to find out what she knows.

They examine Brian's leg in the warm light of the early evening, the edges of the wound curling horribly like a snarl. The blood is beginning to clot, but the gash still gapes, trickles still escaping at the bottom and turning his gym sock scarlet.

"We should sterilize it," Shannon points out, gesturing to the remaining bottles of alcohol from the plane.

"I think it needs stitching," Jessa says, grimacing apologetically at Brian. "You can't leave a wound that big open, it won't heal."

"What are you gonna stitch it with?" Brian asks through gritted teeth. And Jessa disappears to rummage through the jumble of supplies in the overhead bin and returns apprehensively with one of those miniature courtesy sewing kits from the hotel.

"No. No way. You have got to be kidding me."

"She's right, Brian." Elliot peeks again beneath the T-shirt swathing his leg. "If we leave it open like that, it'll be infected within days." And nobody says it, but they're all thinking about Brian's stupid joke about how it'll be an infection that will kill one of them.

"The good thing is that the cut is quite clean, like it slashed you instead of chomping down. The edges look like they could be brought together fairly easily."

Brian swallows heavily, turns his head away. But there's nowhere to go, no escape from this. "Okay." He grunts and lies back on the sand.

"Who's going to do it?" Jessa holds out the sewing kit and they all stare at it, trembling slightly in her fingers. "Who knows how to sew?"

"Well, I'm out, obviously." Jason shrugs.

"May makes her own clothes," Shannon whispers.

May shudders. "Yeah, with a sewing machine. I only do the buttons by hand."

"That's still more sewing experience than the rest of us put together," Jason points out, and they all turn to stare at her as she stands there, crowned with the soft rose of the evening sun, opening and closing her mouth. She reaches out reluctantly to take the needle, as if she's in some kind of dream.

"Wait, put it in here first." Shannon holds out one of the tiny liquor bottles, and they stuff the needle and thread in together, and Shannon puts the cap back on and shakes it for good measure. May takes another bottle and pours it all over her hands, scrubbing them together.

"Here." Elliot hands two more bottles to Brian, who takes them without hesitation and gulps them both down. "This is going to hurt." Elliot takes the last bottle and carefully empties it into the wound, sprinkling it over each section as if he's seasoning some grotesque cut of meat. Brian gasps, his face contorted in pain, and Jason and Elliot sit on either side of him, placing their hands on his shoulders and his thighs, ready to keep him still.

"I'll be as quick as I can," May tells him. "Move out of the light," she snaps at the others. "We've got to get this done before the sun goes down."

But then she stops, needle poised above the glistening edge of the flesh, and Hayley sees her throat move as she swallows over and over.

"You can do this." Jessa is beside her, her voice low and steady. "You are the strongest person I know. You can do this."

And before she can change her mind, May has plunged the needle through the first slab of skin and into the other side, her fingers pinching the two pieces together, and pulled the thread tight.

Brian's screams are guttural and ragged, quickly giving way to wet, heaving sobs. It's not until he finally, mercifully passes out from the pain after the third or fourth stitch that Hayley takes a breath and realizes she has been biting the inside of her cheek so hard that she can taste blood.

It's not pretty. But when May's finished, the lips of the wound are tightly drawn together, puckered and lumpy. There is a horrible purple bruise blossoming across Brian's calf, but it's no longer bleeding, at least. They wrap it tightly in the cleanest T-shirts they can find and elevate it on a pile of stones in an attempt to prevent swelling and keep the wound out of the reach of sand and insects.

And it isn't until Hayley's in bed that night that she hears a sound she never thought she would hear: the quiet, shuddering noise of May crying into the night.

DAY 12

"WHAT THE HELL?"

Brian has spent most of the day resting by the campfire, carried by the others to a nest of clothes and towels they've made by the fire to keep him warm. But now he's struggling to prop himself up on one elbow, his voice alight with fury.

As they crowd around him, he extends his hand, something wet and congealed hanging limply from it.

"What is that?" May wrinkles her nose. "And why does it smell like it's dead?"

"Because it is!" Brian storms. "It's a handful of the fish guts we've been using for bait. And I just found it in the pocket of my swim shorts."

The others look at him blankly, not understanding. "Does someone want to tell me why they sent me out into deep water with literal *shark chum* in my pockets?"

"Whoa, whoa, calm down," Elliot urges. "Couldn't you have left it in your pocket when you were fishing and forgotten about it?"

Brian is breathing heavily. He looks like a tethered bull about to rip the ring out of its own nose and go on a rampage. "No, I couldn't. I always bait the hook before I go in the water to fish, and I leave the spare bait on the beach. Besides, I wasn't even wearing these shorts then. I've only been wearing them for swimming. Which anybody who has been paying attention knows." He glares around furiously, his scowl etched deep into his forehead.

"Enough. Whatever the hell is going on here, it ends now. I could have freaking died." His voice is shaking with fury. "I still might, if we don't get out of here soon."

There's dead silence.

"Whoever you are, this needs to stop. Now. Before anyone else gets badly hurt."

"We need to know what she wants!" Jason sounds hysterical, his eyes skittering from one face to the next. "Whoever's doing this. And don't look at me like that, May, because it's obviously a girl. Everyone who's been seriously injured is male."

"Jason," May deadpans, "you weren't injured at all. My leech bites hurt worse than your sore feelings after you got scared by a few shards of broken glass."

And before Jason can argue, Jessa steps between them, hands raised for calm.

"Jason's right. We can't stop it unless we know who's doing it and why."

"What do you want?" Jason shouts, half laughing, gesturing wildly around the circle. The silence is total. A log hisses and falls in the center of the fire, and Hayley feels her pulse jump in her throat.

"We don't know for sure it's a girl," May says stubbornly. "We all had our blood sucked, too, remember? And I was almost given alcohol poisoning."

"Yeah, I see your leeches and your cocktail afternoon and raise you *almost being killed by a damn shark*," Brian yells furiously, white flecks of spit flying out of the corner of his mouth.

"We don't know what species of shark it was," Elliot says in a conciliatory tone. "It probably bit you by accident, Brian, because it thought you were a seal or something. If it had really wanted to kill you, you'd be dead. There are actually very few species of sharks that are dangerous to humans in these waters; it might have been a lemon shark or a sand tiger—"

"Or a hammerhead or a blacktip," Jason breaks in angrily. "We grew up in Florida too, Elliot. You might know more than most about little fire-starting tricks, but you're not the sole authority on sharks. So we're not doing this anymore, okay?" Jason sounds commanding, but Hayley can hear the frustration in his voice. It's fine making angry threats into thin air, but they fall flat when there isn't any response.

Hayley closes her eyes and tries to put herself in the shoes of whoever might be doing all this. And even though she isn't certain, she has a nagging feeling that whoever it is wants something.

Most of the attacks have had worse psychological effects than physical ones. If the attacker wanted Elliot dead, they could have finished him off while he was unconscious the night he fell.

If they really wanted to hurt Jason, they could've used the glass shards to stab him, not to scare and confuse him. The leeches were more shocking and disgusting than actually harmful. Following the pattern, Hayley decides that the shark bait was meant to create exactly the kind of terror she saw on Brian's face in the sea, not to cause an actual attack. It's like somebody is trying to make them understand something, to send them a message.

If only they had the chance to communicate, Hayley muses as she wanders up the beach. If the person doing all this somehow got what they wanted, the attacks might stop. Suddenly, she is seized by an idea.

"Write it down!" Her voice comes out breathy and high-pitched, her cheeks flushed. She's digging frantically in a pile of stuff that's just inside the hollow tube of the plane, reemerging triumphantly with a ballpoint pen and Elliot's dog-eared sketch-book. She races back to the group.

"Write. It. Down," she repeats urgently, her eyes shining at the expectant faces. "I'll leave the sketchbook out tonight, away from the camp. Whoever is doing this can tell us anything they want. We'll check the book in the morning. And no tricks. Nobody keeps watch. No handwriting analysis—use block letters if you like, whatever. Just tell us what you want. Or what you want us to know. What we need to do to end this.

Okay? Please. We'll do whatever it takes—just tell us what you want."

There's no answer except the incoming tide, which sounds like a mother soothing her baby. *Shush. Shush. Shush.*

Of course, Hayley keeps watch. She places the sketchbook far down the beach, away from their sleeping places, a good distance from the small glowing circle of sand lit by the dying campfire. Like the others, she pretends to go to bed, but she waits, lying in the silence of sticks and leaves for what feels like hours, her whole body tingling with excitement and anxiety, until the sky is black as soft velvet. She creeps out quietly, leaving some clothes bundled up inside in case anybody checks her shelter, then sets off, sneaking along the beach, seeing nobody. In spite of the danger, there's a small, irrepressible part of her that can't help bristling with excitement: her first stakeout.

The sleeping shelters are dotted along the tree line; anybody who wants to reach the sketchbook covertly could melt into the trees, make their way through the forest in the darkness, and emerge onto the beach farther along, unseen and unheard. Hayley continues through the dark gloom of the trees until she is beyond the book, which lies innocently on the sand, just visible in the soft moonlight. She finally emerges when she is level with a big rock about twenty yards farther along the beach, and she rushes to crouch in its shadow. She peeks around the seaward side so she has a good view of the book but can't be seen by anyone walking toward it from the trees.

It takes about half an hour for her electric excitement to fade to a buzz. Then another hour for it to descend into stiff, unrelenting boredom. Her butt feels heavy and numb, her arms ache from pressing against the hard rock, and her ankles are being bitten to pieces by sand flies. She shivers, wishing she had brought an extra sweater, and tries to shift her position quietly, lying down uncomfortably on her stomach, sand prickling her elbows.

After a few hours, she feels stupid, freezing, and exhausted. Did she really believe that someone who has managed to avoid detection this cleverly so far was going to just walk up and write down a full explanation of their actions?

Eventually, Hayley feels her eyes closing. She tries to fight it, digging her fingernails into her palms and training her eyes on the shadowy place where she left the sketchbook, but the weight of her tiredness presses gradually and unstoppably down on her until she can't resist it any longer. With a little sigh, she rests her head in the crook of her elbow and drifts off to sleep.

She wakes at dawn, unused to the thin, early light, her shoulder and hip aching. The beach is deserted. The fire is out, and the trees stand like silent witnesses to a motionless night. Still Hayley races to the sketchbook, grabbing it up and rifling through the pages with trembling fingers, clumsy in their haste. There's nothing but Elliot's drawings. A hastily sketched exterior of Oak Ridge with its imposing bell tower and rolling lawns; a few drawings done courtside during practice on tour; one of the squad on the plane just before they crashed. She flicks through it again more carefully to be sure. The pages laugh at her, as smooth and blank as ever. Her heart rate slows to normal. She tucks the dog-eared book under her arm and starts to trudge back toward the camp.

The sky is fizzing orange at the horizon, fresh-dawn waves lapping at the beach. And that's when she sees it. Letters four-feet long, scraped starkly into the smooth, wet sand.

JUSTICE

DAY 13

A STORM IS BREWING AS THEY GATHER IN THE CAMP LATER that morning. The usual cacophony of the birds is strangely absent, and the island feels still and silent. An unsettling heat weighs heavy on the camp, the humidity in the air almost beginning to crackle with electricity.

Hayley is pacing back and forth in front of the white, crusty ashes of last night's fire, running her fingers through her salt-stiffened hair until it stands up wildly, waiting impatiently while the others assemble, some squinting and yawning, some wandering curiously over to examine the word carved into the sand.

She feels like everything is coming to a head. Finally, she has her proof, confirmation that somebody has been trying to tell them something all along. That somebody has been trying to ask them all a question, or to answer one, perhaps. "Justice?"

Brian yawns widely, his eyes bleary, still sitting in his makeshift bed by the fire where he slept last night. "What's that supposed to mean?"

"No idea." Jason shrugs.

"It has to be about the end-of-tour party," Hayley bursts out, more loudly than she intended. The others look at her, all confused or suspicious except Elliot, who's is quiet and watchful. "It just has to be," Hayley rushes on.

"Look." She points to the word in the sand. "My question was 'what do you want?' And the answer is justice. We know bad things happened that night. We have to figure out what went down and who was involved."

"The night of the party?" May looks slightly panicked. "Are you still obsessing about that? What makes you so sure that the party has anything to do with this?"

Hayley takes a deep breath. There's no byline to hide behind here. She has to speak up, to tell them everything. "I've been think-ing for a while that something must have happened that night, but now I know it, and I think you all do too. For one thing, all this only started once we got here. The party was on the last night of the tour. The night before the crash…" There's something else too, something nagging at Hayley's subconscious. Something in one of the sketches in Elliot's notebook. She's missing an answer that's right there in front of her, but every time she tries to grasp it, it slips further away. "It has to be connected. It's the only thing that makes sense."

"Except it doesn't, does it?" Jessa frowns. "If something happened that night and this is about revenge—" She glances uneasily at the letters on the beach. "Or, okay, 'justice'—they'd be taking it out on the person who'd done that something, right? But it's not just one person being attacked here, is it? We've all been targeted. We can't all be guilty or lying, can we?"

"I don't know." Hayley clenches her fists in frustration. "I just…somehow I just know it's all connected. But I can't prove it because…" She pauses awkwardly, her heart racing. "Well, because I don't think any of you have told me the truth about that night. Not all of it, anyway. It feels like everybody is hiding something." There's a long silence, and nobody contradicts her. She sees Elliot and Jessa quickly glance at each other and then look away. May is chewing her lip, studying Shannon. Jason and Brian are both determinedly looking down at the sand.

"How can you talk about justice when there's absolutely nothing just about this situation?" Brian demands, frowning irritably as he shifts his position and his face creases with pain.

"At least what happened to you wasn't deliberate," Elliot retorts. "That stuff was probably just in your pocket by accident."

"Says the kid who slipped down some rocks and started this whole thing by pretending he was pushed," Jason interjects scathingly.

"According to the guy most likely to have done it," Elliot spits angrily back at him.

"I didn't push you, okay?" Jason is breathing heavily, his cheeks flushing. "Stop putting me on trial!"

"That's it!" Hayley yelps, her voice electric with excitement. "That's it. A trial. A trial to get to the bottom of this once and for all. To find out the truth. And to serve justice."

"Okay, Nancy Drew, what are you suggesting, exactly?" Shannon is sardonic, reclining in the narrow strip of shade thrown by a palm tree, looking supremely unconvinced.

"I think..." Hayley takes a deep breath and tries to sound authoritative. She's been thinking about this since she first saw the letters scraped jaggedly into the beach. "I think we have to sort of testify."

"Testify?" May chews a nail anxiously. "Testify to what, exactly?"

"What happened that night." Hayley lets the words rush out in a jumble, worried that if she doesn't win them over now, her idea will come to nothing. "We think we don't know the answer, but we each have one piece of the puzzle. We each saw different things, did different things at that party. If we put the pieces together, maybe we'll be able to see the bigger picture."

She pauses, twists a foot in the sand, lets the warm grains trickle up soothingly between her toes. She closes her eyes for the briefest moment; she's on a family vacation somewhere else, sometime else, relaxed and happy and worrying only about what kind of pizza to order for lunch.

Her eyes snap open and she takes a deep breath. "I think if we all try and figure out what happened, we might be able to offer it. Justice, I mean. To whoever is asking for it. We figure out what happened, we each admit the part we played that night, and we come to a group decision. If someone is guilty, we admit that. We all agree. Like a jury. Maybe that will offer a kind of closure."

The tide is coming in, little rivulets of swirling, foamy water sliding into the grooves of the letters, already smoothing and flattening their edges, preparing to erase them completely. "Sounds like you know an awful lot about what this mystery person wants," Jason says, eyeing Hayley suspiciously as he tears the flesh away from a mango seed. There is a large, stringy piece stuck between his front teeth, and it waggles up and down when he talks. "How do we know you're not just trying to orchestrate your own weird revenge 'trial,' Hayley?"

Hayley sighs. "I guess you don't. But does that really even matter?" She looks him straight in the eyes. "I'm not the one who's been doing all these things, I swear. But whoever it is, we need to find a way to give them a sense of fairness, a sense that this is being resolved. Otherwise, I don't think they're going to stop. Somebody has been wronged, or they think they have been. They're angry. They're taking things into their own hands. And if we don't make it right, I'm worried the next person might not escape with only a concussion or a badly injured leg."

"I'm scared," Jessa says suddenly. "It's bad enough that we're stuck here, not knowing whether anyone's going to find us, not knowing if the next storm or weird fruit or freak injury is going to be the thing that kills us. But add in someone actually going around hurting people? I agree with Hayley. We have to do something now, before it's too late."

"Yeah, or it makes zero difference, and we all get cannibalized in our beds next," Brian helpfully offers.

"Say you're right." Jessa completely ignores the cannibal comment. "Say it makes no difference. We haven't lost anything, have we?"

"It's a stupid idea," May says stubbornly. "Why are we wasting time obsessing over a boring house party when we have no proof it's linked to what's happening on the island?"

"But maybe Hayley's right," Elliot says. "The timing does fit. Whoever is doing this didn't know we'd be stuck on an island. If whatever caused it had happened sooner, they might have started doing stuff while we were on tour. But nothing happened there."

"Well, I don't want to talk about it." May sounds like a petulant child. "And you can't make me. What if this ridiculous 'trial'"—she sarcastically sketches quotation marks in the air with her fingers—"just creates more division and fighting?"

"Why would it, May?" Jason asks suspiciously. "You got something to hide? You want to get hurt next?"

May glares at him. She doesn't have an answer to this and subsides into reluctant silence.

"Okay, then." Hayley nods excitedly, rushing ahead before anyone else can object. "We'll need some ground rules. No interruptions. Each person gets a chance to take the stand. We can ask them questions, and they have to tell the truth. Don't leave anything out. You don't know what might be important, even a silly little detail."

She is slipping into her role, feeling the comforting

mantle of reporter settling back onto her shoulders, handing out assignments like she would at an editorial meeting.

"And it doesn't leave this island," Brian pipes up, looking suspiciously around at the others. "Whatever we share here stays here."

Later that afternoon, the fire built up and the camp tidied, they sit in a loose circle around Brian's makeshift bed. The hot, heavy air tightens around them as they all look expectantly toward Hayley, waiting for the trial to begin.

She begins nervously, "Elliot, you were the first one to get hurt. Why don't we start with you?"

"Wait." Jessa steps forward, holds out her fine silver chain, the crucifix dangling and sparkling.

"Do you swear to tell the truth, the whole truth, and nothing but the truth, so help you God?" Elliot looks taken aback, but Jessa gives him a little nod.

Elliot shifts nervously and then nods. "Fine. If this is really what it takes to end this." He looks at Brian, propped up on one elbow, his leg motionless. "I'll tell you whatever you want to know." He reaches out to touch the crucifix briefly.

"Everyone," Jessa says firmly, offering it around the circle. Jason scoffs, but he looks at Brian's leg and touches it too.

"We all swear," May says, rolling her eyes.

"Elliot, when did you arrive at the party?"

"Late. I was shooting hoops by myself at the gym after the game ended. I went back to the hotel to take a shower, and I didn't get to the party until around eight thirty, maybe nine. There were some guys out back trying to tap a keg—I remember it spraying all over one of them.

"I wasn't there for long before Truth or Dare started, and after I drank all that stuff they made me chug, I honestly don't remember much. At some point I made my way upstairs, and I spent most of the night on the bathroom floor."

Brian sniggers and makes a loser sign with his thumb and index finger behind Elliot's back. It's actually kind of reassuring, Hayley realizes, because if he's mocking Elliot, he must be feeling a little more like himself again.

Elliot shrugs. "Sorry. There's not much else I can tell you."

"Then what were you and Jessa arguing about in the trees the other day?" Hayley asks pointedly. "I heard you—it sounded like you were covering something up."

Shannon and May exchange a surprised glance; clearly this is the first they are hearing about it.

Elliot looks at Jessa in alarm. "I—"

"That has nothing to do with anything that's happening on the island," Jessa cuts in firmly. "We don't need to talk about it."

"Uh, yeah, we do," Jason counters. "No secrets. That was the deal. Out with it."

Jessa sighs. "You know what, I agree with May. This whole thing is stupid. What do we really think is going to come of this, digging into everyone's privacy?"

Shannon laughs. "Girl, could you make yourself sound any

guiltier? You have to tell us now, otherwise we're all going to believe that you're the…" She waves her hand in the air, gesturing vaguely toward Brian's leg.

"The attacker," Brian mutters darkly.

"The psycho," Jason adds.

"I'm not, I swear," Jessa says helplessly.

"Wow," Elliot mutters under his breath.

"What?" She narrows her eyes at him.

"I just can't believe you'd rather let people believe you might be the one behind all this messed-up shit than admit we were together that night."

Hayley's head snaps up. "What?"

"Jessa and I were together, okay? After Truth or Dare, but before the alcohol caught up with me. I was dancing and I started to feel hot and dizzy, so I went outside to cool off, and Jessa was out there in the garden. And that has nothing to do with what's been happening on this island. Unless you tried to push me to my death so nobody would ever find out," he says with a sarcastic laugh.

"Of course I didn't!" She looks genuinely hurt.

"Well, I can't say it didn't cross my mind," Elliot mutters. "You weren't exactly eager to act like anything had changed between us after the party. You made it pretty clear you didn't ever want anyone to know what had happened."

"Elliot," Jessa says quietly, "you don't understand."

"I think I do, actually. The scruffy scholarship kid doesn't fit in all that well with your usual crowd."

May bursts out laughing and Elliot scowls at her.

"It's not about you, you idiot. Jessa's never been with *anyone*. She's taken a vow of chastity," May intones in a singsong voice.

"Hey!" Jessa looks horrified, but May just shrugs.

"Oh, come on. Shannon and I already know, and if we're doing the whole total truth thing, it's going to come out anyway."

"I didn't know," Elliot mumbles. "I'm sorry. I thought—"

"I didn't even know you were on scholarship, Elliot, and it wouldn't have made any difference to me if I had," Jessa says quietly. "But the other stuff is...complicated."

He holds her gaze, his eyes warm and sympathetic, and suddenly he has crossed the circle and put a tentative arm around her, Jessa looking embarrassed but pleased while May digs her in the ribs.

"You dark horse!"

Hayley stands a few yards away, glad of the warmth of the fire to disguise her hot cheeks, feeling herself deflate just a little before she rallies.

"All right." Hayley's tone is brisk, businesslike. "Brian, you're up."

Brian cracks his knuckles. "Shoot."

"You spent a lot of the evening with the Duke girls, right?"

"Right." Brian grins at Jason and raises his eyebrows. "And not just one of them, if you know what I mean." Jason sticks his tongue into the side of his cheek, crudely mimicking a blow job, and Brian chuckles appreciatively while Jessa gives a loud tut.

"We don't need a rerun of your whole routine, thanks, Brian," May says sourly.

"What were you and the Duke guys joking about at the party, exactly?" Hayley asks, glad of the opportunity to get to the bottom of this.

"That? It was just me and a bunch of the Duke guys messing around," Brian says uneasily. "Just joking, you know? And you have to admit, everyone thought it was pretty funny at the time." He looks toward Jason for support.

"Yeah," Jason says staunchly. "It was just a laugh."

"Oh, it was hilarious," May says acidly. "Really sidesplitting. Go on, Brian," she prompts, smiling a thin smile. "Why don't you tell us one of the jokes again, give us all a lift, since it was so very funny."

"All right, fine." Brian says defiantly. "And I'm sorry if they're not woke enough for you, Comrade May, but they are pretty fucking funny, actually." He looks at Jason. "Strawberry cheesecake, or bucking bronco, that's the funniest. Or the angry pirate." He sniggers in spite of himself. "Nah, come on, May, the angry pirate is funny, it's just objectively funny."

He turns to Elliot. "When you…you know…*finish* in a girl's eye and then kick her in the shin so she hops around with one eye closed going 'Arrrrr.'" Jason is smirking and Brian lets out a snort. "Like an angry pirate," he chuckles.

May looks incandescent, and Jessa wrinkles her nose in disgust. "What's a bucking bronco?"

When neither of the boys volunteer, May turns to her, her voice low and gruff in a crude imitation of Brian. "It's when you're having sex with a girl from behind and you take her in the…you know…without warning and see how long you can hold on."

"Good grief." Jessa sounds completely horrified. "Are you guys saying these are things you've *done?*"

"No, God no!" Jason jumps in, looking at Shannon, whose face is impassive. "They're just jokes, okay? May's not telling it right, it's not…it's not funny like that. It's a…party thing." His voice peters out with uncharacteristic uncertainty.

"Did I tell it wrong?" May asks. "Is that not how bucking bronco works?"

Brian frowns indignantly. "It's not…" He sighs. "It's not *literal*. Obviously, we'd never treat girls like that in real life. What do you think we are, monsters? It's just a fucking joke, okay?"

"What I don't understand," May interrupts him, "is how, after hearing you make those jokes, a couple of cheerleaders, both of them apparently in possession of their senses, actively made the choice to go upstairs with you. How did they know they'd be safe?"

"Jesus, May." Brian isn't smiling anymore. "You don't have to make me out to be some kind of rapist just because I told a fucking joke. What, are you saying I might have accidentally raped someone without even realizing it?" He says it like it's the stupidest thing he's ever heard and looks around the circle like he's expecting everyone to agree with him.

"Yes," May says quietly. "That's exactly what I think." There is a long and uncomfortable silence.

"You and all those other guys were publicly joking about changing places with someone else midway through sex without a woman realizing. About forcing things on a woman during sex that she doesn't want or expect. That's rape. You all literally sat around laughing about rape. Describing rape and laughing. Talking about rape as if—"

"Can you stop saying *rape*?" Brian explodes.

"I need to say it," May continues defiantly, "because you didn't. Because you didn't use that word, and I don't think you necessarily even knew it was what you were talking about. What you were laughing about. I should have said so at the time. And every other time. So I'm saying it now, because it's better late than never."

"There is a difference between talking about something or even joking about it and doing it," Brian mumbles.

"Yeah? Well, we know one of the Duke girls was raped at that party." May's eyes flash as Brian looks in panic at Jason.

"What?" Elliot gasps.

All the boys look completely shocked. If one of them is faking it, he's very convincing.

"So how do we know you didn't rape someone without knowing it?" May demands, her eyes still boring into Brian's. "Since apparently you don't even know what rape is."

"Okay, fine," Brian explodes. "You want to know how I know I didn't rape anyone?" He pushes himself up into a sitting position, panting from the effort. "Because there wasn't any sexual contact at all. Okay?" He is breathing heavily, a fine veil of tiny sweat beads trembling along his top lip. "There. I've said it."

"What do you mean?" Jason asks slowly.

"I mean I couldn't…perform." Brian gestures to his groin area, circling his hands exaggeratedly. "It was a lot of pressure, okay? Those girls had ideas, and everything happened very fast, and somehow it wasn't like I imagined it would be, and nothing…came up."

Jason lets out a raucous snort.

"You choked! You had the dream and you fucking choked. Two girls. TWO GIRLS. Oh man, you better hope we never get off this island, because you will never, ever hear the end of this."

"It is nothing to be ashamed of," Jessa interrupts, glaring at Jason, though Brian looks ten times more scalded by her sympathy than by Jason's jibes.

"Can we. Please. Just. Move on?" he hisses.

"Right." Hayley, who has watched open-mouthed through most of this exchange, tries to regather her scattered thoughts and take control again. "Right."

She turns to Jason. "You left the party early, is that right, Jason?"

"My knee was hurting," he grunts. "I'd twisted it in the last quarter of the game, and I needed to ice it and rest up."

"Huh." Hayley looks at Shannon, whose eyes are glittering

across the circle. "Because Shannon said you went home with a headache."

"Whatever. I wasn't feeling great, so I left. I was not involved in whatever voodoo you're convinced happened that night," he says dismissively.

"And nothing happened before you left? Between you and Shannon?"

"We had a minor disagreement," Jason says stiffly. "Which is not exactly unusual in a relationship as passionate as ours." Shannon says nothing, simply gives the slightest shrug of her delicate shoulders. "And anyway," Jason bristles, "I can't see how that's exactly relevant, since Shannon is obviously not the person running around pushing people off cliffs and trying to feed them to sharks."

"How can you be sure?" Elliot mutters.

"Look at her," Jason scoffs, grinning. "Do you really think *she's* got it in her to cause actual bodily harm?"

Hayley decides to move on quickly.

"May, you had a pretty wild night at the party, right?"

"Whatever you say, Hayley. I guess a fairly tame party where nothing much happens could seem wild if it's the first one you'd ever been to," May fires back, snarky as hell.

Hayley holds her hands up. "So there's nothing you want to tell us? About the party? About anything else?"

"Nope. Someone else's turn?"

"Not quite yet. Because I think you do know something, don't you? Or at least you have a theory about who's behind all this."

May freezes, her eyes locked onto Hayley's as if she's trying to figure out whether she might be bluffing. "I don't know what you're talking about."

"I heard you. Two days ago. Just before Brian's accident. Accusing someone of poisoning you with alcohol and saying you knew why they did it. Because you did something to them, didn't you, May? Was it that night too?"

For a few moments, it looks like May is considering making a run for it. She actually glances around the circle as if she's looking for an escape route, her eyes lingering very briefly on each of them. Is she looking for permission? For forgiveness? Finally, she seems to accept that she is cornered. "Okay, you got me. I did something that night that I never should have done," she snaps at last. "I was angry, and I acted in a moment of spite, and I wish I hadn't done it, okay?"

"Done what, May?" Jessa's eyes are round and liquid, her hand on May's arm. "What are you talking about? Why haven't you told me about this?"

"Like you told me about Elliot?" May retorts.

"What did you do, May?"

May's shoulders droop and her voice becomes very small.

"I spiked someone's drink. Sort of. She asked for a virgin cocktail, but instead I gave her something very, very alcoholic with strong mixers to hide the flavor so she wouldn't realize until it was too late. I just wanted to prove a point, I guess. I wanted to force her to relax for once, to stop being such a priss, being on our backs all the time." She looks up, defiance and embarrassment mingling on her face. "She wanted us to skip the party to go over tapes of our performance—a coaching session on the last night of the tour!" She spreads her hands as if imploring somebody to agree with her. But she knows that it doesn't compare to what she did. She looks utterly ashamed.

"That's why Shannon was acting so weird!" Jessa exclaims, looking at May in horror. "I can't believe you would do something like that." The moment stretches thickly between them, the heat and humidity pressing down like a suffocating blanket as May sits there, trapped in her own shame and remorse.

"I wasn't thinking. I wasn't thinking about it like that, like spiking her drink. You know how I feel about that stuff; I didn't mean it like that. I was just so angry. I wanted her to just chill out for once, you know? And yeah, maybe a small, nasty part of me wanted to see her lose control, see her do something embarrassing or stupid for once. Anything to force her to let down that perfect exterior just for one night."

May starts to cry. "I'm sorry, Shan. I'm really sorry. It's hard being your friend sometimes, you know? I love you, but you're so controlled and poised all the fucking time. It can feel exhausting just to exist next to you. It was so stupid."

Slowly, one by one, heads are turning toward Shannon, who is sitting very, very still.

"Wait a minute," Brian says slowly, his head swiveling from May to Shannon and back again. "That's the same thing that happened to you, May. That day we explored the island. You said your drink had been spiked..." He trails off, his eyes widening.

"And—"

"Then—"

"If spiking May's drink was revenge for her spiking Shannon's drink at the party, then that means the person who's been doing all this..." Elliot looks shocked.

"It was you?" Jessa whispers, turning to her captain and friend in disbelief.

They are all dumbfounded, staring at Shannon as if they've never seen her before. Jason is weakly opening and closing his mouth, his forehead deeply furrowed.

Hayley breaks the circle. It's like the last piece of the puzzle has finally fallen into place. Suddenly, she realizes what she's been missing. It's been right in front of her since the very first day, when Elliot lit the fire. She moves across the sand to grab the sketch-book from the spot where she'd dropped it earlier that morning.

"Exhibit A," she says softly, flipping it open to the picture of them all on the plane moments before the crash. Elliot has captured the whole group as vividly as a black- and-white photograph. May and Jessa tangled together in the back row. Brian looking like he's about to hurl. Jason reclining imperiously, earbuds in. Hayley gazing out the window, lost in thought. And Shannon. Shannon in a two-seat row on her own. Shannon, with the faintest smudge of what could almost be a shadow beneath her left collarbone. Shannon's eyes, piercing and preoccupied. Shannon before the crash, viscerally, visibly in pain.

"That bruise just under your neck the day we landed. You didn't get it in the crash, did you?"

Shannon hesitates for the tiniest fraction of a second. "Of course I did. We were all banged up."

"But it was yellow around the edges. Not fresh." Carefully, Hayley rips out the piece of paper from Elliot's notebook and passes it to her. "You had the bruise before the crash."

Shannon's whole face slips and her shoulders slowly sink. Her collarbones are like blades, pushing out through translucent skin. She lets out a long sigh. She almost looks relieved.

"Why?" Hayley asks her simply.

"Chad Maxwell. All the Chad Maxwells," she answers straight away, her voice neutral, detached.

"Chad Maxwell?" It's not the answer Hayley was expecting, and it takes her a minute to place the name. "The guy from the beach party last year?"

"And every guy like him."

"That guy who was arrested at Anastasia Wahlberg's house?" Brian is trying to keep up. "What's he got to do with any of this?"

Hayley's head is whirling. "But you said—I thought you didn't even know who he was?"

"Yeah, that's what I said. Because that's what everyone says. It's just what you do. You keep quiet. You protect the status quo. Especially when it happens to someone else."

"I don't understand." Hayley is turning the pieces over in her brain, trying to get them all to fit together. She traces a pattern in the sand with her fingertips.

"Star athlete. Division champion. Probably going pro."

The words echo in Hayley's head, reminding her of something. The letter the school paper had received from the Maxwell family's lawyer, warning them off the story. "Star athlete...bright future ahead of him...spurious accusations... ruin lives...no foundation in truth."

Shannon is still staring rigidly into the fire.

"That girl at Anastasia's party, she was drunk off her ass. She was out of control. The whole thing was practically inevitable. If it hadn't been him she might have been hit by a car on the way home or God knows what else. She was a mess. Like I was a mess the last night of the tour. Not the kind of person whose story stands up. Not against star power and a letter jacket."

"But Chad wasn't in Texas..."

"It wasn't Chad at the tour party. Obviously. But it might as well have been. Because the story is the same. Another star athlete. I wanted to until I didn't. There was dancing. Everything was moving so fast. I was angry with Jason, wanted to punish him." She doesn't look at Jason, who is gasping, as if he can't quite pull enough oxygen out of the close hot air.

"I walked upstairs on my own two feet. I wasn't in control, exactly, but I was conscious. I knew, even as we went upstairs...I knew it wasn't what I wanted. But I thought—" She breaks off for a moment, scooping up handfuls of sand and letting it run through her fingers.

May looks absolutely horror-struck, tears rolling down her cheeks as Shannon talks.

Shannon sighs. "I don't know what I thought. It was like I couldn't think, like my skin was electric and my brain was on a carnival ride—everything was spinning and I wanted to get off, but I didn't know how and the music wouldn't stop." She runs a hand over her face, pushing her wild black hair, made wilder by the sea air, out of her eyes. She suddenly looks exhausted and very young.

"He was on me before the door closed. As powerful as he had been on the court. I didn't, couldn't say no. I didn't say yes, either. I didn't move. It felt like I didn't breathe. I didn't look. I didn't feel. It was like he was in there with nobody. He must have known I wasn't there. I don't know if he liked that or if it just didn't matter to him either way. I tried to get up at one point near the beginning. I tried to get away. But he had his whole body weight on me." Her fingertips hover above the pale yellow shadow where the bruise used to be, as if she can't quite bring herself to touch it. "The base of his hand, like this, and his fingers near my throat."

She takes her hand, spread wide, thumb straining one way and her four fingers stretching in the opposite direction, and plunges it into the sand, knuckles rigid. "He was too strong." She moves her hand, and for a split second there are five deep wells where her fingers have been. Then the grains of sand slide in, and the holes disappear. "I waited until he was finished, and then he left. And I just lay there and waited for the feeling to come back again. But it didn't." There is a stunned silence. Somewhere far away the first roll of thunder growls and an unpleasantly humid breeze moves across the circle.

"What?" Jason says stupidly, his jaw slack, his eyes moving from Hayley to Shannon and back again as he tries to process what he has just heard. Like his brain desperately doesn't want him to.

"It wasn't some girl from Duke." May is catching on faster, nodding slowly as she puts it together. "It was you. I'm so sorry, Shan," she sobs, over and over again. "Oh God, I'm so, so sorry."

Shannon nods wearily. "It was me. And no, Jessa, before you ask, I suppose I didn't fight back."

And then the rain comes. It's a rush of tropical fury, slashing across their faces like knives, punctuated by lightning so vivid it seems to split the sky in two, forcing them to scatter. A cacophony of noise and water forcing itself into their mouths and eyes as they race to carry Brian to his shelter and dive into their own, huddling desperately underneath the braided leaves, Hayley's mind racing to make sense of it all as the sky turns black and the storm rages on into the night.

DAY 14

EVERYBODY HAS QUESTIONS. SO MANY QUESTIONS IT'S difficult to know where to begin.

When their scattered circle reforms in the thin morning light, Elliot says, "You spiked May's drink." His voice is pitched low, like he's afraid Shannon might break into pieces if he speaks to her too harshly. Like she's suddenly an alien thing, a fragile exhibit in some bizarre story about female fury.

The tide is out, a vast, glassy slick of wet sand stretching away toward the distant whisper of the waves, just like the day they crashed. The sun has barely breached the horizon and the sky is soft and gray. The storm has cleared the air and the breeze is fresh and cool. Hayley can taste sea salt on the back of her tongue.

Elliot continues. "So all the other stuff was you too? It's been you all along?"

She doesn't answer, but she doesn't deny it either. Just looks down at her hands.

"You were raped?" Jason demands bluntly. He's shaking his

head like he can't accept it, like he's waiting for someone to tell him the punchline, tell him it's all been a stupid prank.

"You were raped." He says it again, as if it will help him to understand. "Raped by who?"

The hair that was shiny and coiffed when they arrived at the airport just days and yet years and years ago is greasy now, clinging to Jason's scalp in an oily slick. His face looks hollower, the usual sparkle in his baby blues replaced with a glinting metallic glare.

"It was you, wasn't it?" He moves toward Elliot like a predator advancing on its prey, arms outstretched, fury written in his tensed biceps as he draws back his arm. "It was you," he half shrieks. "That's why she pushed you, that's why you were the one she started with, you dirty, lying—"

"No!" Shannon is in front of him, eyes blazing, and for a moment it looks as if the blow will land on her instead, but with a visible effort, Jason halts, drops his arm.

"Then who?" His hands are on her shoulders, fingernails digging in, knuckles white. "No more games, Shannon." And there's a warning in his voice.

"Nobody. Nobody on the island. One of the Duke players at the party."

Jason isn't the only one who looks completely floored.

"I don't understand, Shannon. You did all *this*? Because some other guy who isn't here—" He looks around at the others. "It wasn't any of us who hurt you?"

"I didn't say that," Shannon says quietly. And Hayley thinks she is beginning to understand.

"It was all of us," she whispers. "Wasn't it?"

"I thought I could bear it at first," Shannon says, almost under her breath. "Instinct kicked in at the beginning when the crash was so fresh, and it drove everything else away. It was a relief to be that person again, to play the role of that Shannon, the captain who looked after everyone else, who always knew what to do. Like an escape. But later, when it all came back, when I realized we were trapped here, I thought I would die. I thought that I could not physically be here with this group of people who I realized had all been part of it, that it would end me.

"And then it was like…" She spreads her hands, looking up at the vast expanse of the sky as if she's searching for the right words to explain. "Like I slowly started to feel that the island was on my side somehow. Like it knew. Like it would help me hold you all accountable, somehow."

"Hold us accountable for what?" Brian snarls, and Hayley can tell that he has more to say, that he hasn't even begun to unleash his fury, but he's catching up too, slowly piecing it together like the rest of them.

"So, what, you formed a plan to create your own punishments?"

"No. No." Shannon's eyes are liquid, her voice urgent. "I never meant to do it—not any of it. It just sort of happened. It was that night, the night of the storm. We were there on the hilltop, and everyone was shouting at once and the rain was slashing down and my hair was soaked and the airplane was roaring, and it honestly felt like it might be the end of everything, and then suddenly in the chaos, there was this moment when I saw him right there in front of me, his back turned."

"Elliot?" Hayley says. But before she can ask what Elliot had to do with it, Shannon is rushing on, words tumbling out frantically, like she needs them to understand.

"And everyone else was looking up at the sky and I just, I don't know, something just coursed through me and it was like time slowed down and I looked at him standing there for the longest moment, thinking about how he'd walked past me that night, how he'd left me hanging there when all I needed was one piece of solid ground under my feet…one hand on my shoulder to stop me from falling… He *saw* me, Hayley. He saw me going upstairs with that guy, and he must have seen that I wasn't right, that I was out of it, and he just smiled. Smiled. What did he think was happening? And I tried to meet his eyes, because there was still some part of me that sensed he could say something, disrupt the situation somehow, and I tried to signal to him, I gave him a look, and his eyes just kind of slid over me, and I swear it was like he almost winked at the guy. Like some kind of bro code or something."

Her face darkens. "Fucking Elliot. Elliot, who wasn't ever one of the guys. But that was the moment he chose to suddenly try and fit in? The one moment I needed him not to? And I just looked at his back there in the rain, inches from the edge, and suddenly I realized I could make him feel it too. Feel what it was like to have somebody let him just slip over the edge. Feel the ground falling away underneath him, nobody putting out an arm. He was almost there already."

She's pleading, her eyebrows knitted together. "He was this close to slipping by himself. He might have done it, even. And I didn't plan it. I swear. But before I knew what was happening, my arms had done it. They'd just done it and he wasn't there anymore." Shannon draws a deep, shaky breath, as if something has left her body and there's a void in its place

Elliot is standing in front of her, his arms slack at his sides, genuine hurt and confusion on his face.

"I never meant to hurt you badly, I swear." Shannon addresses him directly for the first time. "I didn't realize how steep it was or that there were rocks. I thought you might fall a foot or two, have a scare, that's all. And once you were okay, once you recovered and nothing too serious happened, I couldn't stop thinking about it. I couldn't stop thinking about how I could make you all feel things too. Things you'd never feel otherwise. Things you'd never have to feel at home. And it just took me over somehow. I never meant it to go this far. But I couldn't stop it either. I knew that at any moment we might get rescued and it would be over, and there was some urgent, hot part of me that needed it done before we went back and I had to live with it, carry it with me. Like this could lighten the load."

Hayley puts out a hand. "Wait. Slow down. I'm trying to

understand, Shannon, I really am. But you intentionally hurt everybody, right? You're going to have to walk us through this. Elliot left you hanging. You felt like he had a chance to step in and he didn't—I get that. I'm not saying I agree with you. I think Elliot was nervous and embarrassed at that party. He was trying to fit in, and he'd drunk that disgusting cocktail…but I get it. You wanted him to feel the way he'd made you feel…" She frowns, thinking fast. "And…you spiked May's drink because that's what she did to you?"

Shannon nods. "When I thought back the next day, I realized she must have put something in that cocktail. It was the only thing I drank that night, so it was the only thing that made sense. I didn't realize it at the party—everything was happening too fast, it was like a dream. But the next day when I woke up, I felt so awful…my head was pounding and I could barely open my eyes. That's when I figured it out."

May looks like she wants to sink into the sand.

"I'm so sorry, Shan. I'm so, so sorry. I didn't mean it. I never, ever wanted something like that to happen to you. I was just so pissed at you for forcing us to watch those stupid tapes when the tour was over, and Jessa was all, 'Yes, Captain, of course, Captain, oh Captain, my Captain,' and I guess it made me feel jealous. I never meant to hurt you. Or to let someone else hurt you."

"I wanted you to see what it felt like," Shannon says in a low voice. "To be scared, to feel out of control, like your own body won't do what you want it to do. To feel that confusion and terror."

Hayley frowns, remembering May flopping around the camp the other day, the fear and frustration in her eyes. An eye for an eye?

"It was just one bad day for you," Shannon goes on. "It didn't lead to anything else. It won't affect you forever."

"What about Brian?" Hayley asks gently, and Shannon's face crumples in anguish.

"I never meant for it to go that far. I just needed him to know what it felt like. To be really afraid of something bigger and more powerful than you. To feel physically vulnerable. To feel such visceral fear that you can't even move. I thought he wouldn't make those jokes again if he experienced that. He wouldn't laugh about those things, not if he'd known that feeling. And I couldn't stop thinking about whether what happened later...about whether that guy would have felt so comfortable just taking what he wanted if they hadn't all been laughing about it downstairs just a couple of hours earlier."

Jessa is shaking her head. "But Shannon, he could have been killed. And he didn't do anything to you, you know, *directly*."

Shannon looks down at the sand, tracing patterns around her legs. "I didn't really expect anything to happen. At worst, I thought he might see something small like a barracuda or a nurse shark or something."

Hayley remembers Shannon's white face and shaking hands as they helped Brian out of the water. She hadn't been acting, Hayley was certain of it.

"I just wanted him to know what it was like, to feel that same fear. The fear *we* all feel practically every fucking day. A kind of fear he might go his whole life without ever once experiencing. And okay, I took a risk. But don't we play fast and loose with girls' lives every single day? I never really thought anything would happen, though, Brian. Honestly I didn't."

And for the first time, she looks up and meets the fury in his eyes.

"Shannon." His voice is shaking. Slowly, he starts to peel back the layers wrapping his useless leg. Rusty blood has oozed between May's amateur stitches and dried in dark patches. Around one stitch, the flesh is beginning to swell, standing up hard and angry. The long, dark slit of the wound dominates his entire calf. He speaks very slowly, like he's struggling to keep himself calm. "I will be scarred by this for my entire life."

"Yes," Shannon says simply. "Like me."

"I DIDN'T DO THAT TO YOU," Brian screeches, lurching forward as if he would throw himself at her if he could stand up. "I told some fucking jokes. You don't have a sense of humor? Fine, I can't help you. But putting someone else in danger? That is a completely different thing. What you did is unforgivable. The only monster here is you."

"And the glass?" Jason's voice is quiet and cold as Shannon and Brian stare at each other. "What was my crime, please?" His voice is dripping in sarcasm.

For the first time, Shannon looks uncertain. She hesitates, her angular face turned slightly to meet the cool breeze as it blows in off the distant sea. She looks at Hayley.

"How did the glass make you feel, Jason?" Hayley asks.

"What are you talking about?"

"How did it make you feel when you woke up that morning? And when you came back with the rest of us and it was gone?"

Jason doesn't answer. His eyes flit from Hayley to Shannon and back again.

"I think," Hayley says carefully, not wanting to make things worse for Shannon or put words in her mouth, "I think it made you feel scared, and on edge, and paranoid. Like you were treading on eggshells and couldn't trust yourself. Like something awful could happen if you took a wrong step. I think maybe those are things Shannon has felt in your relationship. I think maybe she feels them every single day. And I think maybe they came to a head that night."

"You have no idea what you're fucking talking about, you nosy, interfering bitch..." He lumbers furiously toward Hayley, but Elliot and Jessa leap forward, each putting a restraining hand on his shoulders.

"I think..." Hayley swallows, deliberately raising her chin, forcing herself to look him in the eye even though her heart feels as if it is about to break out of her chest. "I think that something in her snapped when you treated her the way you did that night, when you argued, and if it hadn't, I don't know...maybe things would have been different. I think that's the part you played."

248 | LAURA BATES

Jason is about to protest again, but Jessa is tired of waiting for her turn.

"What about the leeches? I knew they didn't get out of that pool by themselves," she says angrily, and there's a hard edge to her voice. "What the hell did I ever do to you?"

"I nearly told you," Shannon tells her simply. "In the trees that afternoon. And then there was some part of me that couldn't bring myself to say the words. So I told you the story, but I substituted someone else." Her voice splinters. "But then, when you talked about how it wasn't really rape, how that girl changed her mind afterward, how she was just trying to cover her own mistakes...it made me feel so ashamed. Dirty. Like I couldn't ever wash it off."

"Hence the leeches?" Hayley is nodding, understanding slowly. "To make Jessa feel dirty as well."

Shannon nods.

"And I guess you put them on all of us to deflect suspicion?"

"It would have been too obvious not to. Sorry." She shrugs. "Part of me liked the idea of it, anyway. Cleaning the blood. Removing toxins. Or something."

"Wait," Jason says. "Wait, back up. What did you say? About changing your mind?"

"Is *that* what this is about?" Brian is catching on, his eyes widening as he starts to connect the dots. "That guy you were all over on the dance floor?"

"All over?" Jason's voice is deepening dangerously.

"Are you telling me," Brian whispers, his voice menacing, "that this whole nightmare has been about you regretting a one-night stand with a Duke player?"

"You put out for him?" Jason roars, turning furiously on Shannon. "How many fucking years have I waited for you, Shannon? Jesus Christ, what a cuck." He's looking at her in disgust, as if he's never seen her before. "What do you think you're playing at? You're sick, you know that? I think there's something seriously wrong with you."

"Yes," Shannon whispers. "Something wrong."

"Guys." Hayley is horrified, watching them, their anger circling Shannon like a tightening fist. "We're talking about a rape."

Jason gives a bitter, barking laugh.

Shannon just sits there, looking out at the waves, letting it wash over her. In and out. In and out.

And Hayley thinks that it is Shannon's life, Shannon's injuries, Shannon's pain they should be talking about, but they're focusing on themselves. She doesn't know how to make them realize that they're looking at this all wrong.

Quietly, before Hayley can find the words to say anything, Shannon stands up. She brushes the sand delicately from her fingertips. And she walks away.

"So we know what to do now," Brian says, his voice flat and hard. "We watch Shannon 24–7. Or we lock her up. And if we ever get off this goddamn island, we turn her in to the police."

"Excuse me?" May is standing now too, next to Hayley. "Turn her in? Are you kidding me?"

"No." Brian glares up at her defiantly. "She tried to kill me, May. I literally went swimming in shark-infested waters with shark bait in my pockets."

"It's a deep cut, Brian, I know. But someone's going to find us. You'll live. If we're talking about going to the police, it should be to report that Duke bastard, not Shannon. She's the victim here."

"She's not the only victim," Elliot chips in quietly, rubbing the spot on his head where an egg-like bump had protruded for several days after his fall.

"Right, because a bump on the head is the same as being assaulted," May retorts sarcastically.

"Okay. Maybe this is what we have to decide," Hayley says slowly. "This was never only about protecting ourselves. It was about justice. So we sit here and we talk this through and we make a decision. What we'll do if we ever get off this island. Whether we go to the police. And who we report."

"What's the point?" Jessa looks sullen, tired. "We might never be found."

"All the more reason to decide," Hayley says firmly. "If we're going to survive here any longer, we need to know where we stand. We need to decide for ourselves, to give ourselves a moral code. Who's to say something like this won't happen again, here on the island? We decide this once and for all, for us, separate from home, separate from the law. We make our own decision."

"Like a legal judgment?" Elliot looks doubtful.

"Well, sort of. Majority rules. We all have to commit to that."

"What the hell happened to innocent until proven guilty?" Brian splutters angrily. "We all know Shannon attacked us, but we can't just decide to ruin some guy's life, his reputation, without any proof. We can't just take her word for it."

"Why is it innocent until proven guilty for him but disbelieved until proven true for her?" May snaps.

"It doesn't have to be innocent or guilty," Hayley cuts in, holding up her hands for calm. "We're not convicting him, we're just deciding as a group whether to support Shannon by reporting him to the police. Okay?"

"What are you, her lawyer?" Jason's voice is heavy with sarcasm.

"Yeah, maybe I am," Hayley shoots back defiantly.

"You're talking as if Shannon was ambushed," Brian complains. "That's ridiculous. Why didn't any of us hear her scream? She was only upstairs. If she was being raped up there, we would have known about it."

For a long moment, they all seem to be digesting this, and there is no sound but the white noise of the sea and the swishing of the breeze in the palm leaves.

"She knew exactly what she was doing!" It bursts out of Brian, as if he knows he shouldn't say it but can't help himself. "Well, she did. She did," he croaks at Hayley, and it's almost like he is pleading with her, like he needs this to be true for everything to stay the same. To avoid all the moments of his own past that will suddenly look different, the future he will need a new map to navigate. It would be so much easier if Shannon would just say, "Yes, I knew what I was doing." And the world he has always known could stay the same.

"How did you feel when the shark was closing in on you in the water?" Hayley's voice is trembling slightly.

"What has that got to do with anything?"

"Just answer the question."

"I was scared, obviously."

"Scared?"

"Okay, I was really scared."

"Why didn't you punch it?"

"Oh, come on, Hayley."

"You were scared, right? It was bigger and more dangerous than you, and the last thing you wanted to do was go on the offensive and risk provoking it."

"I—"

"You didn't swim away."

"What?"

"I noticed you were frozen there, in the water sort of waving, for over a minute. Why didn't you start swimming for the shore straight away?"

"I don't know, I was—it all happened so fast."

"You were shocked, right? It was terrifying. You froze. Panic set in. You didn't know what to do. Your body took over—"

"That's not the same."

"Why? What's the difference?"

"Brian didn't dance with the shark before it attacked him," Elliot says quietly. "I mean, Hayley, we all saw her draped around the guy's neck, rubbing up against him. Nobody had a gun to her head, did they?"

Hayley watches a muscle tighten and twitch in Jason's cheek.

"Does it even matter?" May leaps to Hayley's defense. "It wouldn't matter if she'd ripped her top off and started grinding on him. The point is what happened afterwards, isn't it? When he raped her."

"It matters to me," Jason mutters through gritted teeth.

"Of course it matters!" Brian splutters. "You're asking us to make a judgment about what happened that night. I'm sorry, but I'm less likely to believe that someone was raped if I saw her all over the guy like melted butter on pancakes an hour before she claims he forced her to have sex with him."

"Raped her," May repeats. "And it doesn't matter how enthusiastic she might have been earlier. If she changed her mind once they were in the bedroom and didn't want to go through with it, then it was rape."

"But she seemed…" Jessa swallows. "I mean, wouldn't we have known? She seemed okay the next morning." Jessa studiously avoids May's eyes. "Look, I want to support Shannon in whatever she's going through, I really do, but I'm finding it hard to understand why she would've gone upstairs with that guy in the first place if she wasn't, you know, up for it." She shakes her head nervously. "I'm sorry, but it doesn't totally add up."

"Yes! Thank you!" Brian applauds, and Jessa looks away uncomfortably.

"I'm sorry to be the one to say this, but we're talking about someone making an active choice to put herself in a dangerous situation. What did she think was going to happen?" Jessa can't meet anyone's eyes.

"Maybe she thought she was going to fool around. Maybe she thought she'd have a little bit of fun. Maybe she never planned to have sex, but she wanted to do other stuff," May says. "Some of us like to have fun, you know. Not all of us are married to our own fathers in weird, fucked-up ceremonies."

Jessa draws in a sharp breath. "That was a purity ball, and you know it meant something important to me. I can't believe you'd throw that in my face."

May looks guilty, like she knows she's gone too far. "I'm sorry, Jessa. I didn't mean that." Jessa turns away from her, eyes filled with tears. May twists her fingers in frustration. "I just hate this idea that any girl who wants to experience some pleasure on her own terms is somehow asking for trouble and deserves whatever she gets," she bursts out. "You know? In this group of four girls, you're looking at one rape. And how many sexual assaults? Who here has been grabbed, or groped, or had a guy expose himself in front of you in the street?"

Jessa sniffs and raises her hand. May puts her own up as

well. So does Hayley. "Four for four," she says grimly. "Virgins included."

"Any of that happened to any of you?" May looks at the boys, her glare like a laser. They all sit motionless.

"It's officially one in three for women," Hayley adds. "I looked it up for that article. It's one in three in the records, because those are the ones that have been reported. One in three women are physically or sexually assaulted."

"See?" May says angrily. "It's not that you're all just far more cautious than we are. This isn't some awful, rare accident that happens to careless girls who go to the wrong place on the wrong night or wear the wrong skirt or drink the wrong thing. It's literally our day-to-day—you just don't know anything about it because you're not living it."

"Oh, come on, you're not living it, May. I'm sorry that happened to you, but stop exaggerating." Jason sounds like a patronizing dad reining in an overdramatic kid.

"I hold my keys between my fingers every time I walk home after dark," Hayley says quietly. "Have any of you guys ever done that?"

The boys look back at her, blinking.

"I call my mom so she'll hear if anything happens when I'm walking at night," Jessa says. "She can track my location, so she would know exactly where I was if anything happened."

"I never come home through the park after dark," May chips in. "Even though it adds, like, twenty minutes to my walk. And on Thursdays, I wait an hour at school while Jessa has yearbook so we can walk home together."

"We go to the bathroom in groups if we're out." Hayley puts up the fingers of her right hand and starts ticking them off, one by one. "I carry pepper spray. I never wear headphones when I jog so I can hear if someone comes up behind me. I cross the street if I see a group of guys up ahead. I check behind me before I put my key in the lock." She folds down her thumb, leaving a tight fist. "Shall I go on?"

The boys are silent.

"Like I said," May says, quieter now, "it's our whole lives."

May puts her hands to her face as if her head is too heavy for her neck to hold up. "And I made it worse. I did this to her. I put Shannon in that situation and took away her control." She shakes her head miserably.

"I never said a word about those jokes. I just ignored them." Elliot is looking down at the palms of his hands, his forehead creased with guilt. "I didn't think it meant anything. And everything you've just described, it's like…it's like there's a completely different world you're all living in, and I've literally never seen it or heard of it before today. Even though it's the world I live in too."

"And I didn't stop them. I saw him taking her upstairs—he was half dragging her, she was so out of it. But I was so caught up in my own thing…" He looks at Hayley, cringing, as if she can somehow forgive him. "I was so busy trying to get into the bathroom to hide how sick I felt, so preoccupied with the fact that I'd just kissed Jessa…I just gave the guy a grin as he went past. Jesus, I might even have fist-bumped him or something, I can't remember."

"That's just great, dude. Good to know you had my back," Jason mutters.

"*Your* back?" Even Jessa looks indignant now.

"Uh, yeah, Jessa. Mine. She went into the bedroom with that guy. She was laughing and joking with him. Everyone's acting like this is all about Shannon and some guy and Brian's leg, but what about me? I'm the one who had something taken from him that night."

Hayley and May exchange an incredulous glance.

"So what exactly are we supposed to decide, here?" Brian demands. "That we condone revenge? That it's totally okay, what Shannon has put us all through? It's okay that I can't even walk? We all agree that it's totally fine for girls to go psycho on everyone if they get 'raped'?" He does the air quotes thing, and Hayley feels a hot flash of anger. "That guys have to be mind readers, and if they're not, they're automatically condemned as rapists?"

"No, Brian. That's not what Shannon wants. She doesn't want other girls to go out taking revenge on people. She didn't want to do that herself. She wanted justice. But she knew that wasn't an option for her. Because we all know the story of Chad Maxwell. And we know a dozen other stories like it. We know what happens to the girl who accuses the star athlete. Or the Supreme Court judge. Or the president. We all know how that story goes."

"We're supposed to decide that girls' lives mean more than boys' sports," May says simply. "We're supposed to decide that there's something wrong if guys need to be mind readers during sex because we've normalized sex where guys are so busy doing what they want to us that they don't even notice what we're feeling or whether we're into it or not. That it matters if a girl is raped at a party where her so-called friends spent the night joking and laughing about rape, which makes her think nobody will take her seriously." She chokes out a half sob.

"What happened to your leg, Brian, it's awful. The idea that it might get worse, that it could get infected—that's unbearable. But why is it that we can all see that, but we can't see what's happened to Shannon in the same way? Why are we okay with leaving so many girls so badly injured?"

Hayley nods and lets out a breath she feels like she's been holding on to forever. "We should take the scars we don't see as seriously as the ones we do."

DAY 15

THE NEXT MORNING, HAYLEY FINDS SHANNON IN THE QUIET shade of the grove of mango trees, their reddening fruit bulging from the branches, their vivid green leaves moving softly in the morning breeze.

On the way, she passes Jason sitting at the edge of the beach with his back against a tree, staring out at the waves. He looks small and crumpled, like a little boy on a time-out. Hayley knows he doesn't understand. He hasn't had some great epiphany, some sudden rush of empathy or revelation about gender bias. She doesn't know if he ever will. But he knows that everything has changed. The ground has slipped from beneath him whether he changes his mind and his behavior or not. And they did that. They can't make him understand any more than they can force Brian to change. But they can change the reaction. They can change the response guys get to those behaviors. And Jason looks like he's realizing that. Hayley almost feels sorry for him. Everything he knows, everything he's grown up being taught by his friends, his favorite movies, his video games, his online world, even his own parents…it's all falling apart. And that's a scary place to be.

But it will never be as scary as what Shannon has been through, she thinks as she passes him and makes her way into the cool of the trees.

"You're up early."

Shannon nods, quietly turning over a waxy-skinned fruit that has fallen to the forest floor with her toe. On one side, it is perfect, the bright, luscious green slowly developing into a dark red blush. When it rolls over, the other side is rotten and putrefying, its orange flesh darkened and congealed like custard, ants swarming greedily into the gashes in its skin.

"You didn't murder Rocket, did you?" The thought pops suddenly into Hayley's head. Did Shannon try to sabotage their water supply as well?

A wry smile flickers around Shannon's lips. "No, I swear. May he rest in raccoon heaven."

Hayley nods.

"I never wanted to sabotage our survival, Hayley. I could've, if I wanted to. All it would have taken is one of those beach apples. Squeeze the sap into the water we'd collected. It would have been so easy."

Hayley feels suddenly cold. The fact that Shannon has had this thought throws her. Before they got here, she thought she had so much figured out. Standing up for what was right. Fighting for justice. But nothing here is easy or black and white. Shannon is a survivor; she believes that. Believes she deserves justice and support. But is what she did to the others acceptable? Forgivable?

"You didn't do it, though," she says, more to herself than to Shannon. And she realizes how much that matters. How bad Shannon's pain must have been to even have had that thought in the first place.

"We voted on what we should do. About you."

"Oh yeah?"

"Yeah. And we voted in your favor."

Shannon nods again. Hayley feels deflated. She doesn't know what she was hoping for. She suddenly feels very young and inexperienced. Foolish for thinking she could somehow fix things. She felt proud that she managed to get to the bottom of what happened. She advocated for Shannon powerfully enough to get the others to agree. But she can't fix it. It's not really justice for a few of them to realize how fucked up the whole night was and how much they all had to do with it. It doesn't change what happened. Will it stop it from happening again? Will it mean they'll be will be more likely to step in if they see a similar situation in the future, to stop the downward spiral that could become a sexual assault before it happens? The part of the spiral that they don't usually see, the bit that consists of all of them, their jokes and split-second reactions, and the moments when they decide whether to say something or to look away?

Hayley doesn't know. Maybe.

Perhaps just trying to make those little changes in the small moments nobody knows are important...perhaps, Hayley thinks, that's as vital as a big, triumphant exposé. It's not the satisfying ending she's used to in her articles, tying each one up with a neat payoff. It's not the perfection Hayley Larkin is used to striving for. But maybe moving forward has to be messy and imperfect or they'll never move forward at all.

She wishes she were better at this. Wishes she knew what to say. Wishes she had Jessa's easy warmth or May's wit.

She knows enough, at least, to realize Shannon doesn't need to know how close the vote was. That Jason and Brian both voted against and Jessa only came down on her side at the end.

"We'll report him, if we ever go back. All of us. We agreed to stand with you. We'll tell the police what happened and back you up. And nobody is going to mention any of what happened here on the island." She pauses, wondering how to word this delicately. "As long as it's over now."

Shannon takes a slow, deep breath, tilting her pale chin upward. The dappled sun plays over her face.

"No. Nobody is telling anybody anything." She says it with a quiet finality, the tone Hayley recognizes from moments at practice when they were debating a new move or a change to the sequence and Shannon held up a hand and ended the discussion, overruling them.

"What do you mean? I got them to understand. I spoke up for you." Hayley feels stupid, and a slow glow of embarrassment spreads through her stomach as she realizes how hurt she is, how much she needs to make this right. "I don't get it. I thought you wanted justice. That's what you wrote, isn't it?"

Shannon shakes her head. "Justice isn't available. It doesn't exist, not for me, not for this. Not back home. Not without a cost that's not worth paying."

She looks at Hayley. "You know what happens to girls like that. Girls from places like Carsons Park. People will find out where I live. And what my upbringing was. And the story will change. You know it will. You've seen it."

So she does remember after all.

Hayley starts to reach out a hand toward her, but Shannon twists away, turning her back and extending a birdlike arm to pluck plump mangoes from the tree.

"Did you look it up for that article of yours?" She looks at Hayley, that hollow, haunted look on her face. "Did you check what percentage of rapists ever spend a day in jail?"

Hayley swallows. "Two point five percent."

"Exactly. So it'll be my turn. My turn to be the gold digger, the liar, the slut. My turn to be ripped apart online, to be disbelieved because I didn't scream loud enough or because my injuries aren't considered bad enough to prove someone hurt me. My turn to be cast as the vindictive bitch ruining an innocent athlete's chance of a shining college career. It'll become who I am. And for what? His shine won't even be tarnished. He'll just shine brighter than ever. I won't let this define me. If his life won't be defined by it, why should mine?"

"So this was all for nothing?"

"Not for nothing," Shannon says quietly. "The others. What they did? That doesn't even count. There's no punishment, no crime. Even though it might never have happened without each one of them. What they did that night will affect me for the rest of my life, and before this they'd never even have thought twice about it. They wouldn't even *know*."

"But now they do," Hayley says. "Exactly. Now they do."

And suddenly, Hayley realizes that the trial hasn't been going on for just the last forty-eight hours. They've all been on trial the whole time. On the island, at the party—the whole time, they've been living in a world where treating one half of the population like disposable objects is so normal no one even notices it. They were all complicit one way or another. Just some more than others.

"Shannon, can I ask you something? Was I right about Jason? About the part he played?"

Shannon smiles dreamily. "Jason Angel. Jason always shines so bright, always has, no matter what he does."

She closes her eyes, letting the breeze stroke her cheeks. "A guy from the Duke team came over at lunch the day of the final game and asked me if he could borrow the salt from our table."

Hayley frowns but waits.

"That's what the fight was about, at the party. He only wanted the salt, but Jason thought it might be something else. Jason is always seeing things that aren't there."

"He was honestly mad at you because someone asked for the salt?"

Shannon smiles. "That was nothing. When we were fifteen, I wore my hair in a French braid for a varsity game one afternoon. Jason thought I was trying harder than usual with my appearance. He said he suspected me of trying to 'catch the eye' of one of the guys on the opposite team. 'I thought you'd be wearing your hair in a bun, the way you know I like it,' he said, and I knew something was off because his voice was kind of low and flat, but I thought he was just in a weird mood." She sighs. "When we were on our way home that night, we stopped to get burgers. Jason went in to pick up the food, and he handed mine to me in the passenger seat. When I bit into it, there was a pebble in the bun. I chipped my tooth."

She opens her mouth and points to a nick in one of her teeth.

"And Jason just kept his eyes on the road and said, 'It's not nice to find something different from what you expected, is it?' in that same flat voice."

She looks up at Hayley like she's checking to gauge her reaction. Like she's worried she might not believe her.

"He's always liked me being friends with Jessa. Said he thought her chastity would 'rub off on me.' Not that I'd ever so much as looked at another guy. But last year, I went over to study at May's house, and he turned up at the door, all charming and apologetic, telling her mom he was there to drive me home, even though I'd never told him I was going. He'd used an app to track me there. Said he didn't like me hanging out with her alone, that he thought we might be gossiping about guys or planning to sneak out to a bar together. May was too 'loose,' he said. And when I left with him, May's mom was practically swooning over how lucky I was to have a guy so dedicated and sweet that he'd come all that way to get me home safe."

Shannon picks up one of the mangoes and uses a fingernail, grown long and sharp since their arrival on the island, to slit its skin from top to bottom, a single glistening cut.

"It started so, so slowly. When Jason and I first met, I was so new, I didn't know anyone or anything about Oak Ridge, and he sort of took me under his wing, guiding me, introducing me around, helping me. And somehow, somewhere along the way, the guiding became more like controlling. But he always made it seem like he was just doing it for me. Helping me. Letting me know what people would think of me if I wore that top to school…for my own sake. Checking that I really wanted to eat that cookie…because he knew how much I cared about making it onto the cheer squad. And so, for a long time, instead of feeling angry, I felt—" She looks down at the mango, swallowing, forcing her fingernails under the skin and peeling it back. "I felt grateful. And stupid. I didn't know why I kept making so many mistakes. And I felt lucky Jason was there to help me."

She lifts the fruit to her lips and takes a small bite.

"There were times when I did stand up for myself a little. I think. But each time I did, Jason would drop something about

Carsons Park, just in passing, just a casual mention. And I'd feel myself freeze. I'd see everything I was working for sort of hanging in the air above his head, like it was suspended in a bubble and it would have been so very easy for him just to reach up and pop it. Just like that. So I learned how to please him—most of the time, at least.

"I love my mom, I love her so much, but I don't want my life to look anything like hers. After my dad left, she had almost nothing. She had me so young. She never went to college, didn't have any qualifications. She moved to a completely different neighborhood, saved every penny of my dad's alimony for the Oak Ridge fees, worked two jobs to make rent, bought my school uniform secondhand and sat up at night for a week hemming it to exactly the right length so it looked new. I've spent the last decade making up increasingly elaborate excuses for why my friends can never come to my house, all the while working to make sure my story will be different from hers. Mom was never going to be able to pay for college, and I'm not academic enough for a scholarship, but I knew I could get a free ride with cheerleading if I was good enough. And you know as well as I do that being good enough isn't the only thing that matters."

"Jason," Hayley says, finally beginning to understand.

"Yes. Jason. He was my ticket to freedom. But he was also dismantling my freedom; he just did it so slowly and so lovingly that I didn't really realize what was happening until it was too late." She shrugs, licking the juice off her fingers. "It just became a habit, like second nature. I didn't even think twice about it. I dressed the way I knew he wanted me to. Never sent a message I wouldn't want him to see if he checked my phone. Went where I knew he would want me to be and when."

She looks up at Hayley. "I think that night, I just wanted to be free for a little while. After I had that drink, I started to feel out of control, and at first, it scared me. But then I realized it was the first time I hadn't been in control—tight, tight control—for as long as I could remember. It wasn't about the guy. It was about being me, about making my own decisions, the intoxication of being unshackled just for one night. And I didn't want it to stop. Until I did."

She takes a long, deep breath and lets it out slowly. Hayley knows instinctively that this is the only time Shannon has ever talked about this to anybody.

"What are you going to do now?"

"Ask the others to keep their mouths shut. If they could decide to go to the police for me, they can decide to do that instead."

"I mean about Jason."

"I don't know. I thought about trying to end it a few times, especially recently. But you don't know what he's like, Hayley. What he might do. I'm so scared he'll come to my house, or he'll undermine me with the squad somehow. After everything that's happened, I just want it to be over. I don't want this to define my life, and I don't want to let Jason control it either. But I don't know how to get out. I don't think he's ever going to let me go. Even after this. There were times before when he was so angry, like he was disgusted by me, and I thought maybe it was over. But then he'd change after a few days. He'd need to have me again. And he'd flood my locker with flowers or bombard me with love songs and gifts. Everyone else always thought it was so romantic. He always finds a way to trap me."

"We'll do it together," Hayley says immediately. "You can stay at my house for as long as you want—Jason doesn't know my address, and neither does anyone else on the squad...or in the school, for that matter," she realizes, slightly embarrassed. "My mom will be thrilled to think I've got a friend good enough to stay over."

She falters for a moment over the word *friend* and looks up, fearing that dreaded eyebrow, a shriek of laughter, a scathing put-down. But it doesn't come. Shannon has set the mango gently on the ground, her hands in her lap, her face softer somehow. She's crying.

"And if Jason tries anything, we'll fight back. We'll expose him for who he is—we'll tarnish his perfect image. We'll put it on the front page if we have to. He's not taking you down, Shannon. I won't let him."

That's when the shouting begins. They look at each other in alarm, and Shannon shakes her head slightly to answer the unasked question in Hayley's eyes. "I haven't done anything else. I swear."

They move through the trees toward the noise, half expecting another disaster, an emergency with Brian's leg, but instead there's a plane. A seaplane floating quietly just off the beach.

There is no dramatic screaming from a helicopter, no rescuers hanging out and urging them forward. No billowing storm of whipped-up sand. There's barely even a ripple.

And Hayley feels none of the relief, the dramatic joy, the hysteria she imagined when she pictured this moment. She watches as the others stream across the sand toward the plane, splashing through the shallows, Elliot and Jason supporting Brian between them.

Inside the plane, she can see Jessa talking rapidly as she gestures toward her arm, a medic hunched over her. May stroking her hair, sobbing with relief.

And as she and Shannon walk across the beach side by side, Hayley looks back over her shoulder. The island is watching them go. Their footprints shimmer for a moment and then disappear.

AUTHOR'S NOTE

IN THE PAST TEN YEARS, I HAVE VISITED MORE THAN FIVE hundred schools and universities, working with tens of thousands of young people in co-ed and single-sex, private and state, rural and inner-city settings. I have never visited a school where sexism, sexual harassment, and sexual assault weren't problems. In the same period, I have received around fifty thousand testimonies from young people describing their experiences of being harassed by adult men on their way to school, being groped and spanked by peers in school corridors and playgrounds, being abused both on and offline.

The young people I work with feel that sexual harassment and assault is so commonplace that it has become a "normal" part of childhood. They feel that coercive control and other forms of abuse are hallmarks of any relationship. They feel abandoned by adults who tell them that "boys will be boys" or send them home for "distracting" their male peers with short skirts. They feel forgotten and failed by a legal system where conviction rates are so low that rape has effectively been decriminalized. And they are furious at a world where men accused of sexual harassment and violence go on to receive sporting awards and cultural accolades, to be elected to government office and seats of "justice."

This is a generation of girls who are courageous, powerful, resilient, and bold. They are finding their own ways of fighting back, speaking out, and refusing to be silenced. They are eager to redefine our societal understanding of consent and our ideas about what relationships look like. And above all, in the face of a world where they feel that justice isn't available to them, they are absolutely determined to create change. This book is my way of standing with them.

LAURA BATES, JULY 2021

ACKNOWLEDGMENTS

I AM HUGELY GRATEFUL TO THE WHOLE WONDERFUL publishing team at Sourcebooks. Huge thanks to Steve Geck, my wonderfully supportive and meticulous editor, and to Lynne Hartzer, Alison Cherry, and Thea Voutiritsas for their forensic and eagle-eyed copy editing. Thank you to the fabulous design team for the evocative cover and to the marketing and publicity teams, especially Beth Oleniczak, for being the real-life kick-ass cheerleading team making sure this book reaches its readers!

I'm so lucky to work with the incomparable Abi Bergstrom at Bergstrom Studios, the most hardworking, compassionate, and understanding agent a writer could have, and Sarah Williams and Stevie Grace at Independent, who work so skillfully to help my ideas come to life beyond the pages of my books.

I am indebted to a number of experts who helped me with questions about the climate, flora, and fauna of the Gulf of Mexico. They include David Williams and Duncan Allen, who furnished me with fascinating facts on everything from birdsong to pygmy raccoons, and the compulsively watchable Emmy Cho of Emmymade for her very detailed descriptions of the flavors and textures of obscure tropical fruits. Special thanks to Harry Kiely for his encyclopedic knowledge of all things related to aviation and plane crashes.

Thank you to Aileen, Emma, Lucy, Eily, and Hayley for being such kind and enthusiastic early readers, and to Nick and my family for your incredible ongoing support.

Most of all, I am very grateful to every single young person I have worked with in the past decade at schools and universities and the tens of thousands from around the world, including so many young people in the United States, who have shared their stories with me via my Everyday Sexism Project. Your voices and stories matter enormously, and I feel very privileged that you have entrusted me with them. Your courage, your hope, and your spirit of resistance inspires me every day. I promise you that you are not alone, no matter how much it might sometimes feel that way. And I promise you that we will keep fighting together to make things better.

HELPLINE ADVICE

IF YOU HAVE BEEN AFFECTED BY ANY OF THE ISSUES IN THIS book, you are not alone. A 2018 national study found that 81 percent of women and 43 percent of men reported experiencing some form of sexual harassment and/or assault in their lifetimes. A 2015 National Intimate Partner and Sexual Violence survey found that one in five women in the Untied States experience completed or attempted rape during their lifetimes, with one in three female victims experiencing it for the first time between the ages of eleven and seventeen. Young women aged sixteen to nineteen are four times more likely than the general population to be victims or rape, attempted rape, or sexual assault.

I want you to know that change is coming. Every week, I meet young people across the country who are taking action, determined to make things better. From launching campaigns to starting their own feminist societies, a generation of girls is taking matters into their own hands and fighting back.

And for the days when you might not feel able to fight back

(we all have days like those), help is out there. The following organizations provide information, confidential support, and a listening ear when you might need it the most. Don't be afraid to reach out for help. You are not alone, you are not to blame, and you deserve to feel better.

RAINN (Rape, Abuse & Incest National Network)
(rainn.org, 1-800-273-8255) The nation's largest anti-sexual violence organization, which created and operates the National Sexual Assault Hotline

Rape Crisis (rapecrisis.org)
Free, confidential support for women and girls who have experienced sexual assault, recent or historic

National Coalition Against Domestic Violence (ncadv.org, 1-800-799-7233)

National Domestic Violence Hotline (thehotline.org)

National Sexual Violence Resource Center (nsvrc.org)

Love is Respect (loveisrespect.org)
Offers 24/7 information, support, and advocacy for people ages thirteen and twenty-six to prevent and end abusive relationships

MaleSurvivor (malesurvivor.org)

    Support for men and boys who have experienced sexual assault or sexual abuse

StopBullying (stopbullying.gov)

    Provides information about bullying and cyberbullying

Cyber Civil Rights Initiative (cybercivilrights.org, 1-800-273-8255) Support for anyone who is a victim of nonconsensual pornography (also known as revenge porn), recorded sexual assault, or sextortion

National Suicide Prevention Lifeline (suicidepreventionlifeline.org) Free and confidential emotional support for people experiencing depression or suicidal thoughts

Planned Parenthood (plannedparenthood.org/learn/teens)

    Information about sex, relationships, bullying, and more

Youth.gov (youth.gov)

    Provides tools and other resources for young people on topics like mental health, dating violence, bullying, and suicide prevention

ABOUT THE AUTHOR

LAURA BATES IS THE FOUNDER OF THE EVERYDAY SEXISM Project and writes regularly for the *New York Times*, the *Guardian*, the *Telegraph*, and many other news outlets. She is a regular contributor to the *Today Programme*, *Woman's Hour*, *Channel 4 News*, *Newsnight*, and more, as well as working closely with politicians, businesses, schools, police forces, and organizations from the Council of Europe to the United Nations. She has been awarded a British Empire Medal in the Queen's Honours List for services to gender equality.

Her critically acclaimed and award-winning nonfiction for adults includes *Everyday Sexism*, *Misogynation*, *Girl, Up*, and *Men Who Hate Women*. Her first YA novel for teens, *The Burning*, was declared "a haunting rallying cry against sexism" by *Kirkus Reviews* and nominated for the Carnegie Medal.

FIREreads

#getbooklit

Your hub for the hottest in young adult books!

Visit us online and sign up for our
newsletter at FIREreads.com

 @sourcebooksfire

 sourcebooksfire

 firereads.tumblr.com